The Art of Three

By Racheline Maltese and Erin McRae

Avian30
New York, New York
The Art of Three by Erin McRae and Racheline Maltese
Copyright 2017
ISBN 978-1-946192-06-6

www.Avian30.com

First Avian30 Printing: January 2018
Printed in the USA

A woman's life is not defined by what is enough.

Table of Contents

Chapter 1

Jamie forgets about something very important

"How did you forget about the referendum?" Callum asked Jamie, clearly aghast. The two of them had finished a scene and were waiting while the crew set up the next shot.

Jamie was torn between trying not to die of embarrassment and wondering how his twenty-four-year-old life had come to this. He was sitting on the set of a film — in which he was starring — and next to him was movie star and heartthrob-to-middle-aged-women-everywhere, Callum Griffith-Davies. Their seats were tucked to one side of the set, out of the way of the bustling technicians and production assistants who scurried about doing the heavy lifting of making movie magic.

Embarrassment won out. Jamie moaned and sank his fingers into the hair his agent liked to call auburn but in reality was simply a plain brown.

"I've been kind of busy," he said with a little tug of frustration. There was never enough privacy on film sets, but Jamie could not contain his emotions. Not about the vote, not about his own sense of haplessness, and, possibly, not even about his fairly awkward crush on Callum.

Jamie was two years out of drama school and starring in his first feature film. His co-stars were actors so famous he hadn't been sure they were real people until he'd met them. Callum, who was the most famous of the lot, was calm, well put-together, and aggressively genial in addition to being unfairly attractive. The look Callum was giving Jamie suggested he would never forget about something as important as the Irish marriage referendum.

"Don't yell at me, okay? My mum already took care of that." Jamie meant it as a joke but hunched his shoulders in shame nonetheless.

"Your mother yelled at you?" Callum stretched his arm across the back of Jamie's chair. A casual gesture, surely, and one of fondness between work colleagues who liked each other, but it was the sort of thing he did constantly. Jamie felt off balance in the face of it. Having a crush from afar was one thing. Having a crush on someone who touched with easy fondness was utter misery.

Jamie nodded morosely. "She called and asked when I was coming home. Said that if she's going to be perfectly okay with her equal opportunity son that she loses ridiculous amounts of sleep over, I am going to do my civic duty."

"Can't you catch a flight up Thursday night?"

"Nope. I'm working that day like everyone else here." Jamie gestured at the dozens of crew members. "There's no way I'm going to be able to get home. What if it loses by just one vote?"

"It's supposed to pass, you know. Comfortably." Callum was relaxed, nearly disinterested, which only piqued Jamie's interest further. He could make out the faintest hint of gray coming in at the roots of Callum's otherwise light brown hair and loved that proof that the older man was human after all. Not only did he age like anyone else, he was vain enough to hide the fact.

Callum's mobile rang in his shirt pocket, and he fumbled to silence it. Nearby, a tech flicked a key light on. Jamie watched as the illumination caught Callum's profile and brought out the rich hazel color of his eyes. He really was magnificent, leonine almost. He'd fascinated Jamie from their first meeting. Jamie had been hard pressed to look away since.

Aware that he'd gone too long without saying anything, Jamie struggled to recapture the thread of their conversation. "If everyone who isn't awful turns up to vote," he said. "But if you're not awful and you've any sense, you've left Ireland, and you're not going back. I mean, I've got mates flying back in from Canada, and I can't manage it from England. I have bollocksed this up. Royally and in a fashion unbecoming to my people."

"How long are the polls open?" Callum asked, ignoring the fact that Jamie was nearly babbling.

Jamie shrugged. "'Til ten?"

"When do they open?"

"Not sure. Seven, I think. Why?"

Callum looked like he was considering something. His mobile rang again, and yet again he silenced it. He fixed Jamie with a keen eye.

"Who else on the crew is Irish, needs to get back, and hasn't figured it out yet?"

"It's not like we have a club," Jamie said. "But, okay." He ticked names off on his fingers. "Kate, from crafty. Mike, he's a P.A. And Angela, I think, but she's got a plan. I mean there are others, too, but seriously, it's not like I have a list. I'd have to ask around."

"Can you get them all together?"

"It'd take a while, but could do."

Jamie had no idea what Callum was up to. He was about to ask when the man's mobile rang a third time. Callum dug it out of his pocket, glanced at the screen, and then turned to look apologetically at him.

"Do you mind if I take this? Apparently, my wife is trying very hard to get in touch with me."

Jamie waved him off. "Yeah, it's fine." On this set Callum was always the most important person in the room. If his wife was calling, he hardly needed Jamie's permission to cut short their conversation.

While Callum took the call in a somewhat private corner of the set, Jamie made himself look at the floor, the cameras, the ceiling — anything other than the indecent lines of Callum's shoulders. Staring at him was absolutely, positively not appropriate. Callum was his coworker. His A-list, decent, kind, and happily *married* coworker.

Jamie had never met Callum's wife, Nerea, but he'd seen pictures of her here and there in the media. She was Spanish and as beautiful and as uninterested in the camera as Jamie expected of celebrity wives. She and Callum had three daughters, all of whom were older than Jamie. Not that Jamie spent excessive amounts of time looking up the details of Callum's personal life on the internet. Really, he didn't. Well, not anymore. But a year ago Jamie had just been a fan, and Callum had been one of those actors whose charming family holiday photos tended to turn up in *Hello* magazine.

Jamie pulled out his own mobile to text his mum so he wouldn't be tempted to eavesdrop. Although any attempt to do so was rendered difficult by Callum conducting his side of the conversation entirely in Spanish. And wasn't that completely, unfairly hot? Some days Jamie felt like he could barely manage English. The idea of being fluent in a second language was beyond him.

Hey. Maybe you won't have to disown me. I might have a plan. He typed slowly and with great concentration. It was hard to focus. Aside from the general bustle of set, Callum seemed very excited about something.

Eventually Callum finished his call and returned. He beamed at Jamie, at the passing crew members, at the world at large, and said, "My daughter's having a baby."

"Oh my God!" Jamie was delighted for him. "Congratulations! How's she doing?"

"She's well," Callum said, bouncing on his toes. Even with his broad six-foot-two frame he looked appealingly boyish.

"Is she telling people yet?" Jamie asked. "I mean, beside you and her mum and your random nosy co-stars?"

"Yes." Callum frowned slightly in puzzlement. "Why?"

"So I can tell people."

"Why would you want to do that?" Callum seemed mystified.

"Because a nice thing happened at work today? That has nothing to do with my inability to get myself home on my own?" Jamie grinned. "Also, you totally just lost your sex symbol status…granddad."

Callum stared at him. For a moment, Jamie was terrified he had overstepped, but then the other man threw back his head and roared with laughter.

Chapter 2

Callum solves everyone's problems but his own

Having spent most of his adult life in the business, Callum had found that the trick to enduring long days on set was to have a life outside of filming. Which meant limiting his social time with the cast and crew and spending as much time as he could with his friends, family, and flings.

The flings, of course, he conducted within the agreements he and Nerea had for their extracurricular activities. Sometimes they were frequent; sometimes they were few and far between. At the moment Callum was only contemplating such a relationship, with a blue-eyed freckle-faced Irish boy too young for him by half.

Family was also difficult to come by presently. Nerea was at their home in Spain, having learned early in their marriage that her enjoyment of Callum's life on set was inversely proportionate to her proximity to it. Their middle daughter, Devon, lived in Spain too, just half an hour away from Callum and Nerea's house. Leigh, their eldest, and Piper, their youngest, both lived in London, but had their own busy schedules and complicated lives. Which made tonight a friend night.

Thom Abbot was Callum's latest best friend. Callum went through best friends at the rate of one or two a decade, which was far better than the turnover rate on his lovers. They had met while working on a movie and they'd quickly bonded over odd films, obscure books, and the raw incompetence of their first-time director. Now, five years on, here they were at a gastropub of the sort that had recently been taking over London. Callum appreciated the food — few things were not improved by being fried in duck fat — but he appreciated the dim lighting and relative quiet even more.

"God, you're getting old," was Thom's first response when Callum finally told him about Leigh.

Callum was working up to a clever retort when someone approached their table to nervously-yet-politely ask for a selfie. Callum winced but obliged.

Thom waited until the fan had gone to give a heavy sigh. "This is ridiculous," he complained. "How am I supposed to mope with your good news and all your groupies around?"

"They're not groupies; they're not my fault; and it was only one," Callum replied.

"That's how it starts." Thom toyed with a chip. "And you love it."

Callum started to protest, then gave up. Thom had half a point. "Not when I'm eating dinner. Or trying to have a conversation with you."

Everyone Callum was close to teased him about being unable to go without human contact for twenty-four hours. No matter how often he denied the accusation, they weren't wrong. Callum loved people: Their stories, their foibles, their failures.

And yes, he adored their eyes on him. But just as much, he loved looking at them when they were engrossed in their own lives, unselfconscious and unaware. Even Thom, in the midst of a messy divorce that was incredibly awkward for their social circle, was fascinating to him. Sure, he'd been yo-yoing between clinginess and refusal to communicate for months, but Callum loved him all the same.

Thom was nearly as tall as Callum but rail-thin where Callum tended to broadness. Since the divorce process had started, Thom had kept his hair buzzed short to hide that he was rapidly going bald. Callum had wondered if Thom was mourning his marriage or trying to get laid again when he'd made the change, but didn't have the heart to ask. Thom reminded him of the friends he'd had as a boy: Loyal, absurd, and desperately kind. Callum always enjoyed the time they spent together.

&

After their meal, Thom declared a need to escape any further groupie appearances and noted that his own place was far too pathetic and sad to hang out in now that Katherine had moved out. So they took a cab from the pub to Callum and Nerea's pied-à-terre in Covent Garden. Callum was glad he had a late call the next day; it meant he and Thom could stay up as late as they wanted to talking.

Because Nerea and Callum properly made their home in Spain near Cortegada, the flat was tiny. They maintained it more to provide the comfort a hotel couldn't when Callum was shooting or when he and Nerea wanted to spend a few weeks in London. It was on the top floor of the building, under eaves which formed a ceiling Nerea found charmingly slanted and

Callum found dangerous given the number of times he'd whacked his head on a low beam that ran above their bed.

The walls were eggshell white, the floors a bright hardwood, and all the textiles of the furniture and curtains were pleasant red and golden browns that echoed the brick of the exterior. The kitchen formed an odd L-shape perpendicular to the rest of the space and the tiny living area was almost entirely taken up by an armchair and a sofa. The bedroom, such as it was, was merely an alcove separated from the rest of the space by a heavy dark red curtain, insisted on and installed by Nerea herself. The layout allowed them to entertain without the awkwardness of having a bed in the middle of the space, but the flat had never truly been big enough for two grown people.

Callum fetched beers out of the cupboard and handed one to Thom. He had already stretched out on the sofa, his shoes off in deference to Nerea's concern for the furniture.

"Tell me your woes." Callum dropped into the squashy armchair wedged in between the sofa and the window.

"I'm forty-one years old. Divorce sucks. Being single sucks. Dating occasionally sucks, like how we can't go to your club anymore because my brief affair with Eloise at reception was…brief."

"Understatement. That was disastrous," Callum added helpfully.

Thom gave him a wary glance. "When it doesn't suck, it's somewhat terrifying. But I'd guess you'd know that. About dating, I mean."

Callum tipped his head to the side in a vague acknowledgment of Thom's point. "Dating can be good," he said. Honestly, anything that distracted Thom from his misery was a positive. Because Thom was supposed to help Callum with his periodic fits of misery. Which it was very hard for him to do when he was preoccupied with his own disaster of a life. Callum wasn't comfortable with being the well-adjusted one amongst his friends.

"Can be. Theoretically." Thom blew tunelessly over the mouth of his beer bottle. "I have my own life and fitting people into it is hard. Relationships are…complicated." Again, that oddly wary look. Callum wondered why. It wasn't like Thom was trying to date him. *Was he?*

"You'll figure it out," Callum said inanely, mostly because he didn't know what else to say. Relationships came easily to him; he liked people and liked to be liked. That hadn't caused problems for him in at least several years.

"Mmm." Thom blew over the mouth of his beer bottle again.

They lapsed into companionable silence, until sufficient time had passed that Callum was fairly sure it wouldn't be rude to start talking about himself.

"So, I think I have a problem," he said at the same time Thom said, "I need to tell you something."

"What is it?" Callum forced himself to ask.

Thom sighed wearily and waved his hand. "No, you go."

Callum didn't protest. "There's a boy," he said.

"Of course there's a boy. There's always a boy. Or a girl. Or someone." Thom teased.

"There hasn't been one in months," Callum protested. "Not for more than a few hours anyway."

"There's a boy and you think you're serious about him. Heaven help us all. Who is it? And how bad of an idea does Nerea think he is?" Thom's voice conveyed the judgment of the long-suffering.

"I haven't told her yet. I haven't told *him* yet. I'm still thinking. Maybe I won't even do anything about it. Maybe he'll say no."

"No one says no to you." Thom started peeling the label off his beer bottle.

"You do."

"You never ask," Thom drawled. "You never write, you never call."

"I know better." Thom was charming when he felt like being so and smarter than Callum. If he were interested, Callum wouldn't be opposed.

"Yes, and I'm grateful for that."

"It's Jamie," Callum said.

"Jamie who?"

"Jamie the handsome, charming, complete nobody who is now my co-star and is going to be a household name in six months."

Thom's jaw dropped. "Seriously? *Him?*"

"Yes."

Thom thunked his head back against the arm of the sofa and stared at the ceiling in supplication. "Why do you always make such terrible choices?"

"I haven't done anything," Callum protested, mildly offended. "I just want to."

"Good. You should continue not doing anything."

"Why?"

Thom held up a hand and ticked off points on his fingers. "He's new to the business. You'll have undue influence. He'll need you too much. It won't occur to him he can say no. He will drive you crazy." Thom ran out of fingers and held up his other hand. "And then you'll be mean."

"I need to help him get to Dublin. For the referendum."

Thom narrowed his eyes. "You're not listening to me."

"Rather."

Tom sighed. "Fine. Define 'help.' And that is a sketchy way to seduce someone."

"I don't know. That's why I'm asking you."

"Are you going to start paying me your assistant's salary?"

"Hardly. I'll owe you one."

"You'll owe me several," Thom grumbled, but he sat up and looked mildly attentive nonetheless. "So you need to get your boy to Dublin."

"Jamie and a half-dozen other kids who need to get back when they're all supposed to be on set. I should probably offer to pay the union fines for when some arsehole complains about whatever rules our director is going to need to break in the process."

"And he's going to do it because you ask?"

"Probably," Callum said. As far as he was concerned there was nothing to be gained from being oblivious to the combined power of his charm and his box office appeal.

There was a pause in which Thom conveyed with a wordless look just how much he was judging Callum.

"He was very upset," Callum said more weakly now.

"And you have a type. Helpless, confused, and very pretty when they're sad. Which, according to Nerea, was fine when the same could be said about you."

"And now?" Callum was amused and even a little gratified that his wife and his best friend took the time to discuss his foibles.

"And now it looks like a pathetic midlife crisis, frankly."

Chapter 3

Nerea finds a way to irritate all her children

Time alone in her house meant time to paint, to read, to attend to the thousand and one chores of upkeep the old place demanded. On this fair morning, Nerea was in her studio working on a new piece. The room was already warm with the heat of a Spanish spring. There were things that would need attending to once she went downstairs, but here Nerea could be absorbed by her work, by the brushes and paints and canvasses that littered the room.

But this morning, as she stared at her sketches and the pale expanse of fabric waiting to be given form and color with her paints, Nerea's mind wandered. There was so much going on right now, some of it expected, some of it very much not. And it all, in one way or another, came back to this house where Nerea had been born and where she had raised her own daughters. Before this room had been her studio, it had been her parents' bedroom. Before that it had been only an attic. Who knew what it might become in the future, when this house was no longer hers.

When time moves forward it forces people — or at least women — to deal with their past. Nerea's grandmother used to tell her that as she dealt with repairs on this heap of stone.

Money they didn't have and her grandfather's frequent absences for his job had left that work to Abuelita Josefa's hands.

Now, there was plenty of money for upkeep and anything else Nerea wanted. But Callum was in London. As much as their relationship had always flourished in the separations their lives demanded, today she felt it too keenly. Here in Spain, in a little town two hours from Porto in Portugal and five from Madrid, Nerea found herself in an unenviable position. She had to decide whether and how to share her family's good news with the ex-lover they all liked to pretend didn't live down the road. Nerea wanted her husband, not an awkward phone call with her past.

Leaving her brushes, she went downstairs and out into the garden with a cup of tea and her mobile. She wasn't going to get any work done until she figured out what to do.

Callum sounded groggy when he picked up.

"Did I call at a bad time?" Nerea asked sweetly.

Callum muttered something unintelligible. "No," he said after a moment. "I was just getting up anyway."

"I'm sure you were," Nerea said indulgently, in Spanish now. She could picture Callum, warm and cozy in their bed in London, gray morning light spilling in from the windows while he pulled a pillow over his face to block it out. The image made her miss him all the more.

"I have news," she declared, forcing herself to smile out of her melancholy at a bird as it swooped over the back garden. There was dew on her favorite bench, still in the shade of the house, and so she walked along the uneven garden paths with her mobile tucked between her shoulder and her ear so she could use her hands to stir her tea.

"Is Leigh all right? The baby?" Callum sounded anxious and much more awake.

"They're fine," Nerea soothed. "But I've had a phone call, and now I need to make another, and I want to talk to you first."

"Mmm, do tell," Callum said, his voice returning to warm and lazy.

"For one, I've had a call from the Tate Modern."

"Oh?"

"Oh? All I get is oh? I've had a call from the Tate Modern and it wasn't fundraising. It was about my work."

"Are you serious?"

"No, I'm making this up for no reason." Nerea should have been annoyed, but she was enjoying sharing her news far too much. "Yes, I'm serious!"

"Nerea, that's huge."

"I know," she said with satisfaction.

"Tell me everything about it," Callum said. "When did this happen?"

"Yesterday. Late, but with Leigh and everything else...." she trailed off. "I wanted to keep it for myself for a day. Besides, it's mostly boring planning details I'd rather bombard you with after the shine's worn off and it's begun to irritate me."

"Really?"

"No, not really, but I'd rather celebrate with you when we're in the same place." She knew she sounded wistful.

"Topic change?" Callum asked as the pause stretched out.

"Topic change," she agreed. Nerea knew each of them missed the other too powerfully for words.

"What's the phone call you need to make?"

"To shift from one good piece of news to another." Nerea felt hesitant but charge ahead. "Devon is getting married. This winter. At our house."

"That's not news," Callum said, wary and confused.

"Ah, yes. But I had lunch with her yesterday, and we should talk about whether we're going to invite Antonio."

"Does Devon want to invite Antonio?"

"Of course she does."

"Then why do we need to have a conversation?" Callum sounded breezy. That meant he was uncomfortable.

Nerea didn't try to hide her annoyance. "Because if we're going to invite Tonio to Devon's wedding, we can't just mail him a piece of paper telling him she's getting married. Also, he owns the only catering company in town so we're going to have to do business with him at some point. I should see him in person, sit down and have a drink or a meal with him, so that he knows the invitation is heartfelt and he is truly welcome. But before I do that I wanted to talk to you about whether that is going to be a problem."

"Of course it's not a problem. Why on earth would that be a problem?" Callum said.

Nerea could have smacked him. "Are you kidding me?" She stopped in her tracks and stared out at the vineyard. The branches of the vines were a soft warm grey in the early sun.

"No. Of course not."

"After all the drama you caused. After all the fights you had with me — and him! — about being around for the girls. You ask me why that would be a problem."

"I'm not angry about it *now*."

"No, but you were at the time, and a couple decades of my life might have been easier if you'd decided to be this magnanimous back then."

"Are you angry I grew up?" Callum asked.

"I'm upset you're failing to acknowledge the long-term implications of your bad behavior and acting as if it's bizarre I should want to check in with you about this."

"Are we going to have this fight — "

"Callum," Nerea interrupted sharply. "I'm not interested in having old fights again. Which you know very well. I'd appreciate it if you stayed grown up."

"About you having lunch with your ex-lover who was like a father to our daughters when they were little because I was too busy with my career to be a constructive part of their lives," Callum said dully.

"Yes. Exactly."

"When are you seeing him?"

"I'm not sure yet, because, as I said, I wanted to talk to you first." No one could capitulate more passive-aggressively than her husband, and Nerea knew how to retaliate in kind.

"Let me know how it goes?"

"I surely will."

Somehow, mostly through the long practice of having to actually work on their marriage, they turned their attention to the smaller, less fraught matters of their separate days. Once they said their goodbyes — and their I-love-you's — and hung up the call, Nerea sighed. She adored Callum but being married to him was never easy. Perhaps it shouldn't have, but decades later it still hurt, the way she and Tonio had fallen apart. Which was not entirely on Callum's shoulders; Tonio had been just as unwilling and incapable of having an adult conversation with

Callum as Callum had been with him. But the end result was the same: One of the best relationships of her life had ended, and her relationship with Callum had needed desperate repair. Although long stitched up, the edges of that wound sometimes still itched.

These days when Nerea and Tonio saw each other, in the market or the odd Sunday at church, they nodded cordially to each other before turning their attention to their own families. Tonio had been married for ten years now and had two beautiful girls of his own. His catering company was by all accounts very successful. As far as Nerea knew, his experiment with polyamory had ended with her. It certainly wasn't a relationship style that worked for everyone. Even in her own family, there was significant variance on the issue.

Of Nerea's daughters, Leigh was the only one she was certain inclined toward poly. Devon was, to her knowledge, monogamous. She had no idea what Piper's dating arrangements were like, aside from the fact that Piper seemed to date a lot of people at the same time. But whether that meant Piper was poly or just young and having fun, she didn't know. Piper's irritation that she couldn't scandalize her parents with her strings of boyfriends was a source of amusement to Nerea and Callum both.

Nerea's lack of concern over Piper's dating life, however, was no reason not to parent her to the fullest. Especially when she'd been so focused on her other two daughters lately. Nerea had been in close communication with Leigh over the pregnancy announcement. Devon lived in the town down the road, and Nerea saw her often. But she hadn't talked to Piper in nearly a week. Piper may have been neither pregnant nor engaged, but surely she could use some motherly fretting.

Nerea thumbed through her mobile and hit *call* on Piper's number with delight.

Piper answered after the fourth ring, her greeting disgruntled and barely comprehensible. Nerea waited patiently until she managed to get out something vaguely recognizable as "What is it?"

"I've called you to be overbearing so you don't feel neglected," Nerea announced cheerfully.

Piper moaned. "Mum, I don't feel neglected. I promise."

"Are you sure? Because Leigh's pregnant, Devon's getting married, and I'm going to have a show at the Tate Modern — "

"And you should tell me more about that. Later. Please, Mum, I don't feel neglected, I feel hungover."

Nerea sighed. Her people might drink constantly, but the English, they drank excessively and for sport. Especially at Piper's age. Nerea was learning to let it go. That was the beauty of having three children. Eventually they stopped alarming you with their garden-variety woes. Not that it wasn't still annoying. Which she told Piper, in Spanish, because Piper always had trouble switching when she was hungover. Nerea was her mother; it was her job to make Piper's life harder.

"It's Dad's fault," Piper declared in slow Spanish.

"Were you drinking with your father?" It wouldn't have been the first time.

"No. He was out with Thom."

Nerea wasn't sure how those facts were connected. "Have you seen your father recently?" she asked.

"No. Unlike you, he's willing to let me suffer in peace."

"You should see him," Nerea insisted. If she couldn't be attentive toward Piper in person, Callum could. Even if he was busy with filming.

"Mum, I'm going to hang up now, okay?"

"But you sound more awake!" Nerea with almost malicious false cheer.

"Mum. I. Have. Company."

Nerea laughed. On the other end of the line she could hear an inquiring male voice and Piper's muttered answer before the call clicked off. If her daughter was going to insist on getting off the phone so quickly, she apparently had a good reason.

Nerea hummed to herself as she slipped her mobile into the pocket of her sweater and strolled back inside the kitchen. Piper with company over was nothing new. Piper with company she'd hang up on Nerea for, was. Either Nerea had hit a nerve — unlikely — or Piper was not the only member of the family without something new and exciting happening.

She was glad. Nerea rinsed out her mug in the sink and set it to dry on the draining board. Everyone deserved something beyond the ordinary to keep them occupied.

Chapter 4

Jamie somehow makes it to Ireland

Jamie hadn't quite understood the significance of what was happening in Ireland until he, Mike the P.A., Kate from crafty, and Siobhan from accounting arrived at the ferry terminal at Holyhead. There were crowds and chaos like he'd never seen before. They were putting on extra boats, and everyone was talking to strangers.

Mike elbowed Jamie in the side. "You'll never get to do anything this anonymous again. Better enjoy it."

Jamie scoffed. "Better see who I can get it on with in the loo then, yeah?" He laughed, even though he'd never been the sort to do that. No, Jamie fell in love. Which he probably wasn't going to get the opportunity to do tonight.

The boat, as they boarded it, was crowded and the experience communal. Someone handed him a rainbow flag and someone else chucked a handful of plastic beads at his head. Balloons were everywhere. When Kate told them all to check Twitter, Jamie had to sit down on the messy deck of the increasingly exuberant ferry in surprise at what he saw.

They weren't only putting on extra boats; they were putting on extra planes. People were turning up at the airports, and the airlines — at least those in London and Boston and Berlin — were responding.

"I don't understand," Jamie said when Mike crouched down to see what was the matter with him.

"What don't you understand?"

Jamie scrolled through the #HomeToVote tag for another few seconds and then held his mobile up for Mike to see. "Why does everyone care about us?"

It was Ireland. No one cared about Ireland anymore. Not even the Irish.

⁓

By the time the ferry docked at Dublin Port, Jamie was too wound up to feel tired even though it was nearly three in the morning and he'd gotten up at five the day before. Callum had texted him until midnight, keeping him up to date with news coming in and also words of fond encouragement. Jamie wondered for the thousandth time how Callum, not to mention his life, were real.

At the dock Jamie's father met him at the same spot he always did when Jamie came home. Hugh Conway, like Jamie, wasn't a tall man. Also like Jamie, he was all sturdy arms and broad shoulders. His brown hair, now turned mostly gray, was tucked under his knit cap. When he pulled Jamie into a rib-crunching hug, Jamie inhaled the smell of damp wool and the clean air of home.

"Glad you made it, Jamie-boy," his father said into his shoulder.

Jamie loved his father and hoped he didn't make his already complicated life any harder. Hugh Conway had been a Magdalene laundry baby, lucky enough to have been adopted out. Any record of his birth mother had been lost, but he loved the parents who had raised him. He had a wife and four children: Two girls, married with children of their own now, Jamie, and Jamie's little sister, Aoife, who had Down Syndrome. Jamie knew that sometimes people, well-meaning and awful, offered his father sympathy — about his queerness or Aoife's situation — as if his family wasn't the sort anyone would want.

But a family was what you made it; Jamie's father had told them all that their whole lives. His older sisters had careers and families. Aoife was happy, had a job in a bakery and a boyfriend. When Jamie had been bullied as a child, his father had taught him how to punch and then told him he never had to if he didn't want. Jamie's mother, Maureen, had raised her children to do right by each other and the rest of the world, as far as they could. She'd driven Jamie to countless auditions and come to every school play Jamie had ever been in. When he got the part in *Butterflies and Fences*, she'd cried with happiness and then phoned all their neighbors and cousins to share the news. When it came to parents, Jamie knew he couldn't have done better.

"There's tea in the flask if you want it," Hugh said as they got in the car.

"Thanks." Jamie fished the slightly dented container out of the cup holder, unscrewed the cap and gulped a too-hot mouthful gratefully. It had started to rain on the last leg of the ferry ride, and the wipers squeaked on the windscreen as his dad pulled the car out onto the road.

"Good ride?" Hugh asked.

"Yeah."

"Your mother'll be glad to see you."

"Yeah."

Jamie was glad when they lapsed into companionable silence. It was always like this when Jamie first got in. Quiet and easy, his father giving him time to get used to being home again. Jamie had worried the first time he had come back after moving to the UK for drama school that somehow home wouldn't still be home. But as infrequently as he took them, trips to Dublin always grounded him.

Landing a part in *Butterflies* had been a dream come true. On set, Jamie could focus on the work. Away from it, he was realizing that he was scared more often than not. Not frightened, but uncertain of how to behave. What was he supposed to talk to his family or his friends about without sounding like a huge prat? The production office was making noises about a press junket and, ridiculously, attention from random people on the street had already started.

It had been cool the first time and embarrassing the second. Now it made Jamie feel awkward because people wanted some happiness out of meeting him that he had no idea how to give. As the headlights swept the dark road ahead, Jamie was glad for the break. The bustle of London started to fade in his mind. On the monotony of the road he was exactly who he always should have been: Absolutely no one, going home to see his family.

The dog, improbably named Vegetables thanks to the combined efforts of Jamie's nieces, started barking as soon as Jamie and his dad opened the front gate. When his mum came to the door, Aoife peering around her shoulder, the creature bolted out into the garden and ran happy circles around Jamie while the humans hushed him to be quiet before he woke the neighbors.

Maureen pulled her son in for a hug like he hadn't been home for years, then bustled Jamie into the kitchen. The house wasn't large, but it had never felt cramped, not even when Jamie had been in school and he, his parents, and his three sisters had all lived under the same roof.

The kitchen was warm. The old familiar lamp swung gently over the table, making the shadows on the wall sway slightly. The light fell on a needlepoint sampler, embroidered with a prayer, and on the kitchen table with the faint outline of water stains Jamie and Aoife were responsible for as children. The cushions on the chairs were a bit flat from years of use. At the window, lace curtains formed a creamy yellow barricade against the dark May night outside.

"I'm glad you made it back," his mum said, stern like any Irish mother, though the corners of her eyes crinkled with her smile. She had the same blue eyes and thick dark hair as Jamie.

Jamie laughed. "You had several very specific threats as to what would happen if I didn't."

"And they worked, didn't they? Do you want coffee?"

Jamie said *no* and *thank you*, because it was his mum. If nothing else, making movies was teaching him the ongoing value of courtesy. "Don't figure I need to be awake to vote," he added. If he was going to get through the next two days, he was going to need to pace his caffeine intake. "How's Mary? And Beth and the kids?"

As his mum made them all breakfast, Aoife filled him in on the doings of their older sisters. Mary, who was thirty, lived in Cork with her husband and worked in hospitality. Beth was thirty-two and had married her high school sweetheart. She and her husband now lived a few streets over from Hugh and Maureen. Their daughters, Anne and Grace, the nieces responsible for naming the dog, were apparently quite put out that Uncle Jamie was going to be in town but they weren't going to see him.

"You should call more often," his mum reproved.

"I know. It's been busy."

"You want to tell us about it?" Hugh asked.

"Want to," Jamie said. "Don't really know how."

"They nice to you, working you like that?" Maureen asked.

"Yeah," Jamie said distractedly. "Yeah they…well Callum, he — is this weird?" He squinted at his dad. There were half a dozen DVDs of movies Callum had been in on the shelf next to the TV. Jamie knew, because he'd seen them all as a teenager. Multiple times.

"'Course it's weird," his dad said with a fond smile. "Now tell your mother the story."

Jamie took a breath. "Okay, I screwed this up. Bad, like. And I'm totally not supposed to be here. But Callum, I don't know, it's like he feels important when he can do stuff for people, and when I said I was worried about how mad you were going to be if I couldn't get here…."

"I can only respect your interests if you're going to protect your interests," Maureen said.

"Yeah," Jamie blew by his mother's constant bargaining about his bisexuality. She wasn't wrong, and she did accept him, but it wasn't always easy. "He made me get all the Irish kids on set together, figure out who had a plan and who didn't, and then came up with a way to fix it for us. Made the director change the schedule and everything. So yeah. Everyone's nice."

Saying it out loud, Jamie knew it mostly made sense and yet didn't quite. No one was that nice. He wondered, not for the first time, if Callum felt he had some stake in the vote. He wasn't Irish, of course. But there were occasionally rumors about his sexuality if a person Googled hard enough.

The sky was growing lighter and the birds had started chattering up a storm. Jamie's mother looked at the clock. "The polls are opening soon. Aoife, love, get your coat, we can drop you off at the bakery after you vote. Let's get in line."

Chapter 5

Callum makes decisions he probably shouldn't

J amie appeared in the makeup trailer shortly after noon and
nearly asleep on his feet. Callum doubted very much he'd
gotten more than a half hour of semi-unconsciousness on
the plane back from Dublin to London. His hair was a mess,
his freckles stood out against his pale skin, and there were dark
circles under his eyes. The Irish complexion did not hide
exhaustion, but Callum found the rumpled, sleepy-eyed look
appealing in the extreme. Jamie wasn't small or slight — he was
quite solid, really, with the shoulders of a rugby player and a
strong jaw — but seeing him this worn out by the world made
Callum want to cuddle him close.

"You made it," he said warmly in lieu of doing anything of
the sort.

Jamie blinked as if he hadn't even realized the other man
was standing right there, but gratefully accepted the paper cup
of coffee Callum pressed into his hands. He nodded as he
drank and nearly choked on the scalding coffee in the process.
"Thanks to you."

"You're the one who wanted to get home," Callum teased.

"Yeah, but I couldn't have asked. Wouldn't have asked you to ask either." Jamie stifled a yawn with his free hand. "So thank you."

Callum hummed in acknowledgment.

Jamie blinked at him. Then seemed to startle. He dropped his hand. "Hey," Jamie said quietly.

"What is it?" Callum prodded when Jamie didn't say anything else. He leaned closer.

"Can we talk? Just us? Later?" Jamie asked, drawing out the words and the pauses between them. His pale cheeks were now streaked with a bright flush as if he were embarrassed.

"Of course," Callum said easily, but as he straightened up, his thoughts were less calm than his outer appearance. Jamie's request, although not unreasonable, was unclear. Was something wrong? Was Jamie upset? Callum wondered suddenly if Jamie were attempting to flirt. Helping Jamie get home to vote, whatever Thom might say, was one thing. A request for a *just us* talk might be another thing entirely. Or it might be nothing at all. "What about?"

"Nothing major. Just…I need to pick your brain about a thing. Yeah?"

"Sure. Tomorrow? After you've slept?" Jamie needed rest, but Callum also wanted the chance to call Nerea just in case there was a chance of something happening between him and this boy.

Jamie shook his head. "Tonight."

Callum looked at him cautiously. Nerea wouldn't mind hearing about whatever this was after the fact. She might even prefer it that way, although the lack of her good counsel would leave him at a disadvantage. He took a deep breath. "All right. If you think you can remain conscious."

⌒

Jamie, to Callum's amusement, didn't even ask where they were going until they were already in the cab.

"My club." Callum said. "If that's all right?"

"Sure, yeah." Jamie waved a hand, too tired to care where they went.

Still, Callum was grateful his club was hipper than some of its compatriots. Located in a small townhouse in Soho, its only oil paintings were ironic. Callum was fairly certain the massive deer head mounted on the wall in the entrance way was also ironic but had never chanced asking.

At the desk, Eloise — she of Thom's failed dating attempt — greeted them both with a tight smile before ushering them to the pub room.

"Do you want food or do you just want to drink?" Callum asked, as they were shown to their table. Or rather, as Callum sat down; Jamie seemed to melt into his chair as a puddle of weary boy.

"Not sure I'm awake enough to lift a fork."

"Then you certainly won't survive just drinking," Callum said amiably with a hand to Jamie's shoulder before going to the bar to order for the both of them.

The room, half full, was dark. In the far corner, nestled in a black leather banquette, a couple was on a date. Closer by, a collection of friends or business associates relaxed around a circular table. None of them paid the least bit of attention to Callum and Jamie.

"Thanks for taking the time to talk with me," Jamie said when Callum returned to the table.

"Of course." He still wasn't sure why they were here, but he meant it, potential ulterior motives aside. He waited to say more, giving Jamie a chance to gather his thoughts. Jamie's eyes glittered in the dark.

"Jamie," Callum said when several long moments had passed without a word. "You've had an incredibly long day. Are you sure you want to do this tonight? I can get you home."

"No, no. No. Thanks." Jamie sat up straighter. "I wanted to ask you. Well — I mean. I'm sorry if this is going make things awkward, but why did you help me get to Ireland? I know it wasn't just me you helped, but it was because of me."

"Not untrue."

"So I keep trying to figure it out. And either you're too nice to live— "

"Hardly."

" — Or I have to ask this."

"Go on."

"Have you been flirting with me?"

Callum blinked mildly at him and took a sip of water. Before Jamie could do something like bolt in horror or start babbling apologies, he said, simply, "Yes."

"Like — *flirting* flirting, or...." Jamie's voice trailed off.

Callum raised an eyebrow. "Whatever you're trying to ask, Jamie, spit it out."

"I just wanted to know," he said a little defensively. "You flirt. With me. And with everyone. Like. A lot. And there are rumors — and I know, I'm really sorry, I shouldn't listen to gossip, and I'm being horribly rude, and can we pretend I never asked to talk to you tonight?"

Callum shook his head. "Bit late now. What are you asking?" he said gently. "What do you need?"

Jamie looked like he hoped the floor would swallow him up but he soldiered on anyway. Callum admired the effort.

"Are you — maybe not totally straight?" Jamie asked.

"I'm married to a woman," Callum said in a tone of wry amusement. Jamie was far too much fun to tease, even if it was probably cruel to do so.

"I know that."

"And, like the tabloids we all call liars have occasionally said, I've had relationships with men. A lot of them. A few were even serious. Does that answer your question?"

Jamie swallowed. "Yeah," he said. "Yes, I think so. I...sorry. Some people would have been insulted. By the question, I mean."

"Some people don't live in the twenty-first century or make very good dining companions," Callum said lightly as their food arrived.

"I'm a horrible dining companion right now," Jamie admitted, twitching his napkin onto his lap.

Callum shrugged. "I've had worse. Now, was there more to your question?" It was obvious that hadn't been all Jamie was after. At least Callum hoped not.

Jamie stared at his hands for a moment. "I'm not totally straight either. Which I assume you knew or guessed because of, well, the flirting. And not being totally straight, that's always been fine? But that was before all this — the movie, I mean — and it's going to be mad isn't it?"

"It's an experience the first time you see yourself twelve meters high on the side of a building, yes. Which is going to happen." There were things about this situation that were not normal, but their respective sexualities were not among them.

"I meant the thing where I'm not straight."

"Are you gay?" Callum was curious as to how Jamie identified and if he could make himself say it out loud.

"Bi," Jamie half-squeaked. "And people are arseholes about that, you know?"

"I'm going to let you in on a little secret." Callum leaned close.

"What's that?" Jamie leaned in too. Callum wondered if he even realized he was doing it.

"People are arseholes about everything," Callum said. "And if you remember that, when they're giving you trouble about who you date or anything in your life you don't want to share with them, you'll remember their judgments have nothing to do with you and it's not your job to respond."

"I'm pretty sure I've known people were arseholes since I was a kid," Jamie said.

"It doesn't get better when you grow up, so congratulations to you." Callum looked at the boy, who appeared even more uncertain than when they had first sat down, and decided to take pity on him. "How's your family?"

Jamie relaxed at the question. With Callum's assistance, the conversation turned to easier topics. But when he leaned forward to make some point and rested a hand on Jamie's wrist on the table, Jamie asked, "Are you flirting with me now?"

Callum looked down at their hands and chuckled. "I suppose I am. But as you pointed out, I do with everyone. Flirting doesn't have to have intent. It can just be a nice game. Or a diversion. Or a way to make someone else feel good. Which you probably know."

"Maybe," Jamie said cautiously.

Callum couldn't resist playing coy. "So I guess my question is whether *your* question is about whether I'm flirting with intent."

Jamie smiled. "Maybe."

Callum made a decision. "Then I am absolutely flirting with intent. Do you want me to stop?"

A stunned smile bloomed on the boy's face. "Uh. No. It's okay."

"Good." Callum brushed his thumb over the back of his hand. "I'm glad."

An hour later Jamie's eyes shone a bit as Callum slid into the backseat of the cab next to him and pulled the door shut. Callum smiled at him when Jamie twined his fingers into his as soon as he touched the boy's hand again. Jamie was an absolute wonder.

"Wait," Jamie said, his eyes growing suddenly wide as the taxi pulled away from the curb.

"What is it?"

"What about your wife?"

"Points for asking, and it's fine. I'll explain when we're not in a taxi."

"Oh. Yeah. Okay," Jamie said, apparently mollified. He slumped sideways and leaned his head on Callum's shoulder.

Callum's breath caught in his chest. This was going to be absolutely marvelous.

"Do you want anything to drink?" Callum asked as they walked into the flat. He tossed his keys into a bowl on the coffee table and his jacket over the back of the armchair. Jamie unzipped his own coat slowly and laid it somewhat tentatively over Callum's. "Coffee?"

Jamie squinted at him. "It's almost midnight."

"Were you not planning on staying up late?" Callum wasn't going to stop flirting now.

Jamie gave him a shy smile.

Callum dialed back a notch, going for gentle over eager. "Tea, perhaps, then?" he offered. "Caffeine-free?"

"I'm just saying," Jamie muttered, as Callum went to put the kettle on. "I wouldn't need coffee to stay up late with you."

Callum laughed with pleasure. Even if Jamie was shy, he wasn't letting it stop him.

They settled next to each other on the sofa. Jamie seemed cautious of him, as if he didn't quite know where to put his limbs. Finally, Callum set his mug down on the end table. Slowly so Jamie could pull away if he wanted, he wrapped an arm around his shoulders. Far from retreating, Jamie leaned into him even as he looked at Callum sideways.

"Not that I'm not enjoying," he said. "But this is where you start talking about your wife. Because I'm tired, but I'm not that tired — and you're good looking, but not that good looking — that I'm going to let it slide."

Callum chuckled and retracted his arm. He scooted away from Jamie and shifted his body so they could have a proper face-to-face conversation as matters like this deserved. "Open relationship. Has been since pretty much always."

"Whose idea was that?"

Callum appreciated the savvy question. He'd gone to bed with people in supposedly open relationships only to find out their partner didn't quite agree, or that one or the other of them had been badgered into it. It was no fun to sleep with someone and find out later they hadn't wanted him as much as they had wanted to use him as ammunition against someone else.

"It wasn't really anyone's," Callum said. "It just was. She was seeing someone else when we met, I was carrying on appallingly, and our lives eventually consolidated. Then we got married. The relationships we had before we met changed, but they didn't go away. Not right away, at any rate. They didn't need to. We're apart a lot, which we don't love, but it is what it is. Better to know and to trust than not."

It wasn't the full story, of course, but it was still very early. Callum didn't want to scare Jamie.

"Does she know about me, then?" Jamie asked.

"She knows you exist, of course. She doesn't know I have you here tonight. I wasn't sure what this was about when you asked, and I didn't know if you were interested. I wasn't even sure I was going to do anything about it if you were."

"Can I talk to her? I mean, it's not that I don't trust you," Jamie hastened to add. "But I'd feel better. You're hers first."

"People don't belong to people," Callum said. "But you are a treasure." He leaned over to kiss him on the forehead, and Jamie grinned sleepily at him. "Do you want us to call her now?" Callum wasn't going to get laid tonight, when not even the twenty-four year old could stay awake. But he could still put in the groundwork. He was captivated by Jamie's insistence on doing right by Callum and Nerea's relationship.

"Yeah. If she's awake?" Jamie said.

"She should be. She might be painting and ticked off I interrupted her, but she'll be up." Callum levered himself up from the couch to fetch his mobile.

By the time he had it open to Nerea's number, Jamie's head had tipped sideways on the arm of the couch. His eyes were closed and his mouth slightly open, chest rising and falling gently. He'd certainly earned that sleep.

Callum pocketed his mobile and knelt to gently work Jamie's shoes off his feet. The boy didn't even stir. He was utterly exhausted, and Callum felt a pang of guilt that he hadn't insisted on Jamie going to sleep sooner. When his shoes were off, Callum unfolded a blanket from the back of the sofa and tucked it in around him.

Once he was sure Jamie was settled, he padded past Nerea's curtain into the bedroom. He undressed as quietly as possible, left his clothes puddled on the floor, and climbed into the sheets that smelled like Nerea's perfume and their laundry detergent.

Callum smiled at the ceiling. His wife, who he loved and missed very much, was at their home in another country. The boy he was smitten with was asleep on their couch in this one. It wouldn't look like contentment to most people, but Callum couldn't have been happier. What would happen tomorrow, he didn't know. But for now, he lay in the dark, listening to Jamie breathe, enjoying everything he had in this moment.

Chapter 6

Nerea deals with her past, or tries to

Nerea spent too long getting ready for her lunch with Tonio. So long, in fact, that she was nearly late and definitely out of breath when she finally met him at the appointed café.

It hadn't been nerves, exactly, that had made it impossible to choose a dress to wear — not one Callum liked too much, not one he didn't like, not one that looked like she'd gone to a lot of effort, and not one that was so sexy the village gossips would accuse her of stepping out on her husband. Because that was absolutely not what this lunch was about. But there was no chapter in the manual of life that specified how to dress to have lunch with a former lover in order to invite him to her daughter's wedding.

"Tell me your news?" Tonio said after they'd been seated in the sun on the patio.

Nerea liked this place and was grateful for its rare newness in the valley of ancient villages in which they both lived. The buildings, the dust on the street, the golden afternoon sunshine of spring, even the bright blue of the sky — all of it carried the weight of age. But this café hadn't existed when they were dating, and that made things easier now. The past could be a heavy thing to carry.

Nerea forced herself not to fidget with her silverware. "Devon's getting married."

"Oh!" Tonio's smile was broad and, oddly, relieved. "That's good news. Congratulations to her. Who's the lucky boy?"

"Miguel García Serrano."

"Ahh, he's a good young man. They'll be happy together."

"That is the plan."

"I have to say," Tonio said, rolling a water glass between his hands. "That's not the news I was expecting you to share."

Nerea tilted her head. "What did you expect?"

"To be honest? I thought you were going to tell me you and Callum were getting a divorce."

"What, no!" Nerea didn't laugh. Of all their acquaintances, Tonio was probably the only one who had any reason to come to such a conclusion, and she couldn't say he was entirely unreasonable. But he was wrong. "No. Devon wants you to come to the wedding, and I didn't want you to find out just from an invitation in the mail."

"Only Devon wants me to come to the wedding?" Tonio asked carefully.

"I would also like you to be there."

"And Callum?"

"Callum will be fine with it."

"But he's not fine now," Tonio clarified. This was not a skill either of them had possessed — the ability to check in on everyone's wants and desires and comforts, asking the uncomfortable but necessary questions — back when they had needed it. But they had it now, long past the time it would have been useful.

"No, I think he is. How he feels beyond *fine*, I'm not sure yet."

"And therein lies the problem."

Nerea nodded, though it hadn't been a question. She and Callum were a united front against the rest of the world, but she had never been able to be anything but frank with Tonio.

"Also, we'd like to hire your company to take care of food and tables and chairs, and I wanted to avoid any potential awkwardness in that regard."

Tonio waved that concern away with a flick of his hand. "And what about what you want?"

There was something in his tone that made the years instantly roll back. Like her, Tonio was older now, but Nerea could still see the young man he had once been. His dark eyes still sparkled in the sun; his hair was going a little silver at the temples but it was otherwise as black and as thick as it ever had been. Time had deepened the smile lines around his eyes and mouth, but it looked well on him. Life had been good to Tonio. If the thought made Nerea wistful, it also made her glad; she had been in love with him once and had never so much stopped loving him as stopped being able to do anything about it.

"Are you disappointed I'm not getting divorced?" she asked, somewhere between playful and sharp.

Tonio shook his head fiercely. "No! No. I'm relieved. I've been worried since you called me. He and I never...well. You were happy together, you and him. And fought hard for it. I would have hated to think that had fallen apart."

"Thankfully it hasn't." Nerea smiled tightly, every fiber of her being torn between awkwardness and grace. "How is Augustina? And your girls?"

"They're well." That cautious smile again. "Augustina told me to say hello."

"The same to her."

Tonio nodded in acknowledgment. So far as Nerea knew, he and his wife weren't polyamorous. It made Nerea feel better to know that after her Tonio had decided managing multiple relationships with multiple partners wasn't something he wanted to do or was even capable of. If he had wanted it or managed it, Nerea knew she would have been jealous to not be a part of that. She didn't know what to do with that knowledge, but as it was, she could simply be happy that he was happy.

"You look good," Tonio said, resting his chin in his hand.

"You're supposed to say that when we first sit down, not twenty minutes into the conversation." Nerea glanced down at the aqua colored dress she had spent so much time selecting.

"I didn't know if you'd mind."

"I don't know if I mind either," she admitted as her eyes met his again. "But it is nice to see you. I would have enjoyed these last years — "

"Decades — "

"*Years* — if we could have had lunch more often."

"That's hardly on my head," he said.

Nerea let it pass. The battle of who to blame wasn't worth fighting just to invite him to her daughter's wedding. "Devon's not the only news," she said. A topic change would do them both good.

"Oh?"

"Leigh's pregnant." Nerea couldn't help the way her heart fluttered as his face broke into a grin.

"You do have a lot of good things going on. That's wonderful," Tonio said. "Congratulations to her."

"I'm going to be a grandmother," she said somewhat ruefully.

"Not congratulations then on the part that makes you feel old."

Nerea was about to tease Tonio about his own age. Instead, she frowned as her mobile rang. She dug in her purse. "It's Callum," she said, not apologetic, but slightly embarrassed. Her husband always had the worst timing. "Do you mind?"

Tonio waved his hand to indicate that he didn't, but he looked away, his eyes fixed on the middle distance. Awkward didn't begin to cover it.

She answered the call in Spanish out of habit. Callum responded in kind, but then switched to English. Nerea laughed as the reason became apparent.

"I have some company that wants to check in with you," Callum said, his voice playful and still half-stuck in what she recognized as his seduction mode. "I hope this isn't a bad time."

"It's never a bad time for you," Nerea said, also in English, rolling her eyes a little. The English wouldn't give her much privacy — Tonio could certainly follow a conversation — but it would cut down on eavesdroppers to this ridiculousness. "I'm having lunch with Tonio."

"Oh...shit. How's that going? Give him my regards?"

"Fine, and I'll think about it. Now, who and what have you got there and are you going to put them on the phone?"

"It's Jamie."

"The Irish boy? From your movie?"

Callum had nattered on about the boy before, so it wasn't entirely surprising, but Nerea hadn't been aware he'd had any plans to move beyond gazing from afar. But then, Callum rarely planned to do anything with anyone who wasn't her. It just seemed to happen.

"Mmmmmhmmm. He slept on our couch after insisting I take him out to dinner so he could ask me whether I'm bisexual."

Nerea gaped. Tonio turned his attention back to her, his face cautiously curious.

"I assume the longer version of this story makes sense," she said.

Callum chuckled, and Nerea closed her eyes in fondness for the complete bullshit of his bashful charm. "It does," he said.

"Put him on the phone." She looked over to Tonio and mouthed an apology. Tonio shrugged it off.

"Hi ma'am, this is Jamie," said an unfamiliar voice with an Irish accent on the other end of the line.

Nerea had never so wished Callum had been in the room with her for such a call. Because *ma'am*? *Really*? She was torn between delight and horror. But the young man had manners, whatever the rest of the story was.

"Jamie," she said warmly. "It's nice to meet you, such that it is."

"You too. Callum said he hadn't talked to you about me yet, and before we did anything I wanted to talk. To you. And make sure you're okay with it? Not that I think Callum's not trustworthy or anything," he added hastily.

"But, he doesn't always seem to have the best judgment?"

"Well," Jamie began but didn't seem to know where to go from there.

"If you think that, you're not wrong," Nerea said.

She made a face at Tonio, whose own expression rested somewhere between wariness and amusement. He made a face back, though, and laughed softly when she winked at him.

Nerea returned her attention to the young man on the phone. "While I appreciate you calling me, he does have my blessing to sleep with you, if you want, but I'm in the middle of something. Although that's no reason for you not to have some fun."

"Uh. Thank you?" Jamie stammered. Nerea would have bet Callum had an arm around his waist and was kissing his neck. He had a very specific move for people he wanted to get off the phone.

"You're quite welcome. But I really am at a lunch you've just made a little more awkward," she said with another rueful glance at Tonio, who was now laughing outright. "So tell him I love him, and he can tell me all about you later, yes?"

Jamie's response was composed of incoherent syllables.

Nerea laughed. "Have fun. Give him a kiss for me somewhere filthy."

She clicked off the line and dropped her mobile in her bag. Then she fixed her smile on Tonio. "I am sorry about that."

"You're not. And if I didn't think Callum was a mess, I'd think you two planned that."

"We didn't. I promise." Nerea hesitated, then put her hand over Tonio's on the table. "But will you come to the wedding? I think we'd all like you there."

"Even Callum?"

"He may have no idea how to have a conversation with you, but you're a good man and were a good man to our girls. He knows that."

"What would you say if I said I need to think about it?" Tonio asked.

"I'd say that I understand, but that I'd like you to do this for me. And for Devon." Nerea was very good at making points non-negotiable.

Chapter 7

Jamie spends an entire weekend with Callum in bed

After the glory of finally getting their hands on each other and getting off, Jamie had expected they'd lay side by side in bed silently catching their breath. Then, if they were very lucky and not too awkward, at least one of them would pass out.

But that was not what was happening. Instead, they'd been lazily making out for the last ten minutes. Jamie's skin was singing with happiness. Callum wouldn't stop touching him, wouldn't stop smiling into his mouth. Jamie had no idea what he'd done to be the center of anyone's universe like this. But Callum Griffiths-Davies's? This was bizarre. All he'd done was ask for advice about being bisexual in public and then been either very brave or very foolish and asked if Callum had been flirting with him. Apparently, this hookup was the door prize for that, even if he hadn't slept in days and had barely been able to hold up his end of the conversation.

"You are absolutely lovely," Callum murmured into the skin of his neck.

"How long have you wanted to do this?" Jamie asked, enjoying Callum's long legs tangled with his.

Callum's chuckle in response was almost rueful.

Jamie opened one eye enough to give him a curious squint.

"For longer than might be considered decent or strictly professional." Callum kissed him again.

"That's not decent. Or professional in any sense of the word." Jamie stuttered a little as Callum trailed kisses from his mouth to his chest and then down his stomach to nuzzle at his hipbone. It was affectionate, even tender, and Jamie hadn't known that having someone's mouth there could be either.

"Are you complaining?" Callum asked, pressing a kiss to the heated skin and then smiling up at him with such sweetness Jamie thought he might go to pieces.

⁀)

They spent the whole weekend like that: In bed, in various stages of undress and arousal, murmuring too much praise at each other and laughing. To be fair, there was also a lot of takeaway after Callum tried to make them dinner and burnt it because they'd gotten distracted with each other again.

Jamie was grateful for the respite from the world the weekend represented. He wasn't looking forward to going back outside and dealing with people who were not Callum. He didn't want to leave and didn't know what would happen next. Eventually, he was going to have to ask. But it wouldn't be fair to ask Callum what he wanted to do next until Jamie knew his own agenda.

He thought about it intermittently as they sprawled tangled together on the couch; as Callum massaged shampoo into his hair in the shower; as Jamie sat on the kitchen counter, Callum standing between his knees as they shared cold leftover takeout. The casual intimacy was everything Jamie had imagined in a long-term relationship, but this could never, he was sure, be that. Jamie was in the throes of a fantasy, much like the movie they were making together. He tried to tease the source of his romantic notions apart.

Callum certainly wasn't the first person Jamie had gone to bed with, but he was the first person who had any sort of real experience at life. That was appealing, more appealing than Jamie would have thought. None of Jamie's relationships ever lasted long. He'd had fun with people, both boys and girls, but had never slept with someone and woken up thinking about having a future with them. He knew he was ridiculous to be doing that now — appallingly so. Callum was married and had adult children. But Jamie hoped it wouldn't hurt too much to linger in this fantasy just a little bit longer.

⇌

"What's the plan for tomorrow?" Jamie asked on Sunday afternoon as he played with the little locks of hair that curled at Callum's forehead. They were on the bed, the sheets kicked down to the foot. The afternoon sunshine was warm on Jamie's bare skin and made him pine for a beach holiday.

"Mmm?" Callum asked, lazy with Jamie's gentle touches.

"At work. Tomorrow. With you and me?" Jamie said. Callum had two little freckles, right at the corner of his left eye. Jamie hadn't noticed them before this weekend. "I'm not asking for anything," he hastened to add. "I just don't want to screw up."

"I hardly think you could do that." Callum smiled at him, his eyes still closed. "But it's a fair question. And you shouldn't be afraid of asking for things if you do want them."

"Well, yes, but." Jamie shrugged. In the few months they had known each other, Callum had always been generous, but in ways that seemed easy to take advantage of. It made him nervous. "You're married. And have kids older than me. So if this is just for today — "

"Why do those things preclude another relationship? With you or anyone else?"

Jamie wasn't sure how to answer that. The reasons seemed too multitudinous to name. Time lurked at the top of the list.

When Jamie remained silent, Callum opened his eyes and rolled onto his side. He leaned up on his elbow, chin resting on his hand. "Because there's room in my life for a lot of people. Which is not to say that fitting a relationship with you into the rest of my life would be easy," he said. "To be fair, I'm out of practice. It's been a while since I've had anything but flings outside my marriage. But that's no reason not to try, if that's what we both want."

Jamie digested that for a moment, but he needed Callum to ask the question.

"What do you want?" Callum asked.

"To know what is going on," Jamie admitted. "Without me making a fool out of myself, if possible."

Callum curled a hand behind Jamie's neck and rolled them so he was on top. Jamie noted how careful Callum was not to crush him. He thought he was grateful, but maybe he wanted to be crushed, by Callum's body and charm and desire, 'til his fear was gone and there was nothing left.

"Tomorrow at work," Callum nuzzled into Jamie's hair. "We will comport ourselves like professionals, because we are professionals. That's no indication of wanting to keep you a secret," he said firmly. "But people yell at me when I get caught snogging on set."

Jamie laughed. "I'd want to avoid that myself. But I don't mind. I mean, I don't want to be your dirty little secret. But it's nice to have this just be between us. For now?"

Jamie had never said anything like that to anyone. He'd never had anything he wanted to keep secret and sacred before. He bit his lip as he waited for Callum to respond.

"I know the feeling," Callum said. Jamie wasn't sure if the man was just humoring him. "You're quite a nice thing to cherish and keep all to myself." Before Jamie could respond properly to that, he went on. "Which means that tomorrow night, you can come back here, or go back to your flat, as you please. Same for the next night. And the one after that."

Jamie blinked up at Callum from the pillows, hardly able to believe what he was hearing. "So…not just this weekend?"

"Not unless that's what you want," Callum said. For someone with such a massive personality that could so easily bowl over people, Jamie couldn't help but notice how careful Callum was with consent.

Jamie shook his head.

"Thank goodness," Callum breathed.

Jamie was surprised by Callum's relief. "What about Nerea?" Sure, he had spoken to her, but that conversation had been so brief. He didn't have a full sense of all their rules, or the time and space he should give Callum to deal with the priorities in his life.

"Nerea is a remarkable woman and an astounding human being. I've no earthly idea why she's still with me. Though I thank God for every day she is."

"Not to be super nosy, but is the issue you sleeping around?"

"You talked to her."

Jamie hesitated. "Is Nerea seeing other people too?"

"Not at the moment, no."

"But she does?"

"Sometimes. She's much better than I at building relationships. So her adventures tend to last longer and have more space between them. But sex with other people is not the reason I am difficult to live with or why my marriage to her, like any marriage, has taken a lot of work."

"What is then?"

Callum laughed. "You're ambitious."

Jamie spluttered and tried to offer so many denials at once that absolutely nothing coherent came out.

"Shhhhhh, I was joking."

Jamie gave Callum a skeptical look.

"I'm the one who keeps asking you to stay," Callum pointed out.

"Yeah, about that, my driver's supposed to be by my flat in— " Jamie looked at his mobile. " — fourteen hours. Which means I either need to get out of here, make some awkward phone calls, or get up at the absolute crack of dawn."

"Whichever makes you happiest. But there's nothing inherently wrong with colleagues meeting for a coffee before work."

"Really?" Jamie somehow doubted his driver would fall for that.

"Breakfast?" Callum tried again.

Jamie didn't change his expression.

"Another quick tumble?" Callum grabbed for Jamie's waist as their laughter dissolved into another kiss, this time filled with intent.

Chapter 8

Callum has an uncomfortable conversation with his daughter

Ultimately, Jamie was the more sensible of the two of them. He went home, he said, to clear his head and not have to deal with the awkwardness of a walk of shame or a changed pickup location the following morning. Callum worried over it like a loose tooth while he tidied the flat. With Jamie here all weekend details like making the bed or ensuring dirty clothes went in the hamper had fallen by the wayside. Callum hoped he had given Jamie the answers he had demanded. But had he been too forward and effusive in doing so?

He was distracted from his fretting by his mobile ringing. It wasn't, to his brief disappointment, Jamie. It was Leigh, his and Nerea's eldest daughter.

"Hello, sweetheart," Callum answered. "Is everything all right?"

"You know," Leigh sounded amused but also slightly annoyed. "Just because I'm pregnant doesn't mean that everything is a crisis or about to be one."

"So that's a yes," Callum surmised. He gladly abandoned trying to make the bed by himself — he'd be going to sleep alone soon enough anyway — and sank down onto the couch.

"Yes," Leigh said decisively. "And you and Mum both need to stop assuming the worst is going to happen."

"It sounds like there's a story there," Callum said cautiously.

"You think?"

"What's going on?"

"Mum rang me up, out of the blue, and announced she's going to come stay with me and Sam. For some unspecified length of time."

"That's bad?"

"Dad." Leigh sounded exasperated. "Sam works. I work. Mum's already been calling me every day to check in on how we're doing, which is annoying enough. I don't think I can deal with having her in my house for that long. Sam definitely can't. I love her, but that would not end well."

"Her your mother or her your wife?"

"Yes."

"Wait," Callum said, sitting up a bit straighter as something else occurred to him. "Why is she staying at your house?"

"This is why I'm calling! What did you do to piss her off?"

"Nothing! That I know of." Callum was somewhat hurt. He had just talked to Nerea, and she'd mentioned nothing about coming to London. Why on earth would she come to town and stay anywhere but their own flat? He thought about calling her immediately, but supposed it was best to get the full story from Leigh first. Nerea was her own woman and had never hesitated to be clear with him in her own time.

"Can you come over to our place tomorrow? Just so we can strategize the best way to deal with this?"

"You want me to referee between our wives." Callum couldn't lie, even to himself. The prospect was daunting. But he did like to be involved in things.

"Between Mum and my butch wife who terrifies you, yes."

"She doesn't terrify me," Callum protested. Then he laughed. "God, you really are my daughter."

"Mhmm." Callum could hear the smirk in her voice. "And you love me, which is why you're going to do this for me."

"You're lucky you're my favorite."

"You say that to all of us."

"And it's all true. All right. When's a good time?"

"You tell me. When are you supposed to be done shooting tomorrow?"

Callum thought about Jamie and what had been his plans. He sighed. Juggling relationships and commitments was hard, and an evening with his daughter wasn't going to do wonders for his open invitation to Jamie. But Leigh had an absolutely reasonable claim on his time. Polyamory meant more than just managing multiple romantic relationships. Maybe Callum would hand Jamie his keys and see what beauty he came home to; he'd deserve the reward.

⁓

When Callum arrived at Sam and Leigh's snug row house in Chiswick, Sam was nowhere to be seen.

"Don't get too excited," Leigh said when she saw Callum glancing around. "She's just in her office finishing something up."

"Ah."

Leigh was tall like Callum and took after Callum's mother more than she did her own, with a nose and jawline she hadn't inherited from Nerea. She did have Nerea's coloring though: tawny skin and dark hair, cut to shoulder-length and streaked with highlights.

"I don't even get why Mum's doing this," Leigh said as she waved Callum into the kitchen. Callum trailed after her obediently. "Her being here will be useful in six months when I can't see my feet and later, when there's an infant, but now? No. Are you two fighting?"

"No, your mother's just smothering. But — " Callum had a sudden flash of realization. He couldn't believe it hadn't occurred to him before.

"But?" Leigh asked dubiously.

"But she might be coming to stay with you so she doesn't have to stay with me. I'm seeing someone."

"Oh, for Heaven's sake." Leigh rolled her eyes and marched over to the sink to fill the kettle. "Isn't there enough drama already?"

Callum shrugged and didn't bother to look sheepish. That sort of thing never worked on Leigh anyway.

"I know Mum's already talked to Tonio. Is this person coming to Devon's wedding too?"

"That's still pending." Callum hadn't thought that far ahead yet.

'Oh good," Leigh said, clearly meaning that there was nothing good about it at all.

Sam came downstairs just as the kettle started to boil. No matter what Leigh said, Callum was *not* terrified of his daughter-in-law. But Sam was five years older than Leigh, a difference that hardly mattered now that Leigh was thirty, but that had seemed unreasonable and daunting when Leigh had first brought her home. Also Sam was nearly as tall as Callum and, Callum was certain, completely able to take him in any and all fights.

Sam greeted him politely and kissed Leigh on the cheek.

Callum reminded himself that he was a grown man with a successful career and was her father-in-law. Still, he took a deep breath to steel himself.

"Leigh tells me you're having issues with Nerea," he said when they settled into the back garden with their tea to enjoy a fleeting bit of London sunshine.

Leigh and Sam exchanged looks. "You could say that," Sam said.

Callum was grateful that Leigh didn't mention the fact that his new fling was possibly the reason Nerea was coming to stay with them. So now, instead of defending himself, Callum could have a lovely chat about how excited Nerea was for the new baby, how being in Spain while two of her three children lived in London was always hard, and that he would, absolutely, have a word with her about expressing her affection from a proximity pleasing to all parties. Callum did not mention how sexist and appalling man-to-man chats about mother-in-law problems were, even when he was the only man involved in the conversation. Callum didn't think that battle was worth having, and, truth be told, he enjoyed being useful a little too much.

He was, however, beginning to worry. He had too many people to keep happy. He clearly needed to be wooing his own wife more than he was for her to skip over even discussing being in the same city as him. Jamie, meanwhile, was hopefully waiting for him in his flat. With this many things going on at once, it was only a matter of time before he bollocksed one of them up.

⁓

When he pushed open the door of his flat that evening, Callum immediately tripped over Jamie's shoes in the entry. He toed off his own, nudging both them and Jamie's out of the doorway. A lump in the bed stirred and mumbled when Callum dropped his bag on the floor.

He was going to ask Jamie how his evening had been, perhaps even inquire as to how the rest of his day at work had gone, since they'd hardly had a chance to speak to each other. But when he approached the bed, Jamie cracked open one bleary eye and lifted the blankets — not very high, but in distinct invitation. Callum almost tripped a second time as he hurried to get his clothes off and get to Jamie.

After they had sex Jamie fell asleep again quickly. Callum tried not to be disappointed; as delicious as the boy was, he would have enjoyed some conversation with him. But he knew his heart was heavy not because Jamie was tired, but because he and Nerea needed sorting. After a quarter of an hour of cuddling Callum climbed out of bed, pulled the blankets up over Jamie's shoulders, yanked on a pair of trousers, and slipped up the stairs and out onto the balcony.

He took a moment to savor the evening air, to feel secure in his place in the world and his worthiness in the hearts of those who professed to love him. And then he dialed Nerea's number knowing this might be one of those conversations where they both had apologies to make.

She answered the phone in Spanish and sounded distracted.

"Did I interrupt you?" Callum asked.

"No. No, I was thinking about putting dinner together. What do you need?"

"Need?" he asked, sitting down on one of the chairs they kept at the café table up here. "Can't I just say hello?"

"You can...." Nerea hesitated.

"But usually I want something," he admitted.

"You usually do."

"Leigh tells me you're coming to visit," he said carefully. He was hoping Nerea would volunteer whatever was going on. The more he thought about the situation, the more her decision to plan a trip to London without telling him felt like a snub. But he desperately did not want to be unreasonable about it.

"I was thinking about it, yes."

"And that you're going to stay with her and Sam."

"Yes?"

"Why aren't you coming to stay with me? In our flat?" Callum didn't think he'd done anything too egregious lately, but he had his suspicions that Nerea felt as hurt and confused as he did. Hopefully the whole matter was merely a miscommunication.

"I thought you'd want the space."

"Why?" Callum never wanted space. Especially from Nerea.

"Your new boy? The one who's so decent he insists on getting my blessing before he graces your bed?"

Callum wasn't sure if Nerea was trying to start a fight or not. Even after all these years he wasn't always good at telling when she was being direct and when she was being angry. "Jamie?"

"Do you have more than one boy at present?"

"No," he was annoyed at having to be defensive about it. So what if there were two boys?

"Good."

Callum scrubbed a hand over his face. "Nerea. What's going on?"

"I'm giving you space and time to spend with your new relationship. We've been married twenty-nine years, Callum, we don't need to spend every moment together." Her voice was condescending in a manner he had certainly deserved at the beginning of their relationship but probably didn't this many years in.

"No, we don't. But you always stay with me when you're in London." Callum frowned up at the sky, disappointed there were no stars easily seen from this part of London. "Is this about Antonio?"

"Why would this be about Antonio?" she snapped.

"Because not only was I bad at being present in our relationship at the time, I didn't give you the space you wanted or deserved with him once I finally got it together?"

"Are you accusing me of being spiteful by respecting your new relationship energy?"

"I sound crazy when you put it like that."

"That's because it's crazy. I feel like we are arguing, and I don't even know what we're arguing about!" Nerea's frustration was evident, and it did nothing to make Callum feel calmer.

"I don't know either!" If she was going to be snappish, he could meet her tone without trouble.

For a long moment they were both silent. Callum didn't like that they were rowing, but he appreciated their ability to be quiet together, keeping the line open even when things were wrong.

"So I'm gathering you don't want space," Nerea said eventually. There was a tinge of reluctance to her voice, embarrassment maybe at giving up the fight, but Callum was happy to match her in detente.

"No. Not at all," he said, not caring how pathetic he sounded.

"Are you done with Jamie already?" she asked cautiously.

"He's asleep in our bed right now. I'm up on the balcony," Callum admitted. It was good policy to be honest. "But I miss you, Nerea. We never get to spend enough time together. If you're going to come to London, stay with me."

"And Jamie?"

"Is someone with his own apartment." Callum may have been smitten, but he had to acknowledge Jamie was also someone with his own life to balance with whatever they were doing.

"That's not what I meant."

"I know." She was too good at getting Callum to say things he didn't feel ready to say yet. She always had been. "I like him enough I should probably figure out how to date him," he said softly.

"Really?" she asked.

"Really. And on top of the already long list of things I would like, I would like you to meet him. And not while you're hiding out at our daughter's house."

"This is serious then."

"Maybe. Maybe not. Also, you're driving Leigh mad."

Nerea, to his relief, laughed. "I suppose I should have expected that. It seemed like the perfect solution."

"Occasionally I come through with better ideas."

"*Very* occasionally."

"I do miss you," Callum said. "And love you. Rather desperately." Callum stood and leaned on the railing on the balcony though he hardly saw the traffic and bustle of London below; His thoughts were all with Nerea.

"And I you. I'm sorry I misread the situation."

"And I'm sorry we're both revisiting the fact than I was an arse about Antonio. Truly. But next time ask before you want to give me that much space, because I'll always say no."

"Callum."

"It's true."

"Point taken. How does my showing up in two weeks sound?"

"It sounds perfect."

"Done. Now, tell me about Jamie," Nerea said.

"I thought you were going to make food?"

"I can work and listen to you at the same time. And I like hearing about what makes you happy."

Callum could hear the smile in her voice. "Nerea, you'll laugh, but I swear, you're going to absolutely adore him."

Chapter 9

Nerea gets yet another surprise

"**D**ad mentioned you talked to Antonio?" Devon said as Nerea passed her a dish to dry.

"Was that a question or a statement?" Nerea asked. Devon's fiancé, Miguel was doing his level best not to be noticed as he busied himself carrying plates from table to sink to be washed. Nerea assumed he'd stop being intimidated by her eventually, but it didn't seem likely to happen soon. He'd only gotten more twitchy around her since he and Devon had gotten engaged. It reminded her of how Callum had behaved around her own mother, thirty years ago.

Devon sighed. "How's he doing?"

"Your father or Antonio?"

"Antonio. Dad is fine, because he was feeling apologetic about Antonio again. Which doesn't change the fact that he was a prick."

"Language," Nerea admonished gently because it was her maternal duty. Weddings were emotional events, and small wonder that this one was reopening old wounds for so many people. Devon had been the most attached to Tonio of all the girls when they'd been little. She'd resented Callum's absences

63

and his returns the most, and she blamed her father, then and later, for being the disruptive force that removed Tonio from their lives. Leigh had always been Callum's daughter and, like him, ready and eager to forgive any failure of attention or emotional outburst. Piper had been too young at the time to form any opinion.

"Antonio's well," Nerea went on. "He'd like to see you, I'm sure, before the wedding. If you have time."

Devon nodded shortly. "I know. We already have plans to meet for coffee next week."

"Then why did you ask how he was?" Nerea handed her another clean dish.

"It's been a while since he and I have really talked, making plans for coffee aside. And because I wanted to see if you and he were okay."

Nerea wasn't thrilled by all the back channel fretting going on over Tonio, but at least everyone was trying to be aware of the emotions involved.

Once cleanup was done, they moved on to wedding logistics. They spread planning materials over the kitchen table. Nerea doodled out ideas for the invitation design while Devon and Miguel debated the merits of having the reception in the church hall versus at the house.

Devon looked over at Nerea's sketches and took a deep breath. "I need to tell you something."

Nerea was forty percent sure the next words out of Devon's mouth were going to be *I'm pregnant.*

What she actually said was, "I'd like to change what people call me."

Nerea had no response prepared for that. "Say again?"

"Obviously the invitations need our full names," Devon waved a hand at Nerea's doodles. "But, Miguel calls me Margarita. His family calls me Margarita. I think I'd like for everyone to call me that from now on."

Nerea's eyebrows hit her hairline. "Even our family?"

"Yes. That's why I'm telling you this."

Miguel looked like he'd rather dissolve through the floor than be present for the rest of this conversation. Nerea tried to gather her thoughts. This was hardly anything dire, but the hesitance in her daughter's voice had made her uncomfortable. As she looked for more words, her mobile rang. She glanced at it: Callum and his eternally ridiculous timing. It could have felt ominous, but after their conversation the other night, him reaching out, for whatever reason, made her feel hopeful that he could bring a steady presence to this odd moment.

"Hello darling," she said as she picked up. "Guess what?"

"I couldn't possibly," Callum said after a moment's hesitation.

"Our daughter wants to change her name."

"Oh." A beat. "Which daughter?"

"Devon."

"She's getting married. Isn't that what married people do?"

"Not in Spain," Nerea reminded him, as if he could have forgotten. It had caused a scandal with his family upon their own marriage. Nerea had never particularly grown more fond of them for it. "But no, not her last name. Her first name," she clarified.

"Oh. Why?"

She pulled the mobile away from her ear and set it to speakerphone. "Tell your father why, Devon."

"I live a Spanish-speaking life, with a Spanish man, in Spain. It's not complicated." Devon spoke in slow, condescending English, half to Nerea, half to the mobile Nerea now set on the table between them. "And I'm not changing it. I'd just prefer if you called me Margarita from now on. It's part of my name anyway, it's not that big a deal."

"Are you changing your last name?" Callum asked, annoyed, in Spanish.

As Devon stuck to English, Nerea marveled at the capacity of both her husband and her daughter to use their bilingualism in a passive-aggressive battle of wills. "We don't do that here. You know that, and even if you didn't, Mother just reminded you."

Callum merely said, "Huh."

"Was there something you needed?" Nerea prodded.

"Ah, no, not particularly. But Jamie's asleep, and I thought maybe you and I could...*talk*?" The flirtation in his voice was all too clear.

Devon put her head in her hands and moaned. Miguel patted her on the shoulder. Nerea rolled her eyes at the two of them.

"Callum," Nerea said.

"Yes?" Callum sounded so hopeful it was absurd.

"You do know Devon — sorry, Margarita — and Miguel are still sitting right here and that you are still on speakerphone, don't you?"

"Yes?"

Nerea pushed herself up from the table with a laugh. "All right, I'm leaving the room and taking this call privately. And then you can tell me more about what you've done now. Efficiently. Because you're interrupting wedding planning."

"Efficient is no fun. And I didn't do anything," Callum protested. "I mean, other than Jamie."

Nerea laughed. "First things first," she said as she headed upstairs to their bedroom. "Are you calling because Leigh complained about me again, or because you want to gossip about your new toy, or because you are insatiable and want phone sex?" She marveled at how little changed after twenty-nine years of marriage and three children. The banter and the fun and the deep, underlying trust and affection had never wavered, practically since the moment they'd met, episodes like Tonio entirely aside. But then, neither she nor Callum were perfect. More importantly, neither of them expected the other to be.

Chapter 10

Jamie meets Nerea Espinosa de Los Monteros Nessim

"Can I talk to you about something?" Callum asked.

Callum's words were far too close to *we need to talk* for Jamie's comfort. But as he and Callum worked side-by-side in the kitchen at Callum's flat to prepare dinner, Jamie tried to remain calm. Callum was cooking, a simple pasta with pesto, and Jamie was making salad with lettuce he was now trying not to shred too violently.

"Of course," Jamie said as if he weren't half-sick with worry.

"Don't look nervous." Callum kissed his shoulder as he lifted the pot lid to check on the pasta. "It's about my wife."

"Oh?" Jamie wasn't sure how that was supposed to make him less nervous.

"She wants to meet you."

"Really? Why?" This was not where Jamie had expected the conversation to go. He wondered if this was better or worse.

"Because I'm dating you, and you're important to me, and you're lovely. I think she'd enjoy seeing you, and I'd like for you to know each other."

Hope and relief bubbled in Jamie's chest, but he had no idea what to say.

"That is, if you don't mind?" Callum asked. "Relationships like this are usually easier if all involved are at least acquaintances."

Jamie shook his head, probably a little too enthusiastically. "No, I don't mind. Not at all. I'd like to. It just didn't occur to me to ask." Of course, that wasn't entirely true. It had occurred to Jamie many times, but he hadn't thought it was his place to invade the privacy of Callum's marriage that way.

"Good then." Callum drained the pasta. Jamie went back to shredding lettuce, feeling as he had the last several weeks: Stunned, overwhelmed, and with no idea what his life had become.

⬥

Jamie spent the first week leading up to Nerea's arrival feeling like it was years away and the second in a state of rapidly intensifying anxiety. He was careful to hide that anxiety from Callum, lest the man think he was unable to navigate the reality of the situation. But the stakes were high, and Jamie felt overwhelmed. If he wanted to stay in Callum's life, he needed to land himself in Callum's wife's good graces. He just had no idea how to do that.

By the day of Nerea's arrival, Jamie had moved from anxiety to a state of near-panic. He was able to focus when he was working, but only barely. He was far too nervous to eat lunch. During breaks he hid in the makeup trailer and tried to entertain himself with games on his mobile but kept zoning out to think about Nerea's imminent arrival. What if she didn't like him? Would she think he was too young? Too awkward? Annoying rather than charming? Clingy?

He took deep breaths and tried to calm himself before he hyperventilated and passed out on the floor. That would be truly embarrassing. He trusted Callum; Callum had more experience navigating relationship issues like this; and Callum thought Jamie and Nerea should meet. He was, in point of fact, incredibly enthusiastic about it. Besides, Jamie had managed to get this part and make friends on set, so he knew he wasn't utterly devoid of personal appeal. If Nerea didn't like him that was something he and Callum would have to deal with together.

Still, for all his mental preparation, he wasn't ready when a production assistant showed up with a petite dark-haired woman who made Callum light up like a Christmas tree as he strode over to greet her. Even if Jamie hadn't recognized her from pictures, it would have been obvious this was Nerea.

In person she was even lovelier than in photographs. Her bearing was elegant, her long hair was swept up off her shoulders, and her eyes, a pale golden brown and with faint wrinkles at the corners, were bright as she took in her surroundings before her gaze returned to Callum. Jamie's heart did a strange thing when Callum dipped his head to kiss her. He wasn't sure how to interpret that feeling, but it didn't feel like jealousy. It felt like appreciation. And maybe even want. Jamie was still stuck staring when Callum waved him over.

"Jamie." Nerea smiled and held out her hand. Jamie was pretty sure he knew how Callum must have felt the first time he met her, because his own ability to make words, much less coherent sentences, was utterly gone. She was too beautiful, too self-possessed, too sparkling with charisma. And she'd only said his name.

Her eyes fixed on Jamie, warm and curious, as if she were collecting all of Jamie's secrets simply by looking at him. Jamie was overwhelmed with an almost visceral urge to touch her and a near certainty that he would crack like temperature-shocked glass if he did. He stammered a greeting and reached out to take her hand in his. He did not, to his surprise, break. Nerea's skin was cool and delicate but slightly rough. He felt a wild impulse to kiss it, like he was some fairy tale knight and she his queen. But he restricted himself to a smile that felt not at all polished or restrained. "Nice to meet you."

"And you." Nerea turned to Callum. "You're right, he is cuter in person."

Jamie made an involuntary noise of dismay.

Callum laughed. "Get used to it. She's not going to quit teasing you."

"Thanks?" The use of future tense was encouraging, but Jamie still felt off-balance.

Nerea looked from Jamie to Callum and back. "Did you want to have dinner Friday? The three of us?"

Jamie was surprised. He knew, from what Callum had said, that the three of them would likely spend time together socially. But while he was still getting used to the situation, Nerea had hit the ground running.

Jamie stammered. "That would be great," He wanted to kick himself. Now Callum's stunning wife probably thought her husband was screwing around with a very pretty fool. Maybe he needed to practice basic conversational skills in the mirror in desperate hopes of not completely messing up the dinner.

"Excellent." Nerea clapped her hands together. "I'm sure Callum will collect you after you're both done with work. But now I should be going. I have to spend an afternoon annoying my eldest daughter over tea. It was lovely to meet you, Jamie."

Before he had a chance to react, Nerea kissed him on the cheek, Callum on the lips, and was walking away, heels clicking smartly on the floor.

Jamie looked at Callum, dimly aware his mouth was hanging open.

"Don't worry," Callum said, his eyes fixed on his wife as she walked away. "I was at least as much of a mess around her for months."

⁊

That night Jamie went home alone; Callum, presumably, had gone home to his lovely wife. Jamie hadn't spent much time at his own flat in weeks and felt particularly lonely when he let himself in.

Despite the late hour, he considered calling friends to see who he could round up for a pint. Then he caught a glimpse of himself in his bathroom mirror; that was not going to work. Not with hickeys scattered across his throat. On set, makeup had the decency not to comment. But in real life his drama school friends would laugh, purr at him to share details, and give him no end of grief.

But sudden work and incipient fame had made having friends hard. There wasn't time to sit around pubs drinking and chatting anymore. Jamie felt terrible about it, but it wasn't something he knew how to make right. What could he even say about the state of his life now? That there was a guy and that they worked together? But his friends would demand names and details, which was definitely where things would get complicated. What was he supposed to do then? Explain that he was only out drinking with them because his unnamed lover's wife was in town? Would they believe him if he said she was okay with her husband shagging some random kid? And if they did, how was he supposed to avoid discussing her incredible hotness — especially when Callum and Nerea were probably in bed together *right now* having wildly attractive sex?

Jamie made a noise of annoyance at his empty apartment, this ridiculous situation, and his sexual frustration. He was either going to have to get a lot better at compartmentalizing or he was going to have to forgo all unnecessary human contact for a while. Otherwise he was definitely going to ask someone if it was rude to jerk off to thoughts of his lover in bed with his wife.

He grabbed a beer out of the cupboard and opened it. "Congratulations, Jamie," he said toasting his empty apartment. "Your life is a mess."

⏎

On the appointed day and time, Jamie and Callum arrived at the restaurant where they were due to meet Nerea. The place was dim, with little lighting beyond the candles burning softly on each table. The leather seats and dark wood walls contributed to the gloom and added the edge of sex.

Nerea was there already at the bar. When she saw them, she slid off her stool with an elegance Jamie hadn't known existed in real life. She wore a fitted gold dress and her dark hair fell in sleek waves down to the middle of her back.

"Callum. Jamie," she said when her husband bent his head to kiss her hello. Jamie looked away so as not to be caught staring. No matter how much advice Callum gave him, every moment seemed to generate a new situation in which he had no idea what was expected of him. He wondered why there wasn't a handbook for this sort of thing. Like *What to Do When You Like to Watch the Guy You're Sleeping with Kiss His Wife.*

As they took their seats at a table, Callum ordered a bottle of wine. Nerea caught Jamie's eye when the waiter returned to present it. Her expression spoke of long-suffering amusement at Callum's solemn enactment of the tasting ritual. Jamie could relate. Callum's insistence on the proper pairing of wine — even with takeout — was somewhat absurd, and now he looked like he was showing off. For who, it was a mystery. Nerea was hardly impressed, the waiter looked placid and bored, and Jamie was already as far gone on Callum as it was possible to be.

Jamie must have made a face, because Nerea started to laugh, bell-like and girlish. Before the waiter even left — and despite his best efforts and all good sense — Jamie joined her. Which only made everything funnier. Callum looked up at them quizzically; it was like being caught passing notes in school.

When the waiter had gone, Nerea leaned across the table to touch Jamie's hand. "I was terrified you didn't know my husband was ridiculous."

He shook his head. "Smitten, not stupid," he said before slapping his other hand over his mouth in chagrin. He was such a liar. He was smitten *and* stupid, even though he hated to use that word. "I didn't mean...."

"It's fine." Her eyes were wide and bright.

"I was trying to be so good," Jamie moaned. He glanced at Callum who was rolling the stem of his wineglass in his fingers.

Callum looked between them, a wrinkle of curiosity between his eyebrows. "Am I missing something?"

"We're bonding over how much we like you." Nerea gave him a flirtatious look over her shoulder. "You don't need to worry."

"He looks worried," Jamie said, wanting to recapture her attention.

"Should he be?" Her tone was suddenly crisp.

Nerea radiated confidence and perhaps even power. Although she still seemed entertained, Jamie was reminded yet again that he was outclassed in every way. Combined, Callum and Nerea had almost four times his life experience. Jamie, worried, glanced at Callum. Had Nerea's sudden sharpness meant he'd overstepped?

"Nerea," Callum said softly. Not a scold, but something else. A man trying to hold back a horse. Or a storm.

Nerea gave him a reproachful look, and he dipped his eyes apologetically. Jamie wondered how long a couple had to be together before they could communicate so thoroughly in silence.

"I only meant," Nerea spoke tartly as the smile crept back to her face, "that I am sure Jamie and I will have lots to gossip about as soon we can get a moment away from you."

Jamie flushed. "Oh my God." At least he wasn't in trouble.

"Try the wine," Callum said.

Jamie thought he was being rescued from Nerea's teasing. But Callum watched, his eyes fixed on Jamie's mouth, as he raised his glass to his lips and took a sip. If pressed to describe it, Jamie would have said the wine had notes of oak and blackberry. And then, because he was painfully aware of Callum's gaze, he would have gotten lost. Who cared what the wine tasted like when Callum was looking at him like that?

He set his glass back down.

"How do you like it?" Callum asked.

Jamie's cheeks burned. Nerea put her hand over his on the table again. Suddenly, the question felt like it was about far more than the bottle Callum had selected.

"It's good," Jamie gulped. "Not just the wine. All of this." He was desperately trying to be clear, but he didn't have a silent language with either of them yet, which meant he needed to use words as clumsy as they might be.

"I'm glad," Nerea said.

"Really?" Jamie squeaked. He coughed and reached for his water.

"Really?" Callum echoed in Nerea's direction.

"*Yes,*" Nerea said with a laugh. "Jamie, you've charmed me from the time you called me to ask if you could sleep with my husband. Not many people are that brave. Or that polite. I don't always give Callum credit for good taste, but he chose well with you. I'd like very much to get to know you better."

"Oh," Jamie said, awed.

Callum smiled warmly at Nerea and covered her small hand with his larger one. Then he leant over to drop a kiss onto her hair.

Jamie gathered his nerve. "Okay, can you explain something to me?"

"What's that?" Callum asked.

"How do you — how do you two…." he trailed off, hesitant. He took a deep breath. "How did you decide to do things this way?" He gestured to include the table and himself. "Actually," he added, before either of them could respond, "You probably don't want to talk about that with people around."

"I don't mind." Callum shrugged, but Nerea shook her head.

"Later is probably best. Thank you."

Jamie nodded. "Okay. Sure. Yeah." Frantically, he paged through his brain looking for a safe and appropriate topic of discussion. "Will you tell me how you met then? You must have been really young."

"Oh *well* done," Callum muttered.

Nerea shot him a glance Jamie didn't know how to interpret. "Younger than you," Nerea said. "I was, anyway. He was not."

"It's true." Callum spoke with obvious delight. "I'm absolutely terrible."

⁀

Jamie was having the best, strangest night of his life, which was saying something. His life had had a lot of peculiar and wonderful nights in the last year. But none of them had felt as easy, intimate, and kind as this. He rested his chin in his hand, rapt as Callum and Nerea finished tag-teaming the story of their meeting, courtship, and wedding. Callum at twenty-six had been a disaster of a human being, sleeping his way through the London theater scene and making sure everyone knew it. Nerea had been only nineteen. He'd needed less freedom, she said. But she'd needed a lot more.

"I saw her at a coffee shop," Callum said.

"You're kidding."

"Where else would I have met her? It was here, in London. She was in town for a student art show and I was going about the mess of my life. We were in the queue." Callum took another sip of wine. "I wanted to pay for her coffee. She said thank you, but no thank you. Then, just as I was ready to crawl into a hole and never show my face to the human race again, she told me that if I wanted to buy her a drink that night she would be most amenable."

"Really?" Jamie looked to Nerea for confirmation.

She nodded. "Really. You've seen him, Jamie. If a man like that asked you for something what would you say?"

"You're braver than me," Jamie admitted. He flushed a furious scarlet, barely able to believe he'd maneuvered himself into this moment at twenty-four. He couldn't imagine having had that type of self-assurance at nineteen.

Nerea picked up the story. "We went home together that same night. He was living in some horrible little flat in Camden Town, which was awful all the way around back then. But I didn't care. He was there, and that's what mattered. Even though I'd only met him hours ago."

*

Jamie eventually excused himself to the toilet for a few moments alone. As he washed his hands, he wondered how — and what — he was doing. Was he making a good impression? Did Nerea like him? Was he flirting with her? And if so, did he mean to be? For that matter, was she flirting with him? Jamie wasn't sure what he wanted to happen or what he might do to get it once he figured it out.

He got back to them just in time to hear Callum say to Nerea, "Invite him yourself."

"Invite me where?" Jamie hovered at the edge of the table.

Nerea tugged him into his seat. "Sit down. We can keep talking here. Or we can keep talking at our flat." Nerea's fingers — small, slender, and very warm — curled gently right at his pulse point. Jamie flicked his eyes over to Callum, hardly daring to believe he'd correctly interpreted the unspoken invitation in Nerea's voice.

Callum nodded at him in confirmation.

"That would be great. Okay, yeah. Day off tomorrow." He had been rendered incapable of speaking in complete sentences. He hoped Callum and Nerea wouldn't rescind the offer on the spot.

The cab ride to the flat was silent. Nerea sat in the middle. Jamie was acutely aware of her warmth, especially where their thighs were pressed together. At one point Callum shifted, Jamie assumed to put an arm around her shoulders, but Nerea leaned forward ever so slightly. Jamie felt Callum's hand warm on his back. Fingers slipped up under his jacket. Jamie wondered if it were possible to spontaneously combust from anticipation.

When they got out of the car in front of Callum and Nerea's building, Nerea frowned and stepped out of her high heels right in the middle of the sidewalk.

"You're so tiny," Jamie exclaimed. He hadn't realized how high her shoes had been. Or how nice it was to be around a woman who was shorter than him. At five foot eight, most of the actresses and models he worked with definitely weren't.

"I'm not climbing those stairs in these," she said like Jamie hadn't spoken, gesturing at Callum with the shoes. "This is still an annoying flat."

Callum laughed. "You love the flat."

"So do you," Nerea shot back. "Until you hit your head on the ceiling. Again,"

"The place seemed like a good idea when we got it."

It was obviously an old and fond argument. Jamie felt privileged to witness it. He stuffed his hands in his pockets, nervous all over again. Callum and Nerea had decades of physical and emotional intimacy between them. Was he a fool to think there was room for him at all, even for a night?

Jamie put his doubts aside when Callum gestured for him to follow his wife up the stairs. Nerea swung her hips more than was probably necessary, and Jamie watched her magnificent curves as she climbed the flight ahead of him, her shoes dangling from her hand. Below, Jamie heard the now-familiar sounds of Callum locking the front door behind him.

His footsteps were still somewhere down a flight when Jamie got to the top landing and was met by Nerea's smile and a beckoning crook of her finger. His mouth went dry; Callum was all very well and drop-dead gorgeous, but Jamie had never kissed someone as stunning and completely out of his league as Nerea before.

"Do you not want to?" Nerea asked quietly when Jamie hesitated. She wasn't being a tease. She, like Callum, genuinely wanted to know.

"No, no, I really, really want to," Jamie said, nodding with embarrassing amounts of enthusiasm. "I just...." How was he supposed to say that this was a very nice dream but he was afraid he would wake at any moment? Before he could get the words out, Nerea went up on her toes, slid her slender arms around Jamie's neck, and kissed him.

Jamie sighed into her mouth. He had forgotten how nice it was to hold onto someone smaller and softer than him. His arms went around Nerea's waist, and she didn't need the gentle press of his hand at the small of her back to step closer to him and deepen the kiss. Her mouth tasted like chocolate and the dessert wine Callum had insisted on ordering.

By the time Callum reached the landing, Nerea had her fingers in Jamie's hair. Jamie had turned them around so that she was pressed against the wall next to the door as he pulled at her lower lip with his teeth.

"Oi, inside," Callum said as he opened the door. He grabbed Jamie by the back of his jacket to push him through.

He staggered, caught off-balance, and gave Callum a doleful look at being interrupted.

Callum looked at Nerea as he shut and locked the door behind the three of them. "I get to say this so rarely, but you are a bad influence."

Nerea laughed as she walked Jamie backwards, deeper into the apartment. She tugged his collar open and then went to work undoing his shirt buttons.

Well, Jamie thought happily, *straight to the bed, then.*

Chapter 11

Callum realizes his wife and his boyfriend have hit it off really well

J amie rocked in to work on Monday with little more than a nod for Callum and faint shadows under his eyes. Callum could hardly blame him. After the weekend the three of them had enjoyed, he felt exhausted too and without the benefit of youthful recovery. Still, he wanted to check in with Jamie. He knew the hours alone after such a spectacular — and somewhat accidental — date could be difficult, especially on someone new to such adventures.

They didn't get a chance to talk until lunch. Callum slid in across from Jamie at a table in the studio's ancient cafeteria and smiled at him. The boy was twisting his napkin into bits; apparently Callum's concern was not entirely misplaced. Callum was determined to make sure Jamie was okay. And if he wasn't, figure out how to help him be okay.

"How are you?" he asked, trying not to feel as if he were back in school and having drama with any girl or boy who would let him.

"Not quite in a state to be honest in public?"

Callum frowned. That could mean a lot of things, from emotional distress to pleasurable distraction. "Not bad, I hope?"

Jamie shrugged. "Nah."

"You're a terrible liar," Callum observed mildly.

Jamie squinted up at him. "What makes you say that?"

Callum used the excuse of reaching out to take the poor, abused shreds of napkin out of Jamie's hands to finally touch him. He'd been aching to all morning. "Happy people don't destroy the napkins."

"Clearly you've never met my parents' dog. But I'm okay. I think."

In this moment Callum hated that they worked together because the deepest reassurance he knew how to give was physical. After all, he was an actor and often only adept with words when other people wrote them. Still, Jamie needed him to try. "Shall we have dinner this week? Just you and me? And then we can talk?" Callum asked. As wonderful as the weekend had been, he wanted to make sure he and Jamie got some time with each other without having to worry about anyone else.

Jamie's attempt to be brave collapsed. Callum kicked himself as he realized his likely error. Young and uncertain as he was, Jamie thought Nerea didn't care for him beyond this weekend's fun.

"Nerea thinks you're lovely," he said, voice clear and crisp and insistent. "And you should have dinner with the both of us again and soon. But while having her in town changes things with my schedule — and yours — I want to make sure I set time aside to spend with you on your own. If that's something you'd like."

Jamie's smile returned, albeit a bit sheepishly. "I would like that very much."

"Good," Callum said, relieved he'd made Jamie relax and delighted he'd made him happy.

Until Jamie said "Fuck!" and buried his face in his hands.

Callum was alarmed. Had he done something wrong, overlooked something particular that would upset the boy? It wasn't out of the realm of possibility, but he'd been working hard to handle this affair right. "What is it, darling?" he asked.

Jamie peeped out at Callum from between his fingers at the pet name. Which Callum possibly shouldn't have used at work, but the young man was so dear it was impossible to keep himself in check.

Jamie removed his hands from his face. "If we get together — assuming Nerea's going to want your flat to herself — you'll have to come over to my place."

"And?"

"And," Jamie admitted, the tips of his ears flushing red, "my place is kind of a pit."

⁀

Callum spent the rest of the afternoon watching Jamie closely. Jamie was engaged in the work whenever he was actively doing it, but between shots Callum caught the boy worrying his bottom lip between his teeth more than once. That was a new habit and suggested he was working up courage for something. Whatever it was, Callum suspected it was better than his earlier fretting, but beyond that, he had no idea.

Jamie eventually cornered Callum at crafty.

"Can I ask you something?"

"Of course," Callum said, trying to project affection just in case this was another round of insecurity. But Jamie didn't look upset the way he had at lunch, and Callum hoped he would stay that way.

"I'm getting wrapped early today."

"Now you can go home and clean," Callum teased. He hoped Jamie would go home and sleep. Eight hours a night was a rare commodity when working on a film, no matter the schedule the union theoretically promised. And, though the three of them had spent all weekend in bed, very little of that time had been spent asleep.

"Would you mind if I went to hang out with Nerea?" Jamie blurted.

"You can do whatever you'd like." Callum tried to hide his surprise. "So can Nerea." He didn't quite know what Jamie was up to but was curious to find out.

"I don't have her phone number."

Callum cackled and fished his mobile out of his pocket. Quickly, he thumbed a message to her. *The very brave boyfriend I shared with you would like me to share your phone number with him.*

The reply came almost immediately. *You're both ridiculous.*

Is that a yes? Callum keyed as Jamie shifted his weight from side to side.

Yes, of course. Tell him I eagerly await his call.

Callum smiled to himself. He could hear her every word and knew she was likely as mystified by this request as he was. He hit a few more buttons and Jamie's mobile chimed.

"Go have fun," Callum said. "I'll text one of you when I get out."

⁓

Shortly after eight, Callum unlocked the door to his flat quietly, in case Nerea and Jamie were asleep after whatever they'd gotten up to. But while the lights were on, no one was immediately apparent. The bed was made as neatly as Nerea always kept it. Callum frowned and looked toward the bathroom, but the lights were off and there was no sound of water. Apparently they weren't indulging themselves with the only decent water pressure in London, either.

"You are both being very confusing," he muttered as he set down his bag. Then he heard Nerea's laughter from the passageway to the roof.

Callum went up the first few steps that led to their balcony and stopped once he could see them through the open door. They were dressed for the warm summer evening, Jamie in a T-shirt and shorts and Nerea in a pale blue sundress. It was one of Callum's favorites that she'd bought years ago in Madrid. Both of them were laughing, easy and carefree. A bottle of wine, mostly empty, on the table between them may have accounted for some of that, but not all of it.

Callum loitered in the doorway, enjoying their happiness from afar until Jamie turned his head and noticed him. His face split into a grin that made Callum want to kiss his dimples. Nerea turned her head too. She smiled with a deep contentment when he stepped through the door and out onto the balcony.

He kissed them both hello, then scraped a third chair up to the wrought-iron table. "Not what I expected to come home to."

"Callum thought we'd be fucking," Nerea clarified, popping her consonants.

"We didn't," Jamie said.

"You could have," Callum told him.

Jamie and Nerea sighed in almost perfect synchronicity.

"I know that," Jamie said. "But I wanted to have a conversation with someone I don't work with and who isn't as young and inexperienced as me."

"And you chose my wife?" Callum chuckled. Nerea was hardly an innocent bystander to the current state of Jamie's life.

"It was your wife or my landlord."

"We've had a very nice afternoon. And evening," Nerea said. "And if I don't eat something soon, I am going to die." She clutched at her stomach theatrically.

"You could have eaten," Callum pointed out as mildly as he had suggested just a moment ago that they could have gone to bed without him.

"Yes, but we wanted to get drunk instead." She reached out and caught Callum's hand in her own. "Now take us to dinner."

Chapter 12

Nerea, as usual, is excessively good at communication

Lying in bed on a late Saturday morning in London, Nerea listened to Jamie and Callum making breakfast while arguing about a recent review in the *Times Literary Supplement*. Which was when Nerea realized that Callum was into Jamie despite his age, not because of it.

The thought had been creeping up on her the more she spent time with Jamie and the more she spent time with him and Callum together. To be sure, it had only been two weeks, but it had been steady and inexorable. That morning, watching Callum give Jamie a heart-melting smile and a kiss before admonishing him to watch the eggs, she was sure.

She waited — through a day of markets and strolling, a late evening trip to a film that featured absolutely no one they knew, and another glorious night in bed — until Jamie went home on Sunday afternoon to ask Callum about it.

"It's easy with Jamie, isn't it?" She tried to be as casual as she could, though Callum wouldn't be fooled.

"Too easy," he said glumly as they stripped the bed. Sunday was laundry day. Just because they could hire someone to come in to clean didn't mean they wanted that sort of intrusion.

"Why is that a bad thing?" Nerea asked.

"Because things that are easy now tend to lead to decisions that are hard later."

Nerea gave her husband a wary look.

"What?" he said. "I'm not the complete fool I used to be."

"I just hope that's about your choices and not mine." She shook a pillow out of its case before tossing the ecru fabric into the hamper.

"I'm not having a go at you about Antonio, if that's what you're implying."

"Just checking," she said sweetly, starting on another pillow.

"No. It's definitely about mine. I just know where this is likely to end."

"Where's that?"

"With me being sad, Jamie being heartbroken, and you being exasperated with both of us but especially me. Because I have a track record of being unkind when you're seriously involved with someone who's not me, and Jamie at some point will surely want a normal life and a normal relationship."

"We are normal." Nerea hated when Callum said otherwise. Just because other people didn't handle their marriages as they did was no reason to accept their judgments. "We're married, we have three beautiful children. A grandchild soon."

"Those aren't things Jamie can have with us. Not in the same way."

"Maybe he'll have a primary or nesting relationship with someone else. It doesn't have to end because it might get complicated or sometimes make us sad. And Callum, I am not keeping score. You're allowed to ask for comfort in a possible future even if you've been poor at providing it in the past."

"No one likes being sad. And not everyone always wants to do the work."

Nerea could have argued, but there wasn't much point. She pulled fresh sheets out of the catchall closet while Callum went to put the contents of the hamper in the washer. While he was crouched on the floor squinting for the millionth time at the instructions Nerea had written out and taped to the front of the machine, he said, almost to himself, "It was easier when I thought he was only a midlife crisis."

"You never seriously believed that," Nerea scoffed. "You've too much ego to admit to such a thing."

Callum laughed softly. Finally having gotten the settings on the washer correct, he pressed start with satisfaction.

"Fair. But denial is nice."

"And now?"

"And now I'm in love with a twenty-four-year-old I met while working on a romantic comedy."

Nerea stopped in the middle of shaking out the pale grey bottom sheet. It settled slowly into soft hills and valleys on the bed, except for the edge she still held in her hands. She felt light-headed. She'd been essentially polyamorous since she'd started having relationships as a teenager, but hearing such a thing still came with a frisson of fear. Not at the possibility she could lose Callum — they'd been together too long and through too much for that to concern her — but at the reality that love was complicated. Every relationship in a life, whether about romance or not, impacted every other. She reminded herself to breathe.

"Shit," Callum said to the laundry machine.

"Did you just realize that?" Nerea asked, after a long moment.

"You know, I don't even know." Callum levered himself slowly to his feet. The pipes gurgled as water ran to the machine. "It felt— "

"Easy?" Nerea finished for him, echoing the word that had gotten them into the conversation in the first place.

Callum nodded. And then he turned his big, sad-looking eyes to Nerea. "Is that all right?"

"Oh, for Heaven's sake," Nerea started smoothing out the sheet on the bed and tucking it around a corner of the mattress. "Don't ask foolish questions like that about things we agreed to years ago."

"In my defense," Callum said, stepping back into their bed-nook and helping tug the sheets down on the other side. "We never agreed to quite this situation."

"And what situation is that? Other than the obvious."

Callum spoke cautiously. "I think you're in love with him too."

For the second time in five minutes, Nerea stopped moving to stare at Callum.

Callum still looked a little wild about the eyes. "See? Terrifying, isn't it."

"I haven't even said yes! It's only been two weeks!"

"It took you a day to fall for me."

"Yes, your massive ego aside." Nerea found it easier to tease Callum than to talk about those moments of recognition she had experienced when he had first spoken to her in that café and first taken her to his bed.

Callum grinned at her, knowing the game, knowing, she was sure, everything she didn't say. "I know you. And he's very good with you."

She made an irritated sound. "Have the decency to let me say it."

"All right then." Callum's grin turned into a smirk. "Are you in love with Jamie?"

"Maybe," she said before correcting herself. "Probably." Jamie wasn't anything like Callum, but he was curious and kind and could keep up with her without fear. So few people had that ability. She had no idea how anyone could spend an afternoon with Jamie and not fall in love with him. "Fine. Yes!" Nerea threw a pillow at him. "Now, what are we going to do about him?"

Callum gave a vague shrug.

Nerea decided now was not the time to criticize his frequently laissez-faire attitude towards logistics.

"I want to keep being in a relationship with him. And I want to keep being in a relationship with you *and* him, if you both continue to want that," he finally said.

"Even after you're done with the movie?"

"Very much so. I imagine it'll be a lot more fun when we've both had some sleep."

"You and I live in different cities half the year, not to mention countries. And how does he see his future?" It was one thing to talk about what they wanted, but it didn't mean anything without knowing what Jamie wanted.

"I know," Callum agreed. "It's complicated."

"Yes, so what would we do about that? The logistics at least? If he were on board?"

"I don't know," Callum admitted. "It's not a problem yet, but when it is, it's probably going to take both of us to figure it out."

A week later, Callum came home from work with Jamie, takeout, and a frown.

"What is it?" Nerea asked, helping to unpack the food while Jamie excused himself to the toilet, looking subdued himself. Had they fought? Had something gone wrong at work?

"Nothing. Everything's fine," Callum said. "I got the press tour schedule for *Diminished Fifth*."

"I still don't like that title," Nerea noted. It was easier than mentioning how much she hated the way Callum's films never stopped throwing wrenches into their lives. Filming was hard. Sometimes the media follow-up was worse.

"It's a psychological thriller about a serial killer. It's supposed to be unsettling."

"You and your desire to play the villain for once," Nerea teased. But now she understood Callum's moodiness, and Jamie's. Press tours — and the long weeks of intense travel and separation they entailed — were Callum's least favorite parts of the business. As much as he loved travel, meeting people, and playing with interviewers, Nerea knew that weeks on end of that, without her by his side, took their toll.

"When is it?" she asked when her husband stopped unpacking containers and wrapped his arms around her from behind. He rested his chin on her shoulder.

"August."

"So soon?"

Callum hummed. "Middle of August to the middle of September. Almost an entire month."

Nerea stopped working and pressed her hands over Callum's; that was too long. "What do you want to do right now?"

"I want to eat dinner with you and Jamie and then go to bed, also with you and Jamie."

"You're tired?"

Nerea felt the puff of Callum's breath on the back of her neck when he chuckled softly. "No. Not to sleep."

⁊

Jamie wrapped his work on *Butterflies* before Callum did. On his last day he went out with some of the crew to celebrate. So that night Nerea and Callum made dinner together and carried it up to the roof to eat — and talk. About their marriage, about their children, about their lives, and about their future.

Nerea, as was often the case, found herself leading the way, but Callum was attentive and eager, always wanting to do the best for everyone, even if he was, at times, too clumsy for everyone's hearts. They stayed up far too late in the warm summer night, Nerea eventually sitting on her husband's lap as they shared a bottle of wine and discussed their plans from small to large and easy to hard.

At noon the next day Jamie turned up at their flat looking a bit hungover and like he didn't quite know what to do with himself. He hadn't bothered to call or text to say he was coming over, which didn't strike Nerea as best practices. Yet, to her surprise, she didn't resent the intrusion. And Callum, as usual, was too thrilled to be in the presence of affection to really worry about protocol.

The three of them ventured out to dinner at a local place a few blocks away. Sex and an afternoon nap had been a restorative, and Jamie seemed happy to be outside on a gorgeous night and not either trapped on set or desperately trying to catch up on sleep. He walked backward most of the way to the restaurant for no reason Nerea could fathom unless it was that he wanted to look at them both as they talked. Which was adorable, but slightly dangerous. More than once Callum had to put out a hand to grab Jamie before he backed into a post box or a tree.

The restaurant was little more than a neighborhood pub. Small and not at all crowded, it hadn't changed much in the years Nerea and Callum had lived nearby. A German shepherd, curled under a table, gave a friendly wag of its tail as they walked past.

"I still can't believe you go to places like this." Jamie slid into a booth across from them.

"I like a good dive as much as you boys," Nerea said with a smile, "Also, Jamie, you're dressed like a slob."

Jamie looked down at his sweatpants and T-shirt. "Yeah, okay, that's fair."

For a quarter of an hour, they worked their way through greasy pub fare and argued the merits of their various beer selections. But as pleasant as that chatter was, change was upon them. Nerea knew it needed to be acknowledged. She turned to Jamie.

"What are your plans now you're done with the film?" It wasn't an elegant question, but Nerea wasn't sure there was ever a delicate way to inquire as to a lover's potentially disruptive plans.

"Sleep for a week. Then I'm going back to Dublin to visit my parents and sisters for a bit. After that, I'm not sure. It's hard to think that far ahead. Call my agent? See what's next?"

"And your plans for us?" Callum put in.

Nerea nudged Callum's foot under the table. Just because they'd planned this conversation didn't mean they had to let Jamie know. Or conduct it in public.

"I don't know." Jamie looked between the two of them, his earlier ebullience fading. "I mean, I've thought about it, and I know you asked the question. But I don't see how I can give you any meaningful answer here?"

"I think that's fine," Nerea said, so glad that Jamie understood both the conversation that needed to happen and that it probably shouldn't happen here. Callum popped another chip in his mouth. Nerea relaxed as their talk slowly drifted back to the day-to-day mundanities with which it had begun.

They strolled back to the flat slowly through a mild evening humming with the chirp of insects. Nerea had done this walk with her husband hundreds of times over the years. Prime ministers had come and gone, fashions had changed, their daughters had been born and grown, and yet London and their love remained. Jamie by their side was just one more version of the life they had always been living.

Callum reached for Nerea's hand; Nerea reached back for him instinctively. She was fairly certain Callum didn't see the wistful look Jamie gave their twined fingers. She also suspected her husband didn't hear the young man's silence the way she did. In fact, Jamie was quiet the whole walk back to the flat. When they reached the sidewalk outside he hesitated, then seemed to make a decision.

"Tonight was fun," he said, taking a step back despite his words in the restaurant. "But I should probably get home."

Nerea could see that Jamie's pulling away was more than physical and it tugged at her with the hint of pain to come.

Callum must have felt it too, because before she could speak, he did.

"I think you should probably come upstairs with us."

"But you and Nerea — "

Callum took a step toward the boy and wrapped an arm around Jamie's tense shoulders to steer him through the doorway. "We would like to have a conversation with you."

"Are you sure?" Jamie asked. "I do want to, but you probably want time together, and I don't want to make trouble or be a bother for you." He was babbling now. Nerea's heart ached for him.

"We're sure," Callum answered for both of them. "Now come in because if we didn't want to discuss this in a pub we definitely don't want to on the street."

Upstairs, Nerea stepped into the bathroom to change out of her dress and into lounge clothes, not because she needed privacy but because she wanted to give Jamie and Callum space alone for a few minutes. They had been together first, and it was only courteous. When she emerged back into the main living space, her comb in her hand and her hair loose around her shoulders, it was obvious no talking had been done at all. Callum sat at one corner of the sofa, knees crossed defensively and his fingers tight on the arm. Jamie was curled up in the recliner in the opposite corner. Nerea sat down on the ottoman in front of Jamie's chair and started to work on her hair.

"Is everything all right?" she asked the room at large. "Callum?" she pressed, when her husband and Jamie exchanged brief glances and then looked away from each other.

Jamie spoke first. "I have a question." He rearranged himself in the recliner, but looked no more comfortable for the effort.

Callum gestured for him to keep talking.

"I'm done with this movie. Nerea, you're going back to Spain eventually. Callum's going to embark on whatever press he has for his creepy serial killer movie. All of which is fine, except that no one is talking about it except to ask me what I'm doing next. I don't know how to answer that when I don't know why you're asking. Polite curiosity or planning? I don't know where I fit — assuming I fit at all — for more than a shag here and there while we're all still in town. Also the thing where you ask me questions in public about things we can't talk about in public is annoying and yet you keep doing it."

Callum nodded thoughtfully. "That's why we asked you to come up here," he said.

"To shag while we've all still got the time?"

Nerea laughed at that even as she digested Jamie's reasonable criticisms. The boy shot her a conspiratorial grin which gave her hope for this conversation resolving with them all more happy than not.

"No," Callum said. "To talk."

Jamie looked nervous. "But is this a 'we need to talk' talk?"

"Well, don't we?"

Nerea made a noise of disgust. Men were awful. These men in particular, right at this moment. No wonder they were both so tense. They both thought they were about to get dumped. Not that it wasn't tempting.

"What?" Callum asked her, hands out and voice sharp.

Nerea sighed. She was going to have to explain this slowly. "You have the longest relationship with me. And the longest relationship with Jamie. And you're giving him a hard time and putting us in the position of me or him doing all the work."

"Ohhh." Callum had the good grace to look abashed.

"I am rapidly feeling even more incompetent than I am," Jamie said. "I know you two have your very real, solid relationship. And I know I'm ridiculously young and get into everything way too fast. Meanwhile, Callum, I *know* you probably have a habit of shagging your costars — "

"That's the most generous 'probably' anyone's ever given me."

"I'm not expecting to be special or an exception or anything like that. But I need you to tell me how much I get so I can figure out if I can stand to lose it."

Callum shot Nerea a look that was half frantic, half helpless. Nerea resisted the urge to roll her eyes. She and Callum had talked about all of this already. They had a plan. But, somehow, as always, it was up to her to be the adult in the room.

"Do you understand we're talking about three relationships here and not one?" Nerea asked Jamie gently.

Jamie blinked. So that was a no. Which wasn't surprising, but still needed to be addressed.

"You and Callum. You and me. And the three of us. Leaving Callum and I out of this, since I think he and I know where we stand with each other. Plus, we've been married longer than you've been alive."

Jamie blinked some more. Apparently he'd been avoiding that math.

"I should have thought of that," he said. "I've never done this before."

"We know. Which of those do you want to talk about first?" Nerea was a little annoyed she was still doing the work. But Callum was fidgeting with the strap of his watch and looking terrified. Foolish, silly man. Nerea adored him far too much for her or anyone else's good.

Jamie stared at Nerea with a look of mild panic.

"There's no wrong answer," she said.

"Me and Callum, I guess."

"That's fine. Do you want me to go or stay and listen?"

Callum shrugged. Adorable, occasionally useless man. She hoped he would rise to tonight's occasion before she ran out of fondly exasperated adjectives.

"Stay?" Jamie asked, half reaching for her. Then he pulled his hand back. "I mean, I assume we're both going to talk this out with you afterward anyway. Might as well save you the pain of hearing us both retell it."

"Efficient." Nerea smiled. Thank goodness one of them was. "Good."

Jamie shifted in his recliner so he could face Callum fully. "Am I a fool for wanting to date you?"

"Probably." Callum scrubbed a hand over his face. "I don't know how Nerea puts up with me." He shot her a self-deprecating look, but Nerea jerked her head toward Jamie. They needed to speak to each other, not her.

"That's not what I meant," Jamie said.

"No." Callum shook his head. "You're not a fool for that."

"So what's the end game?" Jamie insisted.

"We've been doing this for three months. Why do you need to know the end game?"

"This started as a film fling," Jamie said keenly. "Does it end now that our movie is over?"

"It hasn't yet."

"Not that I have any plans right now, but what if I start seeing someone else?" Jamie asked.

"We have a conversation about it," Callum said. "You make selections from the choices available to you."

Nerea smiled, but didn't say anything. She didn't need to. Her men were finally starting to get to the crux of the issue. They might even have stopped assuming the worst.

"What do you see in me?" Jamie asked reasonably. Not that youth wasn't appealing, but Nerea knew it was easy to take advantage of with only the most casual of interest.

Callum groaned. "I know you're young, but I can't do low self-esteem theater."

Jamie rocked back at that. Nerea willed Callum to get himself together.

"I'm not always nice," Callum said. "You need to know that."

"And I wasn't having low self-esteem," Jamie shot back.

"Then what were you doing?"

"Wondering if I'm your midlife crisis, *Gramps*, because that's a crap basis for a relationship."

Nerea had to cover her smile. Maybe, just maybe, she needed to stop worrying about Jamie so much. He could give as good as he got.

Callum seemed to realize it too as he leaned his chin in his hand and stared at Jamie. "You're amazing," he said. "And very brave."

"And you're not actually scary. I'm just here wanting something. No bravery required."

Not for the first time, Nerea found herself admiring Jamie's courage.

"To answer your question," Callum said, "I don't know if you're a midlife crisis. I haven't had one before and can't be sure I'm not now."

"What about the post-filming breakup scenario?" Jamie asked.

"It's post-filming now," he reminded Jamie. "For you at least. I don't think we're having this conversation to break up. It's logistics. We won't, as you note, always be working on the same films. We won't always be in the same country. As soon as either of us starts another project, this isn't going to be easy."

"You and Nerea do all right."

"We do," Callum admitted. "We also have practice."

"Do you think we could practice, then?" Jamie asked. "Make it work, you and me, long-term?"

He was so hopeful. Nerea wondered if that would be an asset or a hindrance when things got truly hard.

"Of course it could work," Callum said. "But we can't foresee all the ways it might not. It's too early, lovely as you truly are. So you should consider if you want to wait and see. I'd completely understand if you didn't. It's surely the smarter choice. But you and I hardly wound up in this beautiful mess by making the smartest choices."

"Wait, wait, wait." Jamie leaned forward in his seat, almost going up on his knees in his excitement. "You think I want out?"

Finally one of them had figured out what was going on. Nerea was triumphant.

"I had wondered," Callum said. "After all, you're the one discussing return on investment. You might decide to cut your losses sooner rather than later."

"Because I'm twenty-four?"

Callum nodded. "Trust me. One day you'll be stunned by how much you don't know about yourself right now. It's all right. It happens to all of us."

Jamie shook his head with fond exasperation.

Callum smiled softly. "Then come here," he said and patted the sofa next to him. Nerea pulled her legs up out of the way as Jamie brushed past her. As quick as he could, Callum wrapped an arm around Jamie's shoulders and the young man immediately snuggled into his side. Nerea was content to be forgotten for the moment. Callum and Jamie wrapped up in each other gave her a moment to breathe, count to ten, and not be smug about the absurdity of their communication difficulties.

Eventually Callum kissed the top of Jamie's head and then turned his eyes, warm and soft in the lamplight, toward Nerea with a questioning look. He was telling her the ball was in her court now, if she wanted it.

"What do you two still need to talk about, and what do you need to talk about with me?" she asked softly.

"I think we're okay? For now?" Jamie said, twisting to look up at Callum.

Callum nodded. "Should I leave while you have a conversation with my wife?"

"You use possessives a lot," Jamie pointed out. "Did you know that?"

"Look at her," Callum said. "Wouldn't you?"

"Smooth and inappropriate," Nerea said. She could say people didn't belong to other people constantly and mean it; they didn't belong to their partners or parents or jobs or children. But she was still a woman who lived in this world and understood that possession was, for many people, an idea that could occasionally be appealing. With those she trusted, she was even willing to indulge it. Certainly there was a pride she took in being Callum's wife. She only struggled when other people decided it was the most important thing about her.

"You should stay," Jamie said to Callum. "If Nerea doesn't mind?"

Nerea shook her head. "No, not at all. Now." She put both feet back on the floor and leaned forward, her elbows on her thighs. "I'm more efficient than Callum, so I'll keep this short. As you said, I am going back to Spain. I'll be there until my Tate show in November. Since Callum's going to be gone and I'll be left with an empty house...." She let the implication of her offer hang in the air and watched, pleased, as Jamie's face seemed to glow with cautious joy. "So, if you want, and if your schedule allows, I would be delighted if you came and stayed with me in Spain."

"Seriously?" Jamie twisted around to look at Callum and then at her.

"I'm not that sort of tease." Nerea said. Jamie was going to have to learn to take her and Callum at face value, at least during serious relationship conversations.

"And it's okay with you?" he asked Callum.

"I can hardly take you on my press tour. Plus we'll get our own for *Butterflies*. You two should enjoy time together while the opportunity is available."

"Yes," Jamie said instantly, turning back to Nerea. "I mean, I should triple check my calendar, but — yes."

"Good," she said. Jamie may have been cautious and uncertain, but Nerea was still amazed at how quickly he could accept and adapt to new opportunities. How strange his life must be. Of course, her life had once been quite strange too. Like her at nineteen, Jamie at twenty-four seemed absolutely determined to make the most of it. They were fellow travelers, and her heart sang with it.

She stood and brushed her hands together, pleased with all that they had achieved in a difficult relationship meeting. "Then we have a plan," she said. "Now shall we go to bed?"

Chapter 13

Jamie talks to his family, but leaves out some key details

On a warm, sunny afternoon Jamie flew back to Ireland. His dad met him at arrivals. While the motion of the car and the familiar drive to the house lulled Jamie, he felt far less exhausted than when he'd come home to vote. But as he watched the familiar streets roll by, the entire past year of his life — the movie, Callum, Nerea, Callum *and* Nerea — felt like a dream. Jamie was going to miss them both while he was in Dublin, but they had already scheduled a date for the three of them for when he returned to London in two weeks. Soon after that he'd be in Spain.

In the meantime, Jamie had family to enjoy. Aoife would be at work for a few more hours, but his mum was home, and his sister Beth was over with Grace and Anne. Vegetables, of course, was in the thick of it, jumping all over Jamie and whining to be played with.

When Aoife got home she filled Jamie in on all the gossip of the family and neighborhood. Among their extended cousins there'd been two engagements plus a baby he hadn't heard about; he'd been bad at returning his mother's calls.

"How's your boyfriend?" Jamie teased, drawing out the word as he grabbed a dish towel out of a drawer. The question always made her stammer and blush, which was why he always asked it. What were brothers for if not to torment sisters about their love lives? But this time, Aoife tossed her head defiantly and said, "Good. Our three-year anniversary is next month."

"Wait, seriously? You've been together that long?"

"Yes seriously. Not like I can't."

"Didn't say you couldn't."

"No. Not you," she said quietly.

Jamie thought there was a story there that he'd have to prise out of her later. No one was going to stop Aoife from having anything she wanted, as far as he was concerned. "If you've been together that long, this is getting serious. I should probably have a talk with him about his intentions, mm?"

Aoife narrowed her eyes at him. "Are you going to scare him?"

"Maybe. A little. I should set a good precedent."

"Just because I'm the only sister you're older than, doesn't mean you get to scare my boyfriends."

Jamie grinned. "I disagree."

"What's your love life like?"

Aoife had turned the tables on him. Jamie hadn't prepared for this moment and didn't know what to say, but he was glad to be asked. "I'm seeing someone too. Although we've only been together a few months." Jamie knew he sounded smug but didn't care one bit.

"Who's that?" his mother asked, coming into the kitchen. "You didn't mention a girlfriend."

"It's — ahh — not exactly a girlfriend." Jamie had spent a lot of time deliberately not worrying about explaining the current state of his relationships to his mother and now here he was, halfway in without a rubber.

"Boyfriend, whatever. You still didn't mention him."

"It's new." Jamie said quickly. "And kind of complicated?"

"Please don't tell me you're dating someone from work," Maureen said.

"Aoife met her boyfriend at work!" Jamie protested. Patrick and Aoife worked at the same bakery.

"Yes, and she has better judgment than you, Jamie-boy. She also doesn't work in the movies. I worry about you. You're a good boy, but all you have to do is one foolish thing and then your face will be in every paper."

"Mum," Jamie rolled his eyes. "You worry too much."

"You don't worry enough. And you're leaving spots on my nice glasses."

"Can I meet your boyfriend?" Aoife asked Jamie.

"Yeah, I'm not subjecting him to this family," Jamie grumbled. Frankly, he couldn't imagine Callum and Nerea meeting his family. His parents would probably hit the roof. Even aside from the polyamory it would be odd. Nerea was younger than his mother; Callum was the same age, give or take a year, as his father. And that was a thing Jamie was much happier not thinking about, now or ever.

He was relieved when his mother changed the subject to ask him what his plans were for the fall.

"I've, er, been invited. To go to Spain."

"What's in Spain?"

"The person I'm dating." Sort of. But *I'm going to Spain to visit Callum Griffith-Davies's wife while he goes on press tour* was not something he could say to his mother. Possibly ever. Which was strange. Both of his sisters were married, Aoife was in a serious relationship, and here was Jamie, dating two people and unable to tell his parents about any of it. It felt dishonest, which was bad enough. Worse was not being able to share something so important to him.

⤳

With no work to do except the chores his mother gave him around the house, and hardly anyone to socialize with besides his family, Jamie spent a few days luxuriating in relative idleness before becoming profoundly bored. He spent most of his time puttering around the house and thinking about Callum and Nerea. About what they were doing now that Callum was nearly done with filming, too. About what it would be like to be in Spain with just Nerea, and about how that would impact his own relationship with her — and with Callum.

He talked to them nearly every day: Sometimes a quick call on the phone while he was out walking Vegetables, but more often, texts exchanged while he lazed around the house or ran errands for his mum. He wanted to ask them all of those questions and more, but he resisted. Leaning on Callum and Nerea's experience and wisdom was all well and good; they were an excellent resource for him to learn from and always had time for any of his questions. But he was also learning on his own. Like how to let go and let events unfold as they would. Emotions weren't, he was realizing, controllable or predictable, regardless of relationship style. Jamie wanted to figure out how to do this whole dating-a-married-couple thing for himself. At least, as much as he could.

So one night, after he'd sat up late teasing Aoife about Patrick and their anniversary plans, and then talking about his own plans for projects post-*Butterflies*, Jamie found himself browsing the internet looking for books. After a lot of agonizing over his choices and reading way too many reviews, he settled on one about responsible non-monogamy that seemed suitable. The blurb acknowledged there was no one true way to get it right, and Jamie appreciated that hint of flexibility. Even Callum and Nerea seemed to employ different styles in handling their relationships.

Jamie was going to have to wait to read it though. Shipping to anywhere in Ireland, even Dublin, took longer than it did in London, which was annoying. But Jamie didn't feel like he could walk into a bookshop and ask for books about open relationships. He was glad his mum would be at work when it got delivered.

When the book finally came, he snuck the package up to his room as if he were thirteen and smuggling in dirty magazines.

～

"So you're seeing somebody," Hugh said one evening as he and Jamie sat out on the back step together. The sun had gone down but the air was still warm. From the open door behind them came the sound of Maureen finishing up the dishes. In the garden, Vegetables ran and leapt awkwardly in a fruitless attempt to catch the insects that had come out with the twilight.

"Yeah," Jamie said.

"Your mum's worried she's not getting any more than that out of you," his dad said.

"Did she send you out after me to ask?"

"Not in so many words," his dad said. "She wants you to be happy."

"I am." Jamie grinned down at his hands. "I really, really am."

"And this person — whoever they happen to be — you're treating them well?" his father asked sternly.

"Dad! Yes. Of course I am." Of his parents' many reservations about the details of Jamie's dating life over the years, he hoped he had never disappointed in how he strove to treat others. Surely, his mother's lectures on respect and kindness had not been delivered with the notion that, someday, Jamie would be dating a man nearly twice his own age — much less that man's wife too. But that didn't meant those words of advice weren't useful.

His dad nodded. "Good."

Jamie had to fight down the urge to squirm with guilt. He didn't like lying to his family, and omitting the actual circumstances of his current relationships felt like a lie. But he had no idea how to even start the conversation. His book was helpful in a lot of ways, but its clearest message so far was that, for as much guidance as it could offer, Jamie still had a lot of work to do.

Chapter 14

Callum makes an effort to spend time with people he's not sleeping with

C allum was relieved to welcome Jamie back into his and Nerea's bed when he returned London in the first week of August. Jamie may have only been in Dublin and out of physical reach for a fortnight, but his absence had still been too long. As much as the quiet time with Nerea had been a blessing, Callum knew neither of them had expected to miss Jamie as much as they had. That emotional investment boded well for the future of their relationship with him, including Jamie spending a month in Spain with Nerea, but it was also hard. Missing someone was brutal, and arranging schedules so that everyone got the time together they wanted was difficult.

The morning after their celebratory reunion date, they ate breakfast up on the roof; Jamie had declared he'd missed the view. Then Jamie asked Nerea out on a date for the just two of them that night, which left Callum at loose ends. Rather than rattle about in the flat by himself, he decided to make plans with the people he wasn't otherwise going to see until his press tour was over.

He called Thom to schedule one of their semi-regular pub nights, and then called Piper to see if she was up for an impromptu father-daughter day out. It was the sort of thing he'd never had time for when she was small. Callum carried his regrets, but skiving off other responsibilities to make time for each other was something he relished now. A need for mischief and serendipity ran deep in them both.

Today's mission, once Piper had agreed to take the afternoon off work, was nearby London Zoo, for no other reason than it was close and neither of them had been in years. Shortly after one, Callum arrived outside the building of the graphic design firm where Piper worked with two paper cups of coffee.

"Where's Mum?" she asked when she finally came out, swinging her bag over her shoulder and taking the coffee gladly. "I didn't think she'd miss a chance to hover."

"At a gallery," Callum said simply. Although there was surely a way to introduce Jamie as a topic of conversation, he was vaguely aware that this wasn't it. He was going to have to, and soon, but he wanted today to be pleasant and about Piper; Callum knew he had a bad habit of making everything about him.

"The Tate? For her show?"

"Something like that."

As they strolled through Regent's Park, Callum tried not to be conspicuously distracted as he thought of Nerea and Jamie on their date. The boy was asking for things, which was a pleasure and a joy. With so many ways their relationships could suffer from wild inequalities, every move Jamie made to claim what he wanted for his own was a good one.

"Tell me how you are?" he asked, refocusing.

Piper shrugged. "Better now that I'm out of the office."

"You seeing anyone?"

"Daaad," Piper whined. "Did Mum put you up to this?"

"Would I tell you if she had?"

Piper huffed "Can you not? Not everyone does dating as their chief hobby. Or as a spectator sport."

"You mean like I do?"

Piper gave him a look that was so Nerea that Callum had to laugh.

"What am I supposed to do for a hobby instead?" he asked.

"Knit."

"So I'm assuming that yes, you are seeing someone." Callum pounced on the topic again as they turned onto the Broad Walk, which was lousy with tourists.

"Ugh. Dad. You don't want to hear about it," Piper said, gesticulating with her coffee cup.

"I am open-minded and your relationship has to be less stress-inducing than Devon getting married or Leigh having a baby."

"See, you think that, so I shouldn't say anything to disabuse you of that notion."

"I promise not to tell your mother?" Callum tried.

Piper laughed and shook her head.

When they reached the zoo, Callum wrapped his arm around her shoulders and dug out his mobile to take a selfie. "Smile," he said.

"Oh my God, Dad, don't." Piper may have protested, but she laughed and tipped her head onto his shoulder just the same. "Please tell me you're not posting that on your damn Instagram."

"But we look adorable!" Callum showed her the picture.

"Yes, and I don't need thousands of gross messages on my social media when people suddenly remember I'm your daughter again." Piper, of the three girls, looked the most like Nerea and the least like Callum; she was small and slender, with dark eyes and hair and dramatic cheekbones.

"Fair enough," Callum conceded. He'd keep the photo just for himself then. Piper was usually sanguine about the periodic difficulties of being his daughter, but complaints about the social media implications he took seriously, no matter how casual her tone. Online harassment of women could be vile and the thought of Piper having to endure it on his behalf was upsetting.

He refrained from asking further about whoever it was she was dating. Instead they talked about Piper's work, the boss who irritated the hell out of her, and a new project she was excited to take the lead on. When Piper tired of shop talk, they chatted about the programs they were both watching or the books they were reading. In all, it was a stress-free low-stakes outing. Callum knew his life would be better if he did more things like this. He was certainly going to miss her while he was travelling.

⤺

At the end of the afternoon, Callum walked Piper to the tube for her journey home to Whitechapel. He hugged her goodbye and promised to meet her again for another outing, wherever she wanted, when he was back in town after his press tour.

He watched her go through the gate. His heart clenched when she turned around to give him a last wave and an exasperated look, the same way she did every time he waited to leave until she was truly out of sight. Having children had been one of the great joys and, at times, great failures of his life. Even after all of these years, he was still learning what it meant to be a parent to them. Fatherhood was hard, and the world too often encouraged men to meet the task poorly. He was still feeling introspective as he walked through the London haze to meet Thom for drinks.

It took Callum a moment to locate him in the pub. He was sitting all the way in the back, wedged in a corner booth and facing away from the room. He was hunched over his mobile. As soon as Callum came into his range of vision, he shoved the device into his pocket and sat up straight.

"Hiding, are you?" Callum asked as he slid into the seat across from Thom and pushed a pint over to him.

"Preemptively. From your groupies. Thanks," Thom said, taking a healthy swig from the fresh glass.

"What were you doing?" If Thom was going to be surly, Callum was going to be nosy.

"Just giving Alice some advice."

"Which one is Alice again? I can't remember everyone you're dating."

"There's not that many of them," Thom said, annoyed.

"No, but they end so quickly I can't keep track." Callum grinned to lessen the sting of the barb.

Thom refused to take the bait. "I'm not dating Alice. She was my assistant a few years back. She's on her first film as director of photography."

"She's arrived then. Why does she need your advice now?" Callum teased for the sheer fun of needling him.

Thom sighed and pointedly ignored the question. "I haven't seen you a lot lately. We should catch up."

"That's why we're doing this now," Callum said easily, but with a flutter of misgiving. It wasn't like Thom to sound so stilted, do niceties, or skirt around issues, but all three seemed to be at hand now. "What's going on with you?"

"The divorce is finalized." Thom took another gulp of beer.

That explained Thom's mood. "I'm not sure whether I should offer congratulations or condolences."

"Yes," Thom said.

"To fresh starts?" Callum raised his glass.

Thom gave a half-smile and clinked his own glass off of it.

"On that note — "

"Oh God, what now?" Thom asked.

Thom was far too much fun to rile. "Jamie's going to visit Nerea in Spain."

"You're fucking kidding me."

"When I go on press tour for *Diminished Fifth*." He couldn't keep the wistfulness out of his voice. He was going to miss everyone while he was gone. His wife. His lover. His daughters. His friends.

"The entire month. While you gallivant around the world," Thom said, disbelieving. "You told me Nerea was seeing him too but I didn't know it had gone that far."

"It's not quite a month. And it's definitely not gallivanting. It's answering the same exact questions twenty times a day and then smiling for the cameras like it's been the most exciting thing that's ever happened to me."

"Have you lost your mind?" Thom was definitely still hung up on the part about Jamie and Nerea.

"It was Nerea's idea," Callum pointed out.

"In that case everything will be just peachy." Thom still didn't sound convinced.

Callum wondered why he cared so much. Sure, Thom needled him as much as he needled Thom. And his friend was having a hard day. But Callum wondered if his and Nerea's relationship with Jamie was ever going to be the sort of situation other people could simply express their happiness for. "Nerea has far better judgment than me," Callum said defensively.

Frowning, Thom passed his now mostly empty pint glass back and forth between his hands. "Yes, that's what worries me."

Chapter 15

Nerea leaves for Spain with Jamie

The morning they were all due to leave London — Callum for the first leg of his press tour and Jamie and Nerea to Spain — everyone was quiet. For Nerea, this was nothing new. From the beginning of their relationship she had gotten used to being apart from Callum, but the knowledge she would be fine as soon as she was back in their house did not make her feel any better about leaving now. She knew Callum dreaded the separation just as much. He went about throwing last-minute items in his suitcase without saying anything and with a distinct air of glumness.

Jamie was similarly quiet as he sat in a corner of the sofa, his bag, packed back at his own flat, tucked neatly as his feet. Nerea wasn't sure of the details behind his silence. Perhaps he was merely affected by her and Callum's moods. But if she knew Jamie at all — and she thought she'd gotten to know him quite well in the last few months — he wasn't thrilled at the idea of being apart from Callum. Besides, the prospect of a month in a new country, where he knew no one but Nerea and didn't even speak the language, would have made anyone uneasy.

No one said much from the time they met the cab to the moment they walked through the automatic doors into the bright, busy, and overwhelmingly efficient interior of Heathrow Airport's Terminal 1. Nerea frowned as a flight attendant rolling a suitcase behind them did a double take at Callum and then tripped over his own feet.

"Let's get checked in and get through security. Then maybe we can find a quiet corner," Nerea said. People were strange about fame, mobile phone cameras were ubiquitous, and people in airports were always keen for any sort of distraction. Nerea accepted that the three of them would eventually wind up documented against their wishes, but she wanted to put off that moment for as long as possible.

But when they joined the check-in queue, someone muttered to their companion, "Hey, is that what's-his-face? I didn't know he had a son!"

Nerea tried not to sigh audibly. The moment was perhaps closer at hand than any of them found desirable. Callum, with his head down and checking something on his mobile, chuckled. Jamie made a sound of utter dismay. Behind them, someone was making frantic shushing noises at the speaker. *Good.* Nerea pressed her lips together tightly to make sure she didn't react to the particularly erroneous assumption at hand.

At the counter, there was a brief delay when the luggage tag on Nerea's suitcase didn't scan properly and another when Jamie's bag was almost over the weight limit.

"What did you have in there?" Callum asked when Jamie, adjusting his backpack on his shoulders, finally joined them

"Uh. Books?"

"How many?" Callum looked amused.

"I'm going to be there for a while. I wanted to be prepared."

"You know we have books at the house," Nerea pointed out. "English ones even."

"And haven't you ever heard of an e-reader?" Callum put in.

Jamie flushed at the gentle teasing, but he didn't look displeased to be the center of their attention. "I have one of those too. But there's something about books. And I brought other stuff too. Like clothes."

"I guarantee you that was unnecessary," Callum said. "I doubt Nerea is going to let you out of bed."

"Callum!" Nerea scolded. Yes, that was true, but Callum didn't need to say it in public.

Callum shrugged one shoulder and held his hands out, palms up.

"I'm counting on that," Jamie's tone was cautious as he entered the banter. "But I didn't want to assume."

"You're both awful." Nerea was glad that Jamie was rallying a bit.

Callum pulled Nerea's carry-on suitcase behind him as he always did when they traveled together. Meanwhile, Jamie hung a few paces behind them as they navigated the crowds on the way to the security line. Nerea wanted to turn around and tell him that neither distance from them nor deference was necessary; she wanted to grab his hand and draw him forward into her and Callum's conversation. But if the three of them needed to discuss how they were going to handle their relationship in public, this wasn't the time.

"How do you normally do this?" Jamie asked, when they had finally cleared security.

Nerea shook her head and led the way to a bank of chairs tucked out of sight of the main thoroughfare behind a pillar and a rubbish bin.

Jamie slouched into an uncomfortable seat across from Callum and Nerea, "The goodbyes in public thing."

Callum glanced sideways at Nerea. "Normally, we don't."

"What do you mean?" Jamie asked.

"We've never both been involved with someone like this," Nerea said. "Certainly not someone we've taken to the airport. People hardly pay attention to me or my relationships, and most of Callum's relationships" — she made air quotes to highlight exactly how long most of those had lasted — "have been not worth the media hassle and/or involved people in sex clubs."

Jamie's eyes flicked toward Callum.

Callum gave a disinterested shrug in acknowledgment of the truth.

"So I'm a step up for you." Jamie teased.

"It's not a hierarchy," Callum said. "A different set of feelings and desires. But yes, you've lasted longer." How Callum looked so at ease as he lounged lazily in the uncomfortable metal chairs, Nerea didn't know. She was only grateful he hadn't launched into his spiel in defense of sex clubs in public.

"How do you do goodbyes when it's just you two, then?" Jamie pressed.

"Discretely," Callum said. "Especially since the time — oh, it must have been seven or eight years ago now — someone got a photo of us kissing at a gate and it made its way all over the internet before we even got off our planes again. Not world-ending, but annoying. It's no secret that we're married, obviously, but everything we do in public is not for the public."

Nerea watched as Jamie pondered that. Which was good; he'd need that advice soon enough himself. No one should be forced to work for the public's pleasure every time they stepped out their front door. It was, Nerea knew, a brutally hard thing to learn. She'd been by Callum's side as his career had forced them both to struggle with it from the moment they'd met.

When boarding for Jamie and Nerea's flight finally started, Callum pulled Jamie into a one-armed hug appropriate to men who couldn't possibly be sleeping together. Then he kissed Nerea good-bye.

"Travel safe," he told her, ducking his head close to hers.

Nerea replied, as she always did. "You too."

"Call me when you get in?"

"You'll be in the air."

Callum smiled, sad and just for her. "I'll still be here at the airport. In any case, I don't care. I want to hear your voice again as soon as possible."

Nerea took a deep breath against the surge of longing she felt at not being able to stay with him. As they went to the gate, Nerea turned to see Callum wave at them one last time.

As she and Jamie scanned their boarding passes and shuffled along the gangway, Nerea snapped out of her sorrow enough to notice that Jamie's cheeks were red. "What is it?" she asked. She was still learning to classify all the variations of Jamie's often intense, but not always transparent, emotions.

"He gave me a note." Jamie held up a tightly folded piece of paper.

"What's it say?"

"It's not like I can read it out here." Jamie twisted around to see who might be watching them, like a schoolboy caught with a note from his crush. He really was too adorable. "People could see."

Nerea smiled. She thought it extraordinarily unlikely that someone would be able to decipher Callum's scrawl over Jamie's shoulder. Honestly, she wasn't sure Jamie would be able to decipher Callum's scrawl at all.

"He used to do things like that for me when we were first dating and being his girlfriend was making my life difficult," she told him.

"Oh." Jamie's cheeks went, if possible, even redder. His fingers fumbled, displaying an urgency to open it and get to the message it contained. But then he shoved it hard into his pocket and instead helped her with her bags.

Only once they were settled, and the plane had taxied away from the gate, did Jamie return to it. Nerea watched as he opened it with blunt fingers and his eyes scanned across it, once and then twice. When he tucked it away in the inner pocket of his jacket, his eyes were — there was no other word for it — starry.

Chapter 16

Jamie plays house

It was possible that Jamie hadn't entirely thought through this adventure. Flying to Spain to spend a month-long holiday with the wife of the man he was sleeping with? He felt woefully under-prepared. That this only occurred to him twenty minutes into the flight, when Nerea started to doze over her magazine, was perhaps the clearest evidence of this fact.

His impulse was to put an arm around her and pull her head onto his shoulder. At the very least he wanted to twine his fingers with hers while they both napped. He was used to wrapping himself around Callum or Nerea whenever he could, whether at their flat or, occasionally, his. Even on set he had sometimes let himself touch, because no one took the physical affection between performers seriously. In pubs, the presence of alcohol had also given him some leeway.

But now, on this airplane, with someone else's wife, Jamie realized that such gestures were not his to make, not in public, not now and possibly not ever. The sentiment tore him, not with jealousy, but with longing. Even sitting right next to her, he wanted more; needed, even, to feel the softness of her skin, to lean over and bury his nose in the scent of her hair.

Struck by a burst of inspiration, Jamie draped his jacket over his lap and half of hers. Nerea stirred slightly. She cracked open one eye and gave him a smile as he laced his fingers through hers under the cover of fabric. Jamie's heart soared. Maybe this relationship could be less about limits and more about clever, if simple, solutions.

⤳

When they landed, no one gave either of them a second glance as they collected their luggage and dealt with the vague formality of immigration. They were only two hours and change from London and yet, as they stepped out of the airport and into the long-term parking lot, Britain was an entire world away. Here, the air was warmer and the quality of the sunlight different. The faint smell of soil in the air was a marked contrast to the exhaust and dampness of London.

"Which car is yours?" Jamie asked, pulling Nerea's suitcase and his own behind him.

Nerea dug a set of keys out her purse and clicked a fob. She posed with a smug hand on her hip as an absolutely absurd and completely gorgeous hunter green convertible with a cream interior chirped a few yards off.

"Do you want me to drive?" Jamie's mouth was slightly agape. He had meant the words to be an offer, but he knew he was begging. The car was beautiful and would surely be even more stunning if he had its wheel under his hands.

But Nerea was shaking her head. "Oh no, no, no," she said. "This baby is mine."

With a stop for groceries, the drive to the house took nearly as long as the flight had. Soon the city was behind them, and they tore along narrow roads at speeds that probably should have been terrifying but Jamie found delightful.

It was early afternoon by the time Nerea finally turned down a long, dusty, driveway to pull up in front of an ancient stone farmhouse. Large windows overlooked a small vineyard that rolled down the gentle slope before the land gave way to the fields, terraces, and plots of Nerea's neighbors. She pointed out the features of the yard: Behind the house was a garden with a patio, a table and chairs, and a beautiful arbor hung with leafy green plants. To the side of the garage were raised plant beds, practical and filled with vegetables. That garden in turn bordered a thicket where whatever Nerea had once planted with intent had now gone half-wild with vines and brambles. Beyond that was an orchard of fig trees, green and leafy in the summer sun.

"It's beautiful," Jamie said as Nerea unlocked the door and led him inside. The entryway was dim but cool after the summer heat outside. Already he couldn't wait to explore.

"For the amount of time I spend on it, it had better be," Nerea said, reaching up to take her hair down from the massive tortoiseshell barrette that had kept it out of her face while she drove. "But thank you. Now what would you like first — the rest of the tour, food, or fucking?"

⁑

"A guest room?" Jamie was dismayed.

Nerea, in the process of drawing back the curtains, looked over her shoulder at him.

"You don't have to sleep here." Her eyes danced as if he were being very foolish and tripping over his words again, the way he had when he first met her. "But you should have it, in case you want some space to yourself. I have a wedding to plan, the Tate show to start panicking over, and Callum's things have a way of taking over even when he's not here. Believe me, you may want the privacy."

Jamie couldn't imagine how that would be the case. He was here to spend time with Nerea, not hole himself up in a room away from her and all the goings-on of the house. He'd never needed any sort of distance when they were in London. But he also knew it would be rude to protest too strenuously.

"Now, you should take a shower," Nerea said. "You smell like plane."

The bathroom was large and bright, with a window of its own overlooking the flower garden. Jamie had brought his own toiletries, but the bathroom was stocked with soaps and shampoos much nicer than anything he ever bothered to buy and all with a clean, sweet herbal smell. He lingered longer than he expected to in the hot water and fragrant steam, giving himself a chance to clear his mind and soothe his muscles from the long morning of travel. While experience had already told him that Nerea wasn't big on shower sex — too difficult to choreograph, too hard to keep balance, and too likely to end with someone getting accidentally elbowed — he thought this big space with its fancy tile and fragrant soaps would be excellent for that sort of adventure. Maybe once Callum got here.

After he toweled off and put on a clean shirt and jeans, Jamie wandered back downstairs. He heard noises from the kitchen, but on his way there was distracted by a huge expanse of wall between two windows in the living room.

It was covered in photos. In the center, in a large gilt frame, was one of Callum and Nerea on their wedding day. A breeze tugged at Nerea's veil, and they were surrounded by attendants and family and friends, but Nerea and Callum had eyes only for each other. Other photos showed girls, who Jamie thought must have been Callum and Nerea's daughters, as children and young women. There were older pictures as well. Parents, Jamie assumed, and grandparents. The oldest photo, black-and-white and faded in its frame, was of a small dark-haired woman and a tall, spare, but very handsome looking man. Jamie recognized the house behind them as this one. Nerea's grandparents, he guessed.

Jamie wondered what he was doing here. What were Callum and Nerea thinking? When Jamie had thought about relationships before meeting them, he had always assumed he'd be with somebody as clueless and inexperienced with life and dating as he was. Not an older couple, married at that, with big, complex lives and adult children. He probably should have ordered more than one book.

Subdued and uncertain, he made his way to the kitchen. It was massive, bigger than Nerea and Callum's entire flat in London. Exposed beams ran across the ceiling at a height Callum would never need to worry about. The large kitchen island, the cupboards and the counters were all warm, rustic browns and reds. The windows looked out onto the vegetable garden Nerea had pointed out from the front of the house, the plants green and heavy in the afternoon sun. Something pretty and classical, the gentle lilt of strings, played from a small speaker by the brushed steel refrigerator.

At the far end of the room, at the counter between sink and stove, was Nerea. Her back was to him and Jamie took a moment to look his fill without her echoing scrutiny of him. Also freshly showered, her hair was damp and hung down her back in loose curls. The dress she had changed into — gold and green tones in a loose, flowing cut — Jamie hadn't seen before. But more importantly to his rumbling stomach, she was cooking.

"How'd you get down here so fast?" Jamie asked, leaning over the counter to get a better look at what Nerea was doing.

"Magic. Don't touch," Nerea smacked Jamie's hand aside when he tried to sneak a taste.

"Can I help?"

Nerea looked up and seemed to consider him. Jamie hoped she would give him something to do. It was lovely here, but he was a long way from home, from Dublin and London both. Work would help him feel less out of place and perhaps take the edge off the way he felt Callum's presence — and absence — in this house so keenly.

Nerea smiled. "Of course," she said. "Cut these up for me?" She pointed to a heap of potatoes on the island.

When the food was done, simple omelettes of potatoes and herbs, they ate behind the house on a small patio under an arbor of vines, at a wooden table flanked by benches. As Nerea took her own seat Jamie realized, with an odd jolt, that his seat was likely Callum's usual one.

"Tomorrow we'll go into the village to get some more provisions, and you can get acquainted with the town," Nerea told him as they ate. "I'll see if Margarita can come for dinner — I think you two will like each other."

"Does Margarita know about me?" Jamie asked hesitantly.

Nerea nodded.

"How much does she know?" Jamie hoped he didn't sound too alarmed but suspected he probably did.

"That you and Callum started dating at work and now you're coming to visit us here. And presumably whatever else she's read on the internet."

"Except Callum's not here so — "

Nerea cut him off. "My daughter may judge me, but she does not get to judge me more than her father for doing the same things he does."

"Ah." Jamie clamped his mouth shut. Nerea's ferocity reminded him of his mother and his sisters, not that they'd ever had to defend multiple lovers to anyone. But that the world treated women differently for the same choices made by men, he was aware of. He wished it could be otherwise but he felt powerless to change the situation. He was learning, with Nerea's help, that the least he could do was offer them his full support and make sure that anyone within earshot did the same.

"If you have questions, Jamie, you know you can ask them."

Jamie made a sort of despairing sound. "I don't even know where to start."

Nerea smiled at him. "I doubt that's true."

⁓

"I know you explained about me being in the guest room," Jamie said later, after they'd brought in the dishes and were back at the table outside with coffee. The sun hung low in the sky now, turning the green of the landscape gold and pouring long shadows across it. The heat of the day had faded, and the breeze, warm and gentle, stirred the ends of Nerea's loose hair.

"What about it?" Nerea stirred sugar into her cup.

"Is that about giving me space or about giving you space?" Both options were fine, of course, but Jamie's book kept telling him that assumptions were bad. He just had to hope that Nerea wouldn't be offended by, or disappointed in, any of his questions.

"While you're here as our guest — as *my* guest — this house is yours. But it's also still mine. And Callum's. You're welcome in my bed. If you want to invite me to yours, that's up to you."

"You're sure it's not weird? I mean, for me to be sleeping in your and Callum's bed? A lot of men would be uncomfortable with that."

"Callum's not a lot of men. And you've been doing it for months in London," Nerea pointed out. "If the situation were reversed, would you be uncomfortable with it?"

"Honestly? I don't know," Jamie admitted. "But I wouldn't like myself very much if I were."

"We live in the world, Jamie. Some things can be hard even when we don't want them to be. They don't get better by pretending they aren't happening. But no, this is not a problem for Callum and me."

"Okay," Jamie said, cautious but game. "But I feel like London's a flat where you stay when you're in the city. This is your home. I don't want to overstep any boundaries."

"As I keep telling you, the only boundaries you could possibly overstep," Nerea said placidly, "are the ones that exist in your own head, which are a little sexist in that you see me as Callum's property that you're trespassing on, rather than as a person who's inviting you to sleep beside her."

"Oh." Jamie was taken aback, because he hadn't explicitly thought of it in those terms, but Nerea was right. "Wow. I'm sorry."

"You're forgiven," Nerea said with a smile, as she set her spoon aside and wrapped her hands around her cup.

"Did you and Callum ever have separate rooms?" Jamie asked. He wanted to know how they had arrived at their current outlook on the matter.

"Sometimes I sleep in a spare room if he has a cold and is snoring. Otherwise, no."

Jamie let out a bark of laughter. He could imagine it — Callum oblivious and Nerea disgruntled, bundling herself down the hall in the middle of the night. He wondered if she took the duvet with her. Probably.

"So you don't have any space from each other?" he asked.

"You mean other than living in different countries for months at a time? That arrangement makes space less necessary when we are together. But he's not allowed in my studio when the door's closed, and I stay out of his study when his door is closed."

"Callum has a study?"

"He likes the term better than 'man-cave,'" she said tartly.

⁂

As the sun slipped down behind the hills, Nerea brought Jamie to her studio. It was on the third floor of the house with windows on two sides, through which he could see the surrounding fields, now wrapped in a dusky evening blue.

"Are all these for your gallery show?" Jamie asked, examining the canvasses hung on one of the windowless walls and propped up against various bits of furniture.

"Some." Nerea seemed to be inventorying paints or brushes as she shifted things about on a workbench.

"What about this?" Jamie asked, pointing to a canvas stacked against others and leaning against a wall out of the path of the light.

Nerea turned to see which one he meant. When she saw, she shook her head. "No."

"Do you ever show pictures of Callum?"

"Can you imagine? No. It's the worst part of my job." Nerea came to stand beside him. "I'm married to the loveliest model, and I can't share any of my paintings of him."

The painting was of Callum, nude. It wasn't what Jamie might have expected of a nude painting of anyone, but then, Nerea's efforts aside, he didn't spend a lot of time hanging around museums and studios. There weren't any silk sheets or magical golden light or dramatic drapery in evidence. It was just Callum, on a bed with blue sheets, stretched out on his side and reading a book, his knees curled up and his cheek propped on his hand.

What struck Jamie, as his gaze traced over Callum's familiar features, was how Nerea had captured everything that *wasn't* airbrushed underwear-model stunning about him: The bit of paunch that his well-tailored pants and shirts usually hid, his thighs that were sort of pale and were far from fit. Callum was a big man, not heavy, but not muscular when his films didn't require him to be.

All of which Jamie knew, but never paid attention to when they were fucking. Because for all the features some people might consider flaws, Callum was gorgeous. And while all his imperfections were displayed in this painting — and hard to miss, apparently — his beauty was evident too. His ease in his own skin that was so attractive, the warmth of his smile even as he gazed at his book, and his not so occasional melancholy. Beauty was very much in the eye of the beholder, even if sometimes that beholder was the whole world. Nerea had painted this through the lens of her love, and Jamie thought Callum looked absolutely perfect in it.

"Can you do one of me?" Jamie asked, before he was aware he'd given his brain permission to speak the thought. Too much too soon, surely.

Nerea, however, didn't laugh at him or scold; she looked thoughtful instead.

"We'll see," she said.

~

Nerea's bedroom was clearly the one that featured in the painting of Callum. Even the sheets on the bed might have been the same, though now they were neatly tucked under a wonderfully fluffy-looking coverlet.

"Is there more of the tour?" Jamie asked. "Or can I kiss you now?"

Nerea smiled. "Yes, please."

It was sheer luxury to have this huge bed in which to be with Nerea, with no constraints of too-low ceilings or too-early set calls. Jamie and Nerea indulged themselves and each other until it grew fully dark outside the windows, with the stars vibrant pinpricks of light against the black.

Nerea, sprawled out on the pillows, beckoned Jamie to her and let him rest his head on her chest while they caught their breath together. His gaze landed on a book on the nightstand, one he knew was one of Callum's favorites. It was only then that Jamie registered that he still felt slightly strange about sharing this bed with Nerea. Not, he thought, because he saw

Nerea as any sort of possession he was stealing from Callum. But because Callum and Nerea had a history. This had been their home for their entire married lives. They'd slept in this bed together since before Jamie had been born. He knew he wasn't in competition with their history, but it still felt like something he should navigate carefully and honor as best he could.

"I've got one more question." Jamie wriggled off Nerea and onto his back on the soft sheets. He laced hands behind his head. Next to him, Nerea rolled onto her side, her head pillowed on her arm, watching him with an expression he couldn't put a name to.

"Only one?"

"For now."

"What is it?"

"Do you play house with all your flings?"

"You think we're playing house?"

Jamie turned his head to face her, not sure if he was supposed to. But he'd rather face her in the dark than stare at the ceiling and not be able to see her at all.

"Well, we made dinner and did cleanup, and you've got an outing planned for us tomorrow, and now we're in bed together. We both know this isn't a permanent arrangement. I mean, I'm going back to London in a month."

"That's four weeks away."

"Yeah?" Jamie didn't see how that changed anything. His point remained, whether it was critical today or next month.

"I know it's hard when you are young to not always wonder about the future." Nerea rubbed a hand along Jamie's shoulder. "But it's easier to let go if you stop thinking so hard about the rest of the world, or the rest of the year, or the rest of your life."

"But how...." Jamie trailed off.

"Maybe we're just different," Nerea said, her voice soothing. "I do not care about the rest of the world. If I did, I wouldn't live here."

Jamie wondered if he was supposed to have clothes on for this kind of conversation, but being dressed had never been a requisite for serious conversations with Nerea or Callum before.

"Maybe we are," Jamie confessed, nervously. He didn't know how much such differences would matter, in the long-term. "But it's only now, today, that I'm realizing I need to work out what it means, that I'm here. I understand what you're saying about not speculating about the future. But even being with you, here, makes how I see myself and my place in the world complicated."

"How are you feeling about it right now?" Nerea asked.

"Peculiar."

"That's not very specific, Jamie."

"I know. But it makes me feel temporary. Like any moment some alarm I can't see will go off, and I'll wake up, and all this lovely time will be over."

"And you don't want that."

Jamie shook his head, glad that Nerea seemed to understand and that she wasn't judging him for his feelings. "I don't."

⁓

Jamie woke the next morning to birdsong, the herbal scent of tea, and Nerea tossing a pillow at his head. He jerked upright in bed, confused for a moment by not remembering where he was. But then Nerea — slender, quick, and wonderfully naked — pounced on him.

When they did manage to get out of bed, they opted to skip proper clothes to go downstairs and make breakfast. Jamie, despite the excellent morning sex they'd just had, remained distracted by Nerea wrapped in only a pale peach silk robe. But any plan to do something about that distraction was interrupted when, after they'd finished their torrijas, Nerea looked at her mobile. Margarita and Miguel had just texted and would be arriving shortly.

"I'm not telling you to get dressed," she said, tugging the belt of the too-large robe Jamie had borrowed from Callum's closet. "But I would recommend it."

Upstairs, Jamie spent ten minutes agonizing over which shirt and pants would magically combine to convey a message of *Hi, I know I'm dating your parents, but maybe we can be friends?* He was still deliberating it when he heard voices at the front door and then in the downstairs hallway. He grabbed clothes almost at random, dressed hurriedly, and went to meet them.

Margarita's smile when she shook Jamie's hand immediately put him on edge. It was too perfect and too polite, like the girls he met at industry parties sometimes who were way more practiced at networking than he was. Miguel, a tall, lanky man about Jamie's age with a self-conscious slouch to his shoulders, seemed nice enough. Jamie could definitely empathize with the potential awkwardness of the moment.

"You're dating my father," Margarita said without preamble as Nerea chivied them from the foyer and into the living room.

"We met at work," seemed the most politic answer, but Margarita didn't look impressed and likely wasn't going to make this easy for him. She said something in Spanish that

Jamie didn't understand, but it couldn't have been good. Nerea frowned, and Miguel became very fascinated by a painting on the wall.

"Margarita, be nice," Nerea said in English.

"And you're dating my mother," Margarita said to Jamie.

"Um. Yes," Jamie said.

"How old are you?" Margarita asked.

"Devon!" Nerea scolded.

"Don't call me that," Margarita snapped.

"I'm sorry. Margarita. Don't ask questions like that, I didn't raise you to be rude to guests."

For a moment there was silence. Jamie was grateful for a pause in the near bickering.

"You probably looked my age up on the internet before you got here, didn't you?" he put in, attempting to lighten the mood.

Margarita turned toward him with a cool, judgmental look. Obviously, he'd made the wrong choice. Before he could figure out what he was supposed to do, Nerea suggested Margarita join her in the kitchen. It was not a request. Margarita followed her with a last displeased glance back at Jamie and Miguel.

They exchanged uneasy looks. Jamie was pretty sure neither of them had any idea what they were supposed to do in these circumstances. Except sit tight and, on his part at least, not make anything worse.

Miguel, to his relief, spoke first.

"You're dating Margarita's mother?" he asked.

"Yeah," Jamie said. And then because once he had started talking he was not capable of stopping, he added, "And her dad." As if Miguel could have missed Margarita's statement of that fact.

"Ah." Miguel hesitated. "Are you older than Margarita?

"No," Jamie admitted.

"I didn't think so."

"Did you Google me too?" Jamie asked. It was a pathetic attempt at a joke, but Miguel seemed glad to continue a conversation.

"No. Margarita just told me about it. If it helps, she is mostly angry at Callum, not you. Or Nerea"

That was a new wrinkle. "Really? Why?"

Miguel shrugged. "Margarita is usually angry at Callum for something. Which isn't to say he doesn't deserve it. No offense."

"None taken." Jamie said. "You don't have to answer if you don't want, but can you tell me why?"

Miguel darted his eyes around the room as if checking for eavesdroppers. Then he leaned closer. Apparently family gossip was what it took to get him out of his shell. He held up a hand and started ticking items off on his fingers. "She resents the drama Callum made when she was a child. She's annoyed he's coming here flaunting his boyfriend — I mean, you. And she's worried about people gossiping and making life hard for Nerea in the village."

They weren't unfair points, even if Jamie lacked the details behind them. He nodded and wondered, yet again, if he was in over his head.

"And I think Nerea's worried about the Tate and the travel and the wedding planning," Miguel continued, seemingly unburdening himself from his own stress. "She's been trying to help us long-distance, but there's only so much she can do. She likes London, but it's not easy for her always to be away from home."

"Oh." Jamie hadn't known London was difficult, logistically or emotionally, for Nerea. All the time he had spent with her had felt like a holiday, but perhaps that was the problem. He felt like a fool for not realizing it before. Of course she had obligations, cares, and worries beyond just himself and Callum.

As Nerea and Margarita's awkward absence continued, Jamie wondered what it was like when Callum and Nerea fought. But more than that, Jamie wondered what it would be like if he ever had an argument with one or both of them. Would they join forces and scold him like a child? Or would it be something else? Jamie didn't have much experience with disagreements in relationships. Most of his hadn't lasted long enough to encompass such. The ones that had, hadn't survived them.

Apparently done with their conversation, Miguel pulled out his mobile and started reading something on it. Jamie, with nothing at hand to distract himself with, got lost down a rabbit hole of worry about all the ways he could screw up his current relationships. He was jolted out of his reverie by Nerea appearing in the door to the kitchen.

"Would you boys like something to drink?" she asked.

Jamie blinked and looked up at her. She looked as composed and cheerful as she had when she got out of the shower that morning. Beside her, Margarita looked more than a little sulky.

Chapter 17

Callum restrains himself for a change

Press tours were the one part of his job Callum was reliably a diva about. They were grueling under the best of circumstances, and he was fifty-six years old, which was definitely not the best of circumstances. Neither was being six foot two. Airline seats were not built for people with long legs. And so he insisted that his tours be spread out enough so that he could sleep in a proper bed in each city. If it kept him away from home for another week or two, such was the nature of the beast. Thank God he had the clout to get what he wanted and a marriage that didn't mind how much he liked strange.

Singapore, the second stop after Tokyo, was not necessarily his favorite place to be on press tours. Yes, it was a glorious international city-state, but the traffic was a misery and the torrential rain never seemed to stop. At least the Mandarin Oriental was divine. And even if it wasn't, Callum would still sit in its bar. Hotel bars were uniquely well-suited to casual hookups. No one ever worried about running into anyone they knew, and the time between closing the deal and getting to a bed was mercifully short. No small talk if you didn't want it; lots of making out in elevators if you did.

While on the road hotel bars were a nearly nightly ritual for Callum. Not always with intent — far from it — but always with possibility. A bit of flirtation, or more, was always appealing. The potential to discover someone new, or something new in himself, was deliciously sexy, even when he went to bed alone. Sometimes, especially.

The hotel's bar was chic, with rich red sofas and cream-colored chairs clustered about the lounge area. Floor-to-ceiling windows offered a view of Marina Bay and the glittering lights of the city. Tonight, a woman down the other end of the sofa Callum had chosen was making eyes at him. She was in her mid-thirties, had light brown hair cut into a neat bob, and was well put together enough that Callum wanted to take her apart. She kept looking his way. She would smile, make eye contact, glance down, turn away, and then start the cycle over again. She knew exactly what she was doing. Callum wasn't the only one who appreciated the opportunities of a hotel bar, apparently. Better, she either didn't know who he was or didn't care.

Callum eventually nodded his acknowledgment of her smile and thought about sending a drink over to her, the drink an invitation for conversation, the conversation inevitably an invitation for more. Perhaps she would even ask him upstairs first.

But he felt off-balance. The chase was moderately engaging, but tonight anything more seemed flat. Eventually he shook his head at her, a look of self-directed disappointment on his face. He settled his tab and headed up to his room alone. He was lonely, tired and very far from home. Which had been true an hour ago, but now he also felt jarred by his own reaction to the woman downstairs. His ultimate lack of interest in the possibility of the encounter had brought him up short and left him with a sense of mingled frustration and self-doubt.

He wanted to call Nerea and Jamie — he had never been any good at simply sleeping off his moods — but he worried about that, too. Callum didn't always speak to his wife much when he was away. They'd always found it easier to have faith in their marriage and exchange a few texts and call occasionally than to reopen the wound of longing night after night. But right now, he didn't know how to be without Nerea, despite thirty years of practice, or without Jamie, despite that relationship still being far too new for that to make sense.

Callum also worried — with all the recent discussion of Antonio — that if he called it would turn into an argument. Even if it didn't, there was a reasonable chance the three of them were going to wind up having a serious discussion about their relationship because he was feeling melancholy. Skype would be terrible for that, but right now there weren't other options. And, as Callum continued to learn, situations only got worse the more he brooded about them.

So he called.

When the line clicked open, Callum was treated to a view of Nerea and Jamie in bed dressed in slouchy sleep clothes. Newspapers and books surrounded them on the duvet; Jamie had made himself at home in his few days there. It was dark in Singapore, but the bedroom in Spain was still bright with late afternoon sunlight.

"Am I on the big giant screen?" he asked without preamble, settling back against the pillows of his own, otherwise empty, hotel bed. He and Nerea had gotten a wall-mounted flat screen with a camera in it for their bedroom a few years ago. Nerea had spent half a day figuring out how to route her computer through it, ostensibly to watch movies, but in practice mainly for Skype sex when Callum was on the road.

"Of course you are," she said.

"It's pretty weird." Jamie laughed, his body easy next to Nerea's.

Callum made a face. "Can you put me on your tablet instead?" he asked. "I'm in a mood and I feel pathetic thinking about it projected across our bedroom."

Nerea reached for the tablet. Jamie sat up straighter.

There was a brief flicker of the video and the angle changed as Nerea transferred him to the smaller device. From experience, he knew she had propped it on her knees. Jamie leaned into her side, but only two-thirds of his face made it into the frame.

"What's going on?" she asked.

Callum gave a heavy sigh. "I miss both of you."

"What else is going on?" Her voice wasn't exactly sharp, but his wife had always known when he was holding out on her.

"I was just flirting with a woman in a bar."

"Was she cute?" Nerea looked bored.

"More elegant, less cute. Cute smile though."

"She shoot you down?" Jamie asked. There was a tension in his voice that caused it to wobble slightly. It was everything Callum had expected, except for the part where he found it enchanting instead of irritating.

"No." He shook his head. "She wouldn't have, either. I just — she wasn't what I wanted right now, and we hadn't talked about it."

Nerea breathed his name to herself, a combination of pity and affection that made him feel incredibly and undeservedly loved.

But other than that, no one said anything. Callum soldiered on. "Nerea and I have our agreements. Jamie, you and I met in the context of them, but we never talked it all the way through. Normally this is what I do when I'm away, but suddenly I realized I was making assumptions. I know how Nerea feels about me sleeping with people who aren't her or you, but I don't know how you feel about it."

Jamie blinked at him rapidly several times. Even through the mild pixilation of the video call, Callum could tell his heart was racing. He always responded to everything like a test. It meant he handled life well and excelled constantly, but it still broke Callum's heart.

"I don't want to make a decision about how you live your life," Jamie finally said.

"You're not," Nerea murmured next to him. "You're giving him information so he can make a decision."

Jamie frowned, the space between his eyebrows crinkling almost comically. "I don't think I mind you having other relationships," he said, sounding uncertain. "But I don't think I'm a fan of the casual hookups."

"Can I ask why?" Callum decided a question was far better than addressing the hint of smugness on Nerea's face.

"I understand how you can care about more than one person or how someone you care about can fill a need because someone else you care about is far away or just different. But the other stuff I don't get. It's not a deal breaker for me, but I'd have to think about it a lot. Remind myself that I'm not trivial too."

"This is an awful conversation to have over Skype," Callum said, dragging a hand through his hair.

"You're the one who called," Nerea pointed out.

For a moment they were all silent.

Callum shifted against his pillows. "I think I'm not going to be sharing beds — or anything else — with anyone on this junket."

"I really don't want — " Jamie began.

Callum and Nerea shushed him simultaneously.

"My decision," Callum said. "And I feel better already for having made it. Yes?"

Jamie nodded. "Yes."

"And we can all discuss this in detail when I get home," Callum added. He wondered what he had done, in this life or any previous one, to deserve these two wonderful human beings in his bed, waiting for him. "Now," he said, turning onto his side on top of the covers thousands of miles away while his lover and his wife snuggled together. "Tell me what you two have been up to. Preferably with all the goriest details."

Chapter 18

Nerea scandalizes the neighbors

Jamie was a joy to spend time with. He was eager to investigate all the corners of the old house and take long, rambling walks around the countryside, but also happy to curl up next to Nerea on the couch of an evening while she read or sketched.

Nerea started teaching him Spanish too, at first just words and phrases here and there. As Jamie caught on to those, she chatted to him, narrating whatever she was doing while she cooked or worked in the garden or painted. Whatever she did, Jamie was right at her side, watching her, helping her, and taking it all in.

After several days of such narration, Jamie blinked in the middle of reaching for an ingredient she had asked him for in Spanish. "This is what you do with babies, isn't it?" he asked as he closed his fingers around the bowl. "Keep talking at them so they learn how words work?"

Nerea smiled as he handed the garlic to her. "Sí. Muy bien."

Jamie grinned at her, looking exceptionally pleased with himself.

The inescapable downside to Jamie's visit was the interest the rest of the village took in Nerea's guest. The whole town, of course, had known about the Tonio affair. That had been a long time ago, but no one had forgotten. And the neighbors could hardly fail to notice the handsome young man Nerea had staying with her while her husband was gone. Especially when Jamie loved sprawling out in the grass of the garden and playing with the fingers of Nerea's left hand while she balanced a sketchpad on her knees and drew with her right.

On one such afternoon Jamie put his head down on his folded arms and fell asleep. She put her hand in his hair, ruffling the soft sun-warmed strands while she worked. It was Jamie she was sketching, for the painting he had asked, so sweetly, if she would do. She wanted to capture him just like this — drowsy, happy, unselfconscious.

She looked up, she wasn't sure how much later, to the odd sensation of being watched. This bit of the garden was right near the fence line that marked the boundary between Nerea and Callum's property and their neighbor's land. And right now one of their neighbors, Sra. Astorga, who had lived in the next house over since Nerea was a girl, was peering directly over the top of the fence and at Nerea and Jamie. She wore an expression of profound judgment and disapproval. Nerea stifled the reflexive urge to pull her hand out of Jamie's hair.

Instead she called out, "Can I do something for you?" As Nerea stared at her, Sra. Astorga ducked out of sight on the other side of the fence. Nerea sighed. That was not going to be the last she heard about this from anyone. Jamie stirred.

"It's all right," she told Jamie, running a hand through his hair. "Go back to sleep."

"Wasn't sleeping," Jamie said, but his eyes were closed before he even put his head back down.

Nerea bent over and kissed his forehead in case anyone was still watching.

Two weeks in to Jamie's visit they went to the coast, for no other reason than that they could. Jamie dove gleefully into the surf. Nerea sat on the beach under a big umbrella, reading or watching the sun and the sea accentuate the fine cut of Jamie's muscles like some youth depicted on an ancient amphora. He was so lovely, an artist's dream and a middle-aged woman's fantasy. But for Nerea, unaccountably, he was also real. The two of them stayed up each night nearly until dawn talking and listening to the sound of the waves on the shore.

It was a wonderful few days, but there was a melancholy to it that Nerea couldn't put her finger on until they were packing up what little they'd brought to return home. There was beauty in falling in love with someone new and making them a part of her life, but there was a certain sadness to it, too. Even if Jamie continued to weave himself perfectly into her and Callum's life — which was far from guaranteed — there was still a loss to be had if the three of them were to turn into something new together. No longer would it just be her and Callum, decadent and against the world. Or, for that matter, just her and Jamie enjoying luxuries and a companionship their lives were never quite supposed to have.

She wanted to talk about all of it, with Callum, with Jamie, with the world through the fibers of her paint brushes. But she also wanted to keep it close, a secret not even those involved would truly understand. They were men, and the story of what they were all doing together was different for them. It was, Nerea realized, not unlike her first pregnancy and Leigh's birth. To a one, new things in life, no matter how wonderful, came with a cost. Even those closest to her could not fully share in that experience.

On the way back from the shore, Nerea and Jamie stopped in the village to buy groceries. Because the world seemed determined not to let her forget all that was both beautiful and sad in her life, they ran into Tonio. Jamie, in fact, ran literally into him, stepping aside in the street and apologizing in imperfect Spanish. Nerea looked up from her mobile, on which she'd been texting Piper, and came to an abrupt halt.

In other circumstances, Nerea would have stopped and chatted. Perhaps she would have inquired whether Tonio wanted to meet her for lunch again, since she was going to be in Spain for a while still. But with Jamie next to her not knowing any of this history — and how could she have failed to prepare him and herself for this eventuality? — she could only say hello.

"Nerea," Tonio shot a questioning glance at Jamie, who hovered nearby.

"Hello Tonio. This is Jamie," Nerea said in Spanish. She tucked her hand into Jamie's elbow and drew him forward into the conversation. Trying to pretend they weren't there together would only make the discovery more horrid. "Jamie, this is Antonio."

Jamie said hello and looked confused.

"New friend?" Tonio asked, his voice teasing but hesitant, as if he wasn't sure how to proceed. Which made two of them.

"The boy on the phone who interrupted us at lunch."

"Ah." The information did not make Tonio look more comfortable. "It's nice to meet you," he told Jamie even as he kept a wary eye on Nerea.

Jamie responded hesitantly, but correctly, in Spanish. He looked between her and Tonio, putting pieces together.

"I'll see you later," Tonio said in a rush to Nerea. She didn't blame him; the moment wasn't going to get less awkward. He nodded to both of them before walking off down the street.

"Who was that?" Jamie murmured, as they stepped out of the bright, hot street into the cool interior of a shop.

"A very long story," Nerea said. Out the window, she could see Tonio scoop up his little daughter and press a kiss to the cheek of his wife, who had just emerged from another store further down the street.

Jamie took her hand, heedless of the people around them. "Do you want to go home?" he asked. "We can get food later."

Nerea nodded. "Yes, thank you." An evening at home, curled up with Jamie and perhaps an easy exchange of texts with Callum, was exactly what she wanted.

⊸

Their last weeks in Spain slipped away. The worst of the summer heat passed, and the days grew shorter, the quality of the air clearer. Autumn was approaching.

On their last Friday alone before Callum was scheduled to arrive, Nerea watched as Jamie announced they should have a romantic candlelit dinner together, then stood on tiptoe to swipe a pair of silver candlesticks down from the top of one of the kitchen cabinets.

"Do you know what those are?" Nerea asked. She needed a step ladder to reach them.

He stared at them, testing the weight of them in his hands. "No?"

"Put them on the table, and I'll tell you a funny story. Which is not actually funny, but that's generally how stories work here."

"Your house?" Jamie asked, still holding the candlesticks.

Nerea took them away gently and set them down. "No," she said. "Spain." She fished in a drawer for the tapers that fit them. It was easier than looking at Jamie while explaining something about her family that was the sort of secret not everyone took kindly to. But minding the gap between what her family was and what it should have been was something that mattered to her. Family, tradition, and the old stones of the house all demanded it of her. So did Jamie, finding those candlesticks.

"You know my name?" she said.

"Which part?"

"Nessim. It's connected to both Arab and Jewish families here." She waited to see what Jamie would say, if there was any hate lurking there. It was too easy to be surprised. But he said nothing, merely looked at her curiously, a child waiting for the rest of the story. "There are a dozen ways to spell it and who even knows when it became my family's name. Or why. It's hard to be sure sometimes in a place like this."

"Like what?" Jamie asked.

"Spain has been through many things. We were not even a democracy when I was a child," she said simply. "Now, when I was very little — and we had food even when we were poor because we had a vegetable garden and because we had our fruit trees — every Friday night my grandparents lit these candles. My grandfather would pass his hands over his eyes. I asked why did he do this. It was different than how we used candles at church, and I assumed it was some sort of magic."

"I'm going to be really disappointed if you tell me it's not magic," Jamie said.

Nerea shushed him gently. "No. Not magic. No more so than anything else. He did it because his family before him did it. It was, simply, what was done." She finally found the candles and laid them on the counter. "But it seems, from these candlesticks, and from my grandfather's stories about his own grandparents and their grandparents, that this family — my family — is converso."

"I don't know what that is," Jamie said.

"At some point, before the Inquisition, we were Jewish," Nerea said as she lit a match to melt the bottom of one candle before setting it into its holder. "At some point afterward, having done what was necessary to survive, we forgot that. But we remembered this."

"How did you figure it out?" Jamie asked, as Nerea secured the second taper and adjusted the two candlesticks so that they were side by side.

"This is where the story gets odd," Nerea said. "When I met Callum for the first time — and went home with him to his terrible flat to have very good sex — the next morning I got up and put on his bathrobe and went to get some water. I opened all his kitchen cabinets just trying to find a glass."

"Bad housekeeper?" Jamie guessed.

"Terrible housekeeper. No glasses. One sad coffee mug. And a pair of silver candlesticks."

"What the…?" Jamie breathed.

"This was my reaction! Was the whole world filled with people who lit silver candlesticks for reasons they could not recall?"

"You asked him?"

"Yes. What else were we going to talk about that morning? The other people we were seeing? His desperate need for kitchenware? How quickly I should get out before it got awkward? I had no idea if he felt as easy with me as I did with him."

"So you accosted him about candlesticks," Jamie said, his mouth turned up in a delighted smile.

"I did," Nerea said with a shrug. "His father's mother was Jewish. When she died, Callum inherited the candlesticks when his father — who is the most priggish atheist I have ever met — rather coarsely expressed his lack of interest in such superstitions. Callum was sheepish when he told me the story. Whether that was because he had dragged the candlesticks from flat to flat out of some affection for his grandmother or to spite his father, I am not sure. I told him my story. And he told me the word for it, that there is a Sabbath prayer that should go with the candles, and why when our families were something else, some of us covered our eyes. All things about God are about magic in a way."

"Are you religious?" Jamie blurted. "I never thought to ask."

Nerea shook her head. "Callum may like family lore, but he's English. Where's the spirituality in that? Me, I go to church so the neighbors don't talk. My religion is my art, my family, this house, these candlesticks."

"Which sometimes you light," Jamie pointed out.

Nerea struck another match. "There's certainly no reason to stop now."

⇖

That night after they had gone to bed, Jamie stretched out under the blankets that covered them both now that the evenings had grown cool and said quietly, "I keep thinking about those candlesticks."

"Ah?" Nerea had been on the edge of dropping off, but Jamie apparently wanted to talk, so she rolled over to face him. He had his pillow bunched up awkwardly under his head, and the moonlight fell across his face in pale streaks. He was frowning.

"I hardly know anything about my own family. I mean we're Irish and Catholic — I know that much. But my dad was adopted — "

"His parents, the people that raised him, are your grandparents," Nerea said curtly before Jamie could get any further. Biology could be fascinating but was often overrated. Family was what you built.

"Oh, I know. And they're great. But my dad's mum, the one he was born to, she was in the laundries. I don't think she wanted to give him up, and I wonder, sometimes, about cousins or aunts or uncles I might have and don't know about. I have my mum's family, of course, and none of it bothers me, but you can talk about a tradition of centuries, and I can talk about what's lost. It felt weird, sometimes, when I was growing up."

"It's hard to be different." Nerea knew enough to understand that the circumstances of his father's adoption were likely fraught. Jamie didn't spend a lot of time talking about his family, but when he did it was always with evident fondness. That was what mattered. "But you have plenty of stories to tell," Nerea said. "A loving family that chose to be together. That's good, and it's more than many people get."

"I know." Jamie nodded his agreement. "I do know, but if I ever have kids of my own I'd want them to know their history. All of it — my father's parents that raised him and the ones that didn't. But finding any of that out would be hard. And it would probably hurt."

The world was full of difficulties, Nerea wanted to tell Jamie. He only twenty-four, and there was still so much time for life's lost and founds to break his heart. She wondered if she would still know him when he had children of his own; she wondered how much it would ache if she did. But now was not the time to sort that out, not within herself, and certainly not with him.

"It can seem hard to have lost history," said carefully, glad they could barely see each other in the weighty dark. "But all families do. True, only some know it or the terrible reasons for it, but we do the best we can. We make new traditions, and we go on." She touched a finger to the tip of his nose. "There's a freedom in that," she said. "Choose wisely."

≈

Jamie spent the entire morning Callum was due to arrive up in his bedroom. He claimed he was packing his suitcase for his return to London in a few days, but Nerea wasn't fooled. He was nervous and eager and those bedroom windows had the best view of the road as it came out of the valley. He saw the car before Nerea knew it was close and ran down the stairs announcing that Callum was home. But he hung back, lurking in the entry hall, when the car stopped in front of the house.

Nerea stood in the open doorway as Callum retrieved his suitcase from the boot. Homecomings could be hard. They were emotional, draining, and — more often than not — came at inconvenient times of the day or night. But they were also one of the sweetest parts of Nerea and Callum's life together.

Nerea remembered them all, or liked to think that she did: All the many iterations of Callum appearing in the road, looking much the worse for wear after whatever flight he'd just disembarked from, his jacket folded over one arm, pulling his suitcase with the other.

"You made it," Nerea told him when he was close enough that she could see how deep the lines of weariness were around his eyes and how much his smile brightened the closer he got to the house.

Callum didn't respond; he never did, not in words. He dropped his suitcase and his jacket right there on the front step and swept her into his arms — there was no other word for it. Her feet left the ground as he kissed her, long and deep and like the existence of the rest of the world depended on it.

They broke apart slowly, her feet returning to the ground and Callum's fingers warm on her face and her throat as they did.

"It's good to be back," he said softly. His eyes were gentle. They lifted over Nerea's shoulder to Jamie, who was still hidden in the house's shadows.

"Do I get a kiss like that?" Jamie said, or started to. In two huge steps Callum was on him and kissing him too. And just as enthusiastically. Nerea laughed and left the two of them to it while she retrieved Callum's things from where he'd dropped them.

Three minutes after Callum finally walked through the front door they were all in bed. Upstairs, the slightly solemn intensity of their greetings downstairs gave way to laughter. Callum was frantic, his hands and his body trying to be everywhere. Nerea knew much was changing in their lives, and yet so much more was exactly as it had always been.

⸙

Sweet, stunned and nearly submissive in the face of all that sensation, Jamie fell asleep forty-five seconds after he came. Callum chuckled as he crawled carefully around him on the bed to stretch out next to Nerea.

"He usually has more staying power than that." Nerea laughed softly, as if Callum didn't know that perfectly well himself. "He's glad to have you back."

"And you?"

"You know I'm glad to have you back. Stop fishing for compliments."

Callum smiled and kissed her forehead. They had switched to Spanish, not to keep the conversation from a sleeping Jamie but because it was easier. Callum's Spanish was far more polished now than it had been way back at the beginning, when his grammar had been atrocious and his talent for picking the words he absolutely shouldn't had been the horror of the village. Now, choosing Spanish was a way Callum indicated he was fully present in their shared, private life. They had built such a wonderful home here, Nerea thought, as she lifted her head from the pillow to accept the kiss Callum pressed to her lips. Even if the neighbors never minded their own business.

Nerea stopped worrying about the neighbors — or indeed anything else — when Callum kissed her again, so gently she thought she would weep from it. As he shifted them so he could slip inside her, she sighed at the relief of it. Nerea wrapped her arms around Callum's neck as he began to move. She'd been at the house for weeks, but now she was home.

⸙

They made the most of every moment they had with the three of them in the house together. On Jamie's last day before he flew back to London they pulled themselves out of bed long enough for him to pack for real this time. Callum spent most of that afternoon in Jamie's room and then trailing after him whenever he had to venture downstairs to find some book or article of clothing. From what Nerea could overhear whenever they appeared, Callum was giving Jamie advice about his auditions and the two of them were comparing their schedules and making dates. Their plans surely encroached on her schedule, but she didn't mind and would double-check everything later.

On the morning Callum was due to drive Jamie to the airport, Nerea asked Jamie to take a walk with her behind the house. She brought him into the wild area that started at the edge of the vegetable garden. The paths may have been overgrown and in some places visible only to Nerea, but they were still there. Jamie gave her his hand instinctively, as the trees and vines closed off the light pouring down over the hills.

"You have to know," she said, "I don't want you to go."

"You have Callum," Jamie said quietly.

"Don't start with that again."

"I just mean that he'll take care of you, when you're sad."

"But who is going to take care of you?" she asked.

"London, I guess. You'll be back soon enough. For your big show and everything."

Nerea took a deep breath. *And everything.* Jamie had helped her think about it less, but as it drew closer the idea was becoming overwhelming.

"Do you remember when I told you I was afraid I was going to wake up and this would all be over?" he asked.

"Yes?"

"Here is what you should have told me," Jamie said, stopping in the path and turning to face her. "That you can't know if you are dreaming if you don't wake up once in a while. So I'll be fine. And you will too." He laughed softly to himself. "Hell, even Callum will probably be fine."

Later, as Callum and Jamie drove away, Nerea caught herself watching down the road where the car had disappeared. She shook herself. Being in love with Jamie — who was too young, too eager, and needed too much approval — was complicated enough without worrying at the wound of his absence.

The house was terribly quiet. Nerea tried to keep herself busy, but again and again she found herself watching the road and waiting for Callum's return. For the next two weeks they would lose themselves in each other and the isolation of this house. As much as Nerea was looking forward to seeing Jamie again in London — and oh how she was — these hibernations in Spain with Callum were always some of the best weeks of their lives.

Chapter 19

Jamie does his research

Jamie had never particularly considered London home — that was Dublin and his parents' house — but it had never felt so strange and alien as it did when he returned from a month in Spain. Being surrounded by his own language was suddenly odd, the air had an unseasonable chill for the end of September, and his flat was dark and cold. As he dumped the contents of his suitcase on the bed, Jamie found it hard to believe that he'd been packing his last things at Callum and Nerea's house a few short hours before. Spain already seemed like a lifetime ago.

For a few days he didn't hear much from Callum and Nerea, other than affectionate texts here and there and the occasional business email from Callum connecting him with a producer or director. Mostly, Jamie tried not to worry. They'd warned him that these two weeks were for the time they needed together away from the world. Jamie had found that easy to accept in theory, especially when they had already given him so much. But in practice, he missed them desperately.

He still had the keys to their flat and even thought about going there under the pretext of making sure everything was in order. He didn't, though; there was a vast difference between having a key and being told to make himself at home. If his own flat felt odd, he couldn't imagine how dismal and lonely theirs would seem.

Thankfully, his schedule kept him busy enough that he didn't have much time to mope. He had auditions to go to and, thanks to Callum, meetings to attend. When Jamie had protested — he hadn't started sleeping with Callum because of what he could do for him professionally — Callum had shaken his head and gone about setting up meetings for him anyway. Even his evenings weren't empty. He finally met up with his drama school friends and even got together once or twice with the Irish kids from *Butterflies* to have a pint and talk over politics at home.

In all, the two weeks passed faster than Jamie expected. The day before Callum and Nerea returned, he let himself into their flat. He'd brought a bouquet of wildflowers from Borough Market — sunflowers, Jersey lilies, and anemones, along with other blooms he didn't know the names of — a card, and some basics for the refrigerator.

Having finally given into the temptation he'd been so nobly resisting, Jamie felt vaguely guilty. But as he found a vase for the flowers and cut the stems, he told himself that he had reasonable cause. He left the flowers on the table, scrawled a note on the card, and turned on the lamp next to the bed. It would hardly do for them to come home to a dark flat.

Jamie had appointments all the next day and so only knew that Callum and Nerea had arrived safely when Callum texted him a gorgeous picture of Nerea standing at the table in the flat, her dark hair curtaining her face, leaning forward with her nose buried in the flowers he had left.

Thank you from both of us, Callum texted. *Especially for the provisions. Now get over here.*

To Jamie's dismay, he didn't get there until nearly nine. His last meeting ran late, the Bakerloo line was out for planned work while the Hammersmith & City just wasn't cooperating, and that was before he got stuck between stations on the Circle line for twenty minutes. By the time he emerged onto the street again it was raining viciously. Sometimes he hated London.

He was sopping and uncomfortable by the time he sprinted up the steps of Callum and Nerea's building and banged on the door of their flat, laughing with happiness and relief. Cold and wet didn't matter now that he didn't have to wait to see them any longer.

Nerea pulled open the door to reveal a room full of light and warmth. She took one look at him and reached a hand out to pull him inside. The curtain was pushed back and Callum was lounging in his underwear on the bed, his tablet propped in one hand.

"Undress. Now." Nerea ordered.

"You could say hello first," Jamie teased even as he unzipped his jacket.

"That wasn't about your body. That was about you dripping all over my floor. Callum, he's as bad as you."

"You say that like you didn't know," Callum said languidly, not looking up from his tablet.

"Why don't you have pants on?" Jamie asked. Under the force of Nerea's gaze he hung his jacket on the back of the door and toed off his squelching shoes.

Callum looked down at himself. "Oh. We got soaked coming home too. And then it was too much bother to get dressed again."

"So the romance is over?" Jamie asked.

Callum swiped past something on his tablet. "You've spent the last month in my bed with my wife and you let yourself into our building with your keys," he said, distracted. Jamie wondered what book he was reading. Maybe he could be coaxed into sharing or, better yet, reading aloud to Jamie as he drifted off to sleep. "While both of those things mean we have many obligations to you," Callum went on, "neither of them mean I have to get dressed when you come over."

Jamie turned to Nerea. "How is he so charming even when he's a bastard?"

~

And so, Jamie embarked on his Adventures of Leading a Somewhat Organized Polyamorous Life. They made a schedule that Callum dutifully punched into his mobile, Nerea wrote in her beautiful looping cursive in her leather-bound day book, and Jamie scrawled on whatever scrap of paper he had at hand. To Nerea's delight — and Jamie's no small amusement at her delight — they stuck to the schedule. If two of the three of them had a night marked off for themselves that was exactly what happened. If Jamie and Callum went out, Nerea worked on her Tate show, visited with Leigh and Sam or Piper, or just relaxed. If Jamie and Nerea were together, Callum visited the girls or stayed in and read. And when Callum and Nerea went out together, Jamie sprawled across his own bed for a nap and enjoyed having enough room for once.

Jamie savored his one-on-one time with each of them. Those date nights invariably wound up back at his own place. His flat still wasn't glamorous but he'd finally managed to clean and organize it. There was something wonderful about having Nerea spread out on his own sheets in the middle of the afternoon or lounging about naked with Callum watching rugby on his laptop after he'd pounded him into the mattress.

But as special as all that was, Jamie's favorites were the nights that hadn't been claimed by any pair of them. Those invariably turned into the three of them at Callum and Nerea's. Jamie was welcome and expected there — in their flat, in their bed, and in their lives. If he thought about it too hard, it was overwhelming.

"I got a book," Jamie blurted one such night. Nerea, in the middle of pressing kisses all the way down Callum's body, turned her head to stare at him. Callum made a disgruntled noise.

"A book about what?" Nerea asked, somewhere between surprised and amused. Callum shifted his hips in a clear attempt to get her to continue, but she ignored him.

"About polyamory."

Now Callum stared at him too. "Why?"

He might have been asking about the book. He also might have been asking why Jamie was blurting ridiculous things during sex. But it probably wasn't that. In the last few months Jamie had learned that people definitely blurted ridiculous things during sex, even when sex was a hot threesome and everyone involved was a celebrity.

"'Cause I wanted to get it right with you."

"That's why he's so bloody good at relationships," Callum said to Nerea. "He's cheating."

"I'm not cheating. It's research."

Nerea burst out laughing and buried her face against Callum's stomach.

Callum, after a moment, started laughing too. "You really got a book?" he asked through the feathery breath of his mirth.

Jamie gathered the blankets up around himself to hide the fact he was blushing.

"Oh come here, darling." Callum reached out one of his big hands and wrapped it around the back of Jamie's neck. "We're not laughing at you."

"Yes we are," Nerea said.

"Okay, yes, maybe you are. And we appreciate the effort you're putting into this," Callum said. Jamie opened his mouth to protest, but Callum pressed his fingers over his lips. "But please shut up now so I can kiss you."

Chapter 20

Callum realizes there are some conversations they should have had sooner

The day of Nerea's Tate show opening dawned cold and gloomy, the worst of London in November. It was the sort of ominous, depressing day that made Callum wonder if the sun had even risen behind the sheets of gray cloud that scudded across the sky.

This evening was going to be an experiment of sorts. Callum was happy to ignore random noises in tabloids and on the internet about his private life. But if the three of them were going to continue together in any capacity they needed to get used to being together in public and responding to whatever the result of that might be.

At Callum's insistence — and over Jamie's own objections that he'd be in the way — Jamie got ready for the evening at Callum and Nerea's flat. Nerea, despite having far more to do to than Callum or Jamie to prepare for the evening, was ready first. She wore a sleeveless emerald green gown. Her hair was piled high on her head and long gold teardrops dangled from her ears. She spent the rest of the afternoon fluttering around the flat, handing Callum his cufflinks when he was sure he'd misplaced them and doing Jamie's tie for him when he couldn't quite manage the full Windsor she demanded.

"Is she normally this worried before these sorts of things?" Jamie muttered under his breath, as he surreptitiously tried to loosen his tie.

"She's never had a show this high profile before," Callum whispered back. "Most artists only get shows like this when they're dead. Let her fuss."

⌐

Nervous as Nerea might have been back in the flat, Callum marveled when he handed her out of the car outside the Tate. She exuded nothing but calm and poise. When she turned a dazzling smile on Callum and wrapped her hand around his arm, he lost his breath. What on earth had he done to deserve such a rare and remarkable woman?

As she greeted photographers along the step and repeat banner and answered questions from arts reporters, he felt as awed as he had the first time he met her. She was all sly steel and warm confidence, her smile never faltering, even as she knew some of the media attention was simply a product of who she was married to. Callum expected she would curse to — or at — him about that later.

Jamie hung back, discreet but close at hand. Callum admired the way he was handling tonight. If their places had been reversed, Callum was sure he would have made a hash of it himself. But as the two of them waited on the sidelines for Nerea to catch them up, Jamie was charming the reporters. Each time they asked him too many questions about his own work, Callum watched admiringly as he deftly redirected their attention back to Nerea.

The three of them entered the part of the Tate hosting the show side-by-side. Callum had been to dozens of his wife's exhibits before, but to see her work hung here was breathtaking. She may have been nervous earlier but he had no idea how she was so calm beside him now. He was grateful he got to enjoy his triumphs sitting down in the dark.

She looked up at the walls and walked in a small circle to take the moment in, and then looked at him with a smile, giddy and young. "Thank you for being here with me," she said.

"Always." He kissed her briefly, and she squeezed his arm.

Then she turned to Jamie. "There's some people I'd like to introduce you to," she said. "If you're interested?"

Jamie beamed and offered Nerea his arm. Callum was sure Jamie would be interested in anything, so long as it involved Nerea. Callum smiled to himself and turned to pursue his own required networking.

Half an hour later he finally escaped an immensely dull conversation and nearly tripped over his best friend.

"Thom! How good to see you. I wasn't sure you would make it."

Thom took a gulp from a flute of champagne Callum suspected was not his first. "Neither was I. Give Nerea my regards, will you?"

"Tell her yourself, she's around here somewhere." He grabbed Thom by the elbow in hopes of steering him towards her, wherever she might have gone.

"Oh." Thom stopped in his tracks. "There she is."

And there Nerea was, standing in a little cluster of people. Jamie was at her elbow, looking charming and attentive. Piper was there too, as were Leigh and Sam. And, laughing at something Sam had just said, was Katherine, an artist herself, Nerea's friend, and Thom's ex-wife.

"Ah," Callum said. Perhaps this was not the best moment for them to join that particular conversation.

Piper glanced in their direction. Her eyes widened as she caught sight of them. Nerea had no doubt filled her in on the drama. Or perhaps Katherine had herself.

"I'll catch up with you later?" Thom was ready to bolt.

"Yeah," Callum said, dropping Thom's arm. "Yeah, that's fair."

~

An hour later Callum, Jamie, and Nerea huddled together in a corner. Nerea popped an hors d'oeuvre in her mouth from the plate Jamie had filled for them all. She still looked radiant, but Callum could see that the public performance of the event was wearing on her and Jamie both. Before he could say anything about it or ask what he could do to help, a man invaded their space. His suit was expensive but ill-fitting, and there was a sour expression on his face. He was a critic Callum vaguely recognized because Nerea had complained about him once. Too prone to gossip, she had said sharply. Nerea didn't mind it about the movies, but she felt it was ridiculous regarding fine art.

"I didn't know you had a son," the man said, glancing between the three of them.

Unlike previous questions about his presence which Jamie had been able to answer vaguely, this was different. Unlike when it had happened at the airport, here, it required a correction, and it was going to be tricky.

"He's not my son," Nerea said easily.

The critic turned to Callum. "Is he yours?"

Callum was equal parts horrified and amused. "Ah, no. All three of my daughters are also all three of her daughters. Jamie is…."

The moment of truth had arrived, as clear as it was unexpected.

"My date," Nerea said calmly.

Well, then. *Forward we go.*

The reporter's eyebrows went up. So did Jamie's. Callum smiled into his drink. As much as the three of them should have had more of a plan going into this evening, Nerea shocking people was always a delight.

A moment later, though, he wasn't smiling and nobody was amused. Callum missed what, exactly, the critic had said. He just knew that Jamie's face had darkened and Nerea looked alarmed.

"Would you have asked that question if she were a man?" Jamie asked. "Come to think of it, would you have asked Callum that if he said I was his date?"

The critic mumbled something, only somewhat abashed, but Jamie had just started to work himself into a full fury. Callum had never seen him like this. Maybe he should have intervened, but he was too entranced by Jamie's more than justifiable anger.

"Her kids are grown, so why does she have to worry about whether people think she's a good mother?"

"Jamie," Nerea said urgently. Callum could see her hand tightening on his arm, warning him, but Jamie either didn't feel it or didn't know what she meant.

He went on, his face flushed with anger. "And why should she worry about people calling her a whore 'cause she's good at relationships?"

That was Callum's cue to step in.

"Jamie," Callum leaned in as if he hadn't heard any of what had just happened and wrapped his arm around Jamie's shoulders, a smile on his face. "There are some people I want you to meet."

He steered Jamie bodily away; Callum was certain that without intervention, Jamie would have taken a swing at the critic. Loyalty and honor were all well and good, but there were some things that were never acceptable no matter how deserved.

He watched with relief as Nerea, pale, moved from the scene of the confrontation to fold herself into another group of their friends. Reassured that she was taken care of, Callum continued to steer Jamie through the mingling crowd and out into a quiet, mostly abandoned corridor.

"What are we doing out here," Jamie asked when Callum drew them to a halt. He blinked in the dim light as if he'd only just realized they were no longer in the middle of the exhibit and he was no longer yelling at someone.

"I appreciate what you're trying to do," Callum said, trying to keep his own rising anger in check. "But that is not how you deal with people like that."

"But — "

"I heard what he said," Callum said, even if that was — strictly speaking — not true. He could guess well enough. He'd heard most of it all before. "And you need to not react that way."

"I — " Jamie said.

"I understand that the world is terrible to women," Callum ran right over him, because this was not a debate. Or even a discussion. This was a statement about Nerea and how she needed to exist in the world.

Jamie still looked belligerent, so Callum let his own anger and disappointment come through in his voice and his bearing.

"I understand that Nerea's life, in particular, in public, can be very hard. But you cannot call people out like that. That is not what we do."

"What do you mean, not what we do. I can do as I like. Just because you're not willing to stand up for her in public and risk pissing people off. And you both just outed me, to everybody, saying I'm dating her. So don't tell me what I'm allowed or not allowed to say."

Callum went very still. His emotions warred. He was furious with Jamie, worried about Nerea, and now wracked with guilt. They had all made errors, and what the consequences of those errors would be, Callum did not know. Now, however, was not the time for apologies. Jamie needed to calm down, and the three of them needed to get through this as a united front. Everything else would have to wait.

"This is not about me," Callum finally said. "This is not even about Nerea. This is about she, and I, and the unit we have been in public and in private for the last thirty years. The one that has allowed us to live the life we want to live. You now share that unit with us, but that doesn't change how Nerea and I are together or how she and I deal with these matters. And I'll thank you not to make a scene that only puts her more in a spotlight that she doesn't want and doesn't deserve."

"But — " Jamie said again.

"And if you didn't want to be outed, you shouldn't have accepted our invitation tonight."

"That's not fair!"

"Most things aren't. We'll talk at home." Callum spun away before his own anger got the better of him.

⌒

The rest of the party, not to mention the cab ride back to the flat, was tense, but Callum hoped they could go upstairs, hash matters out with Jamie, and go to bed. The less they dwelt on this mess, the better.

What he was not expecting was Jamie to march up the stairs and into the flat, whirl around on his heel, and glare at them with the air of an angry puppy. It was adorable, but that didn't mean the situation wasn't serious.

"You don't get to talk to me like that in public," he snapped at Callum.

"I didn't talk to you like anything in public. I took you aside and we had a private conversation because you don't get speak to anyone the way you did," Callum said. "But it will be better for all of us to let the matter drop until we're all calmer and can discuss it rationally."

"Calmer! You're the one who yelled at me in a corridor at the Tate Modern. After outing me!" Jamie turned to Nerea, his voice pleading. "You heard what he said about you, I couldn't let him — "

"When a man says those things to me," Nerea interrupted him, "Callum draws him off to the side of the room and talks to him, quietly. He tells him that he understands where he's coming from, but that there are ways one talks to a lady, and

175

that is not it. I know it may seem gendered and unfair to you. That's because it is, but it is what works. And it frightens them."

"You gave me this whole speech about how you're not Callum's property!"

"I'm not," Nerea said calmly.

Jamie turned to Callum. "But you want me to just roll over when people say terrible things to her face."

"You're not listening!" Callum snapped. His patience had limits, and Jamie had finally surpassed them. Jamie trying to play him and his wife off each other was also profoundly displeasing.

"I don't want to be a poster woman," Nerea said. "For polyamory or open marriages or politics or anything. I want to paint, as I did before I met Callum, as I did before any sort of normal life became impossible. I couldn't even finish university! But I don't need your protection, or Callum's. I want to do my work and have my loves and deal with these things quietly."

"I can't believe you! If you want to live quietly, why would you say I was your date?"

"Because you were. Because it needn't be a big deal," Nerea said.

Callum bit his lip so he wouldn't comment harshly on Nerea's reasonable but completely wishful thinking. He didn't need to be fighting with her as well.

"Well it doesn't fucking work like that, does it?!" Jamie hollered at her.

"Not when you make it harder," Callum said.

"I am not the problem here." Jamie looked at Callum, looked at Nerea, and then strode to the door.

"Where are you going?" she asked, standing from where she had leaned, nearly slumped, against the arm of the couch.

"To make trouble elsewhere, I guess." Jamie's usually sunny face twisted in anger as he yanked the door open. When he slammed it after him, a picture frame on the counter toppled over.

Chapter 21

Nerea deals with a very worried Callum

"Why isn't he home yet?" Callum demanded, pacing back and forth in the narrow space of the flat. Nerea, in the armchair and still in her dress, uncrossed and recrossed her legs. It was very early in the morning, long past when Nerea would have liked to collapse into bed, but Callum was far too wired for that to be an option.

"He'll come home when he's ready," she said. She didn't say that might be never. Jamie could decide that this type of bullshit from the outside world — or from Callum, who should have known better — was more than he could handle. She didn't want to frighten her husband any further. It didn't seem like that big of a fight to her, despite the level of drama. But she couldn't be sure. All she could do was be optimistic and wait to berate whoever needed berating until this was fixed.

"Where did he go?" Callum stood abruptly from the kitchen chair he'd fallen into and started to pace again.

"His flat, probably." Nerea tried to sound bored instead of irritated, but it was the third time Callum had asked in as many hours.

"He left his keys here. And his mobile. We couldn't get in touch with him if we wanted to. He still doesn't know the city that well. Anything could have happened to him."

"He knows the city perfectly fine. Jamie's a big boy who can handle himself in London. He's been living here nearly a year! He probably just went to crash with a friend." She was worried, too, but that was a motherly reflex she was not planning to indulge, considering the remark that had started this whole mess.

"I should look for him," Callum patted his pockets as if checking for his own keys. "I'll find him, apologize, explain everything...I'll bring him home — "

"Explain what?" Nerea said.

"That we love him."

"Callum."

"What?"

"You're being ridiculous. He knows that. And it didn't stop him — or us — from fighting," Nerea closed her hands around the keys Callum had dropped on an end table, next to Jamie's. "Feelings don't fix logistics. They don't eliminate the fact that we all made mistakes tonight. Let him sort himself out."

"I still have to try."

"Where are you going to look?" Nerea said. "You don't know where to start, and the last thing this night needs is someone tweeting about you running around the city in distress."

"I could start — "

"No. No, stay here, love. I know you want to find him. But all we can do is wait, and I don't want to be alone." It was a cheap shot, and she knew it, but it worked to keep Callum from tearing all over London on his own.

Waiting was easier said than done. By the time the London sky had started to lighten, almost imperceptibly, into morning, Nerea had nearly shouted at Callum herself. His pacing was unbearable and his nerves were contagious.

"I want to invite him to Christmas," Callum said out of the blue.

"You what?" Nerea asked, as startled by the sudden break in the silence as she was by the words themselves.

"If he ever comes back and if we can fix this." Callum sounded tired. "I want to invite him to Christmas in Spain and to Devon's wedding."

"Margarita," Nerea corrected automatically before she completely registered the suggestion. "Are you sure that's a good idea?"

"No." Callum gave a weak chuckle. "It could be disastrous on any number of fronts. But we love him. We want him to be a part of our lives. If that's true, why shouldn't we include him in family holidays and celebrations?"

"For one, I imagine Jamie's family may have some objection to us stealing him for Christmas," Nerea pointed out. To be honest, her heart leapt at the idea of having Jamie in Spain again so soon and for the holidays no less. She wanted to immerse him in the sights, scents, and traditions of Christmas in the old house. He would also be a wonderful companion at the wedding. Assuming no one said anything judgmental and set him off. Which was, at the moment, far from certain.

"Our children rotate their holidays between various in-laws," Callum said. "His parents can hardly expect different from him."

"Yes, but I have no idea what, if anything, he's told them about us," Nerea pointed out. "We shouldn't make it more difficult for him."

"We should ask," Callum said. "Because we can't make that choice for him. Unless you don't want to?"

"I very much want to," Nerea said. "Besides, he's twenty-four and left his mobile here," she said, attempting poorly to inject some levity into the situation. "He'll be back."

Chapter 22

Jamie takes a walk

As soon as Jamie got to the street he realized he'd left his keys and his mobile at Callum and Nerea's. He wasn't getting home to his flat tonight, and there was no way he was going back upstairs. The lack of a mobile also made crashing with a friend difficult; he didn't want to show up at somebody's door unannounced in the middle of the night. And finding a pub to sit and drink in until morning seemed pathetic. The only option left was to walk. Which he did for hours until he had worked off his rage.

He slowed his pace but didn't stop moving as worry overtook anger. He kept his head down, not wanting anyone to see that his eyes were wet although there were few people on the street at this hour. Tonight he had very possibly screwed up absolutely everything that had been good and magical in his life: Not only his relationship with Callum and Nerea, but his career, too.

His mother had been right that one wrong move could follow him forever. Jamie's outburst tonight had definitely been a misstep, but so was Nerea exposing their relationship without having checked with him first. Dating his co-star's wife looked ugly, and anything truthful Jamie could say to make it look less ugly wasn't his to say. Jamie wasn't sure he liked that scenario. If he was going to be open about his relationships he wanted to be open about all his relationships. Assuming things between him, Nerea, and Callum were fixable, would they be amenable to that? And if they were, what would the wider consequences be? Every choice opened a massive can of worms, and this mess wasn't just about his public life. What would his parents think?

He turned onto the Strand and stayed with it as it became Fleet Street. He passed St. Paul's Cathedral and drifted down Cannon toward the monument to the Great Fire. The light shone on the wet pavement; the windows glowed even in the small hours of the morning; and the fog wound its way through the streets. He walked until he was too tired to feel scared and too preoccupied with the city to feel sad.

By the time he reached the middle of Tower Bridge the sky was beginning to grow light. Jamie stood watching the river as it turned from black and gold to a gray streaked with blue. London wasn't ever going to be home in the way the Dublin of his childhood had been. But he was absolutely in love with this city and his life in it. On some level he was still a scared little boy wanting to run back to his family for comfort, but right now that wasn't about his relatives in Ireland. It was about Callum and Nerea and their odd too-small flat under the eaves. It was time to go home.

Jamie wasn't sure if his lovers would accept his apology when he got there, but he knew he owed them one. And if they did forgive him, Jamie had demands of his own now. After all, he deserved an apology too.

By the time he got back to Covent Garden, the businesses that catered to the morning's first commuters were starting to open. He stopped into Costa for coffee and a bag of pastries; ten minutes later he was standing on the sidewalk in front of Callum and Nerea's building. He hit the buzzer with his knuckles. Even if he had remembered his keys, after their argument waiting for them to answer only seemed polite.

He startled when the door swung open and Callum, still wearing last night's clothes, stood before him. His jacket was gone, his tuxedo shirt was nearly halfway open, and his tie, undone, hung creased around his neck. His hair was a mess and there were deep circles under his lovely hazel eyes.

"Oh thank God," he breathed as he pulled Jamie inside and wrapped him up in a hug so tight he could scarcely breathe.

Jamie wriggled awkwardly to save the pastries from being crushed and then buried his face in Callum's shoulder, inhaling the familiar, reassuring scent of his cologne and Nerea's shampoo. When Callum finally let go, he held Jamie's shoulders tightly as if he was afraid he was going to run away again. It was then that Jamie noticed Nerea at the top of the stairs, barefoot but still in her dress from the gallery, looking tired and yet more lovely than he'd ever seen her.

"Are you going to come up?" she asked.

⌘

Upstairs, Jamie bounced on the balls of his feet. He had a script prepared of everything he needed to apologize for and ask about and explain, but Callum put a steadying hand on his shoulder before he could even open his mouth.

"Clearly, we all need to have a conversation," he said gently. "But just as clearly, we all need a nap. And a shower."

He gave Jamie a somewhat worried smile, looking his rain-soaked hair and clothes up and down.

Nerea nodded her agreement. "So we are going to hold off on the discussion until we are all clean, no longer tired, and have completely devoured that lovely heap of sugar and carbs," she said, indicating the bag of pastries with a nod of her head.

Jamie felt himself relax. Apparently he was not done learning tonight. With ease and gentleness, Callum and Nerea had made it clear that the conversation they desperately needed to have could keep, and none of it had to be handled with anger and panic. The three of them were going to be okay. Even so, Jamie wasn't sure he'd be able to sleep with so much left to solve. But as soon as he got out of the shower and crawled into bed in his usual spot between the two of them every muscle in his body seemed to give out at once. He thought he said something about being glad to be back. But he was asleep before he could be sure.

When he woke the sky outside was overcast and it was hard to tell the time of day. He groped around until he managed to get his hands on someone's mobile. Early afternoon.

Nerea woke when Jamie tossed the mobile back down on the bed. She cracked an eye open and smiled at him.

"Feeling better?" she asked quietly.

Jamie nodded, even though he felt nervous all over again. "Yeah."

"Good. Now poke Callum. If we have to be awake, he has to be awake."

Callum was much more reluctant about returning to consciousness, but eventually got out of bed to bring them all coffee. As Nerea and Jamie propped themselves up against the headboard Callum sat cross-legged in the middle of the bed facing them.

"I want to apologize to you," Jamie said as soon as they were all settled.

Nerea tried to interrupt, but he held up a hand.

"No, let me finish. I said some things to Callum that were unfair, and I put you in a bad position, Nerea. It was your night, to be handled on your terms, and I made it about my reaction to someone's bad behavior toward you. For that, I'm sorry."

"Thank you," Nerea said with a gracious nod of her head.

"That said," Jamie continued. "I am not a mind reader. And I should not be told 'this is how we do things' only after the fact. I'm twenty-four, I've never been in the public eye before, I don't know anything, and all I did was read that damn book."

Callum put his hand on Jamie's knee and squeezed, which didn't solve any problems, but it felt nice.

"Also," Jamie added, "We need to talk about the things I am and am not going to be out about. Just like I need to engage your lives on your terms, you need to engage me on mine. It wasn't your place to publicize my relationship with Nerea without asking how I felt about that first."

"I'm sorry too," she said.

"Thank you."

"So am I," Callum said. "You're right, we should have talked about this all weeks ago."

"Well, what's done is done," Jamie said with an awkward smile.

For a moment everyone was quiet, but it was the quiet of peace and ease, not of tension and brewing argument. Jamie let himself breathe for a while, enjoying a world that seemed far more stable than when he'd wandered London last night.

"What happens now?" he finally ventured to ask.

"I suppose," Nerea said with a glance at Callum, "We say out loud what we've been hedging around for some time. The relationships between us are not casual, not simple, and, as the events of last night make clear, can't be private forever. What I am going to say is that, Jamie, I love you, and I am very glad you are back here, and we are going to figure out that and so much else together."

Jamie nodded without being able to make words. For him this had never been something casual, not with Callum, not from that first day; and not with Nerea either, a thing cemented somehow, when they'd been at the beach, and Nerea, always so confident, had made a self-deprecating remark about her one-piece black swimsuit. *To hide the evidence of all those babies*, she'd said, as if she weren't perfect, as if any of the movie industry bullshit they were all wedded to mattered. Jamie was constantly honored that she'd trusted him with any part of the rich history of her life or her body.

"Okay," he finally found his voice enough to say. "I love you too. Both of you." He looked back and forth between them rapidly, all overwhelmed emotion. "Very much."

"As do I," Callum put in, looking a bit stunned.

"Now that's settled," Nerea said, "We have something we'd like to ask you."

"Yeah? After all that?"

Nerea smiled. "Oh yes. If we're doing this seriously and without an expiration date — and if we're making scenes in public — there's no reason not to invite you to come with us to Spain for the holidays. And Margarita's wedding."

"Is she going to be okay with that?" Jamie asked. Margarita had not been thrilled with him dating her parents when they had met. He imagined she would be even less thrilled about him being at her parents' house for Christmas and her wedding.

"We'll talk to her," Callum said. "But I'm sure she'll be fine provided you don't upstage her. Thank you for asking; it's good of you."

"As for Christmas," Nerea put in. "There are going to be a lot of people around. Whether that's a positive or a negative is up to you. But our girls are all coming and thanks to the wedding there will be more friends and relatives hanging about than we'll know what to do with. We'd very much like you to be a part of that."

"I'd love to," Jamie said breathlessly. He reached to grab both Callum and Nerea's hands. He was overwhelmed both with relief and with excitement that he got to continue this incredible relationship. Not only theoretically, but with concrete plans and arrangements. "I have to —" he stopped himself, his happy mood deflating.

"What is it?" Callum looked alarmed.

"I have to tell my parents. That I won't be home for Christmas. And that I'm dating you. *Both* of you. Especially before they read about it in the papers. That's okay, isn't it?" he added. If nothing else this whole mess was a lesson in the importance of not making assumptions.

"Of course it is," Nerea said.

"What do you need from us?" Callum asked.

"I don't know. Yet. It's not going to be an easy conversation. But if we're going to be together, I really need to have it."

Chapter 23

Callum tries to make things right

A week after what Callum now privately called The Great Gallery Debacle and Reconciliation, he went over to Leigh and Sam's house. It was a gray November afternoon, with an edge of cold that seemed to sink into his bones. When he walked into Leigh's warm sitting room, leaving the gloom and damp outside, Sam didn't seem to be at home. Callum was relieved. The conversation that he needed to have with his daughter would be easier to have alone.

"How are things with your mother?" Callum asked. As ever, he quickly gave up the attempt to share the big squashy armchair with Leigh's cat and settled instead onto the couch.

"More than fine. She's been lovely. From a very helpful distance. Thank you, by the way." Leigh smiled and sat down next to him. At eight months along she was moving with the kind of irritated heaviness Callum remembered from Nerea's pregnancies.

"It was no problem at all."

"I saw some reviews for her show," Leigh said. "They were all glowing."

"Yes, indeed." Callum fairly glowed himself at the thought of all those articles praising Nerea's talent, her eye, her composition. Nerea was wonderful, and she deserved the world knowing and celebrating that. Callum had gone out and bought multiple copies of the papers and magazines that carried reviews, and Nerea had carefully clipped out the articles and pinned them up on the wall in the kitchen. It had been an extra relief that, in all the buzz about the show, there had been no buzz about the artist's personal life. Apparently the journalist who'd overheard it all didn't care about who an artist was sleeping with other than, or in addition to, her husband. Perhaps a sensible editor had intervened, or maybe there'd not been enough space or time. Whatever the reason, Callum thanked God for it. Jamie, in particular, had been relieved to have a bit more time to sort out how he was going to discuss the matter with his parents.

Callum and Leigh sat in easy silence for a moment. In the armchair, the cat stood up, turned around, and flopped down again to curl up on its other side.

Leigh sighed. "All right. What do you need?"

"Was I that transparent?" Callum asked.

Leigh gave him a look that said he was fooling exactly no one and that he was being tiresome. "You invited yourself over, asked if things were okay with Mum when they've been fine for months — and you know she and I would have told you if they weren't. You're not talking when all you ever do is talk. You think you're getting better at covering when you want something, but you're not. So what is it?"

"A lot of things." Callum looked at his hands.

"Do you want me to respond to your request, or do you want me to pry the request out of you like a bad tooth?"

"It's about Jamie," Callum confessed.

"Margarita told me she met him," Leigh said carefully.

"What did she say?" Callum couldn't help asking, more eagerly than was probably useful. But he wanted to know.

"That he seemed like a nice enough kid," Leigh said. "But that he's younger than she is. Also she thinks you're dragging Mum into your midlife crisis and has zero patience for any drama that's going to come of this, but you probably knew all of that already.'

"Yeah. Thanks, though, for reinforcing it."

"No problem."

"To be clear," Callum said. "I'm telling you this despite your fair and stated preference to know as little as possible about my extracurricular activities because this isn't extracurricular anymore."

"What does that mean?" Leigh asked. "Do I want to know what that means?"

"The relationship with Jamie is serious. For both your mother and I."

"Serious how?" Leigh looked skeptical.

"Serious, we're making long-term commitments to each other."

"Are you moving in together? Are you telling the papers?"

"Maybe? Yes? At some point in the future at any rate. We're doing the kind of work that's probably going to lead to those sorts of things." Callum knew he was jumping the gun a bit; the three of them hadn't had conversations about any of those topics in particular. But they were headed in that direction.

"Okayyy." Leigh still looked dubious. "How does this impact my life? Just because Sam and I are poly in the sense

191

that we occasionally have joint girlfriends, doesn't mean that I need to know about your poly drama."

"You could tell me about your poly drama," Callum offered.

Leigh grinned smugly. "I don't have poly drama. Drama doesn't come with poly. That's all you."

"Jamie's coming to Christmas and to Devon's wedding."

"Margarita!" Leigh laughed disbelievingly. "And he's doing *what?*"

"Coming to the wedding. And Christmas."

"Jesus, Dad."

"Antonio's also coming to the wedding," Callum said, faltering a bit in the face of Leigh's less-than-promising reaction.

"Yes, I know. Mum told me ages ago. Which has what to do with Jamie, exactly? Other than making this the most awkward get-together ever?"

"I was hoping you might have a word with your sister for me. For us. To…smooth over things about Jamie. And Tonio."

"No. Absolutely not," Leigh said decisively. "I am not going to get in the middle of you and my sister and whatever it is you both need to sort out."

"But you're the one who understands — "

Leigh cut him off. "Me getting along with you, does not give me a direct line to understanding choices you have made in the past. And even if it did, it does not obligate me to play go-between because you can't figure out why Margarita's been angry with you most of her life. I'd been hoping you could figure it out yourself but since you're sitting here asking me to intercede with my sister, that's not going to happen. So I'm going to tell you why, and you're going to decide what to do about it without my help."

"All right," Callum said. Leigh was pragmatic in her anger, which was unsettling because it meant he deserved her wrath. As prepared as he was to hear her out, that was still hard.

"Do you remember when Ana and Carlos's daughter got married?"

Callum tried to recall the name and the event. "That was twenty years ago."

"More than that. Do you remember it, though?"

"Other than that it happened? Not particularly."

"You had just come home. You'd been off somewhere on a project for six months. We'd seen you maybe an odd weekend or two. Piper was just a toddler. In any case, at the reception, Margarita tripped and fell, the way kids do, and knocked out a baby tooth. You and Tonio were both there, Mum was off somewhere else. And Margarita ran to Tonio."

"Oh. Oh God. That wedding." Callum took a deep involuntary breath. He remembered now. He could see it all, twenty years past: The garden decorated for a reception, the milling crowd chatting in its wedding finery, little Devon in her sky-blue fancy dress and white patent leather shoes tripping and falling and Callum hadn't been able to get to her in time.

"Yes, that one. You yelled at her. For going to the man she rightfully expected to comfort her. Which wasn't you."

"No wonder she hates me," Callum said. All the shame of that day was flooding back to him.

"She doesn't hate you. She just doesn't trust you. Not entirely. But you get it now?"

"That's why your mother ended her relationship with Tonio, you know," Callum said. "She was furious with me. Tonio was furious with everyone. He told your mother to dump him or dump me but either way to make a goddamned choice."

"And she chose you."

"She almost didn't." Callum looked at his hands again. It felt strange to talk about. So much of his life was public record, and yet, so much of it was only known to himself and Nerea. And Tonio. "It took a long time for us to be okay again, but we did a lot of soul searching and a lot of work and managed to stay together. And Devon — Margarita, sorry — I've never felt more wretched in my life than I did as soon as I'd finished hollering at her. I was exhausted and jetlagged and I felt like I was losing my family. And then I very nearly did."

"Dad," Leigh said. "I'm not the one you have to explain this to. Or apologize to, because I assume there was an apology somewhere in there. We've always been alike, you and me, and I understand how you make your mistakes. Piper doesn't even remember those years. But Margarita — you owe her an apology. You can't change what happened or fix what you did. But you can apologize. And maybe be less prickly around her very legitimate sore spots."

Callum nodded slowly. He felt like he'd been kicked in his ribs. He somehow hadn't thought, hadn't considered, that Margarita would have been so affected by that incident. She deserved to be, and Callum deserved all of her mistrust. That didn't make him feel better, but it did make him understand.

"All we wanted then was for you to be around," Leigh said. "Not to come crashing back into our lives full time by breaking all the systems we had finally got in place."

Callum nodded again. He didn't trust himself to speak; this was a reckoning a long time coming.

Leigh bit her lip. "It's great that you and Mum have someone to add to the happiness that you have now. But if Jamie is somebody you're serious about, then I presume you're not going to keep him separate from my life with Sam. And our baby."

"Part of the family, yes," Callum mumbled, still shamed by Leigh's ongoing fierce clarity.

"What I'm saying then, is that if Jamie becomes a part of my kid's life, and then you and he or Mum or whatever fall apart, you do not get to make my kid's life miserable the way you made mine and Piper's and Margarita's miserable. Though obviously Jamie's not going to be a parent figure."

"I'd hope not, he's younger than you."

"Ugh, yes, you don't have to remind me," Leigh said, laughing at an absurdity Callum could recognize too. "But the point remains. Don't do the same stupid stuff twice, because I'm not going to be on your side this time and I've got a bigger mouth on me now."

⌒

Callum was glad he'd arranged to meet up with Thom weeks ago. Although he wasn't much in the mood for company after his showdown with Leigh, time with someone he adored who was neither blood family nor lover would do well to shake him out of his funk. If he was very lucky, Thom might even help him figure out how to make things up to Margarita going forward.

Coming in out of the freezing drizzle of the rain was a deep relief. The sky was already dark even though it was barely four o'clock, and Callum needed to lose himself a bit in the warmth of dark wood and ale.

Though he'd been at the gallery and witnessed most of that drama in person, Thom dutifully absorbed Callum's relation of those events and his conversation with Leigh without adding much in the way of commentary.

"One thing's for sure," Thom said when Callum had finally finished. "Your daughters are all way smarter than you."

"I knew that," Callum said proudly. "And now, I would like to extend my and Nerea's formal invitation to spend Christmas with us."

"Really?" Thom looked taken aback. And possibly wary. Both were strange.

"Definitely! Unless you have other plans. But we've been inviting you for years and you've never come. So this year you and whoever you're bringing to the wedding are."

"I get a date?" Thom looked faintly green.

"Of course you do. Let me know if you're not bringing anybody, though — Nerea wants a final headcount soon. You did get the invitation, right?"

Thom nodded. "Probably. I haven't looked at my mail in a while. I've been busy."

"Are you seeing anyone?"

"What makes you think that?" Thom looked downright nervous now.

"You just said you were busy when I know for a fact that you don't have any urgent work projects right now. So I assumed." Callum wasn't sure what to make of the look on Thom's face.

"Some people have hobbies other than fucking people," Thom said.

"So you're not seeing anyone?"

"I didn't say that."

"So you are seeing someone."

"I can, in fact, be seeing someone and not want to talk to you about her," Thom said.

"Where's the fun in that?"

"Believe me, both of us will be happier if I don't."

"Really?" Callum didn't believe him. He was also disappointed. Gossip, especially about a friend's happiness, could be such good fun.

"Definitely." Thom was firm. "And you can tell Nerea I won't be bringing anyone that will increase her headcount."

"No? That's a shame."

Thom shook his head and lifted his glass to drain it. "You have no idea."

Chapter 24

Nerea plans a wedding

On the first of December, Jamie left for Dublin, and Nerea and Callum flew back to Spain. Nerea loved this time of year there. They both missed Jamie immediately but there were other pleasures to compensate while they waited for him to rejoin them. The air in Spain, in contrast to London's, was soft and mild. The sharp brightness of winter hadn't fully set in, and mists threaded their way through the trees in the morning and evenings. The woods and fields were soft browns and tawnies, the sun mellow and gentle.

There was plenty to keep both of them busy. The wedding was scheduled for the day after Christmas in the village church, and the reception would be at the house. Which would make the day of the wedding hectic in the extreme but there was something proper and fitting about the party being held in an old house that had been in the family for so long. Until then, there were flowers to arrange, tents and heaters to plan for the back garden, and negotiations to be made with the church ladies about schedules. Margarita had settled on a lovely dark green and gold for her wedding colors, and in the evenings Nerea sketched different ideas for what to do with the heaps of pine boughs and gold ribbon they'd acquired while Callum sat reading aloud to her from a book.

⁂

"Tonio called," Nerea told Callum after they'd been at the house for a week. They were getting ready for bed: Callum was in the bathroom brushing his teeth while Nerea undressed and sorted her clothes into the proper laundry bins. It was dark outside, but over the fields Nerea could see pinpricks of light from their neighbors' home. In here, their bedside lamps glowed warm and golden.

Callum made an inquisitive sound around his toothbrush.

"He offered to come by and make sure that all the tables and chairs we rented for the reception would work."

"What did you say?" Callum asked.

"I said it was more kind than necessary. But he insisted that everything should be perfect for Margarita. So I told him I would talk to you and see if it was all right." Nerea pulled on an old shirt of Callum's — long-sleeved and worn soft — that she loved to sleep in.

"You don't need my permission to have him come over," Callum said. Nerea thought he sounded rather embarrassed.

"I know I don't," she said with more patience than her husband deserved. "But before my ex-boyfriend who we nearly divorced over, whose catering company we are getting food and tables and chairs from, shows up at our house without the buffer of a crowd, I want to make sure you're going to be okay."

"It was a long time ago."

"It was and so you keep saying. But are you going to be okay? And don't do me the disservice of pretending, again."

"It will be fine," Callum said as he emerged from the bedroom. His brown hair was mussed and the fabric of his T-shirt showed the strong lines of his chest and the softer curve of his belly. Nerea found him devastatingly attractive, not least because of all the work and love and care that had gone into making their life together possible. Callum was gorgeous in both body and soul in a way the public world that sustained him would never understand. For all he had infuriated her in the past and surely would continue to in the future, Nerea counted herself one of the luckiest people in the world to have a love like this. A love that, now, she got to share with Jamie as well.

"Leigh told me about the conversation you two had. About him," Nerea said.

"Ah. She did?"

"I'm not going to ask for details and I'm not going to ask if you've talked to Margarita about it yet. But I want you to know that I appreciate it. Rather greatly."

"I should have apologized long ago," Callum said as he climbed into bed. Nerea slipped under the covers next to him and was happy to be wrapped up in his arms, one of his long legs draped over hers.

"You did. To me. But not to the girls."

"And it's my intention to repair that. And not only because Margarita is still a bit annoyed we're bringing our boyfriend to the wedding."

"It's a wedding," Nerea said as Callum pressed a gentle kiss to her hair. "It wouldn't be proper if one of our daughters wasn't annoyed at us for something."

Tonio stopped by the house the next day. Nerea was in the kitchen experimenting with dessert recipes when he arrived. She wouldn't have planned it so, but Callum was the one who answered the door and let him in, asking after his wife and girls as he led him down the hall to the kitchen.

It had been years since Tonio had been in the house. As he and Callum entered the kitchen Nerea couldn't help but remember when he used to be here nearly every day — and usually overnight — walking into the house with groceries he'd picked up or with laundry he'd helped bring in from the line, or just with himself, happy to spend time with her and her girls. She could tell, as he looked around at the room, that he was thinking the same thing.

Tonio said hello when she looked up from where she'd been pretending to concentrate on her cookbooks.

"Hello, Tonio."

"Not much has changed," he said quietly.

"Some things have. Some things haven't."

With Callum standing there trying and failing to appear non-awkward, she wondered again if letting Tonio come by was a mistake. But then Callum, as he occasionally did so magnificently, rose to the moment. "Can I show you the garden?" he asked.

Tonio startled, like he'd forgotten the other man was even there. "Yes. Thank you."

As they left through the back door, Nerea caught Callum's eye and gave him a warning look.

Don't worry, Callum mouthed back.

Nerea waited. Whatever was about to happen, she was glad for the moment alone. That was the downside of the wedding, of three children, of a husband, of Jamie. Never quite enough time alone, not to prepare for all the messes and moments they made.

She didn't hear any shouting for a quarter of an hour but also didn't manage to make any progress at all with her desserts. She gave up waiting, wiped her hands on a dish rag, and crept through the house toward her own garden.

If any work had been accomplished — and she didn't know that it had — it was already done. Tonio was lounging in a chair, his legs crossed. Callum was perched on a low wall that separated the rose bushes from the orchard beyond. Of the two of them, he looked the more tense, but not angry. Ashamed. He was leant forward, eager to be understood.

He turned and saw her in the doorway, and his face instantly softened. In love with her like always. But Nerea wished he hadn't seen her watching. Especially when Tonio followed Callum's gaze and lifted a hand at her in acknowledgment.

"The life we should have had," she said softly to herself, not loud enough for either of the men to hear. She smiled at both of them before taking her leave. Maybe this reconciliation meant they all could be friends and Tonio could bring his wife and their girls over; they could eat meals under the fig trees. Today was not yet that day, but it was closer than it ever had been before.

⤝

"What are you thinking?" Callum asked, stroking a hand through Nerea's hair. She was lying half on top of him in their bed, his arms wrapped around her and his heartbeat a steady pulse in her ear.

"I don't know." She rubbed her wet face into Callum's chest. Wordlessly, he flailed for a tissue from the night table for her. He even tossed it toward the waste basket when she was done blowing her nose. He missed, as he usually did. "That I didn't think this was going to be this hard, and I thought it was going to be hard."

Callum hummed, a small, soothing sound.

"Screw you for getting along with him now, you know?" Nerea wasn't truly angry, but awkward avoidance had been better than this wrenching melancholy. She was glad Jamie wasn't here to see it.

"I know. I'm sorry."

"Why are you so good at sorry all of a sudden?" Frustrated, she pushed at his shoulder.

"The world in which our three children and our twenty-four-year-old lover were all more mature than me was becoming depressing."

"It's very annoying," Nerea said after a breathless pause. "That after twenty-nine years of marriage you keep finding new ways to impress me."

"Sorry," Callum said with a chuckle and a kiss to her shoulder. "But very much not sorry."

"There's something else I keep thinking about," Nerea said after a quiet moment. "And since you're feeling so very capable, maybe you can see a solution."

"What's that?"

"This house. We can't live in it forever. Not with just us."

"Why not?"

"It's too isolated. It takes hours to get here from the airport and it's half an hour to the nearest town. It's always a little too cold even in the summer. And don't even get me started about all the time and money it takes in upkeep." It pained her to admit it, but it was all true. Her parents had given her this house long before they'd been too old to care for it themselves. Not a wedding present, but much later, perhaps forgiveness for all the drama around her marriage. It had taken years before her mother had forgiven her not only for being married in London, but for not having a Catholic service.

Now she could only think about her age and Callum's, their daughter who was so insistent on being Spanish and having a Spanish life, and the boy from Ireland they were both in love with. While they had always had a flat in London, Spain had always been her only home. And suddenly, because Callum had finally gotten his act together, she felt like she was going to have to say goodbye to it.

"What do you want to do?" Callum asked.

"I don't know yet."

"Can we figure it out together?"

"Always."

"Just checking."

They lay in bed for a long time after that, not speaking, enjoying the stillness of the house and listening to the occasional ruffle of wind round the walls.

Chapter 25

Jamie tells his parents everything

As Jamie's plane landed in Dublin, he was aware he had put off having a conversation with his parents about his relationships for far too long. He had justified it, at first, by telling himself that since he'd come out to them as bi when he was fourteen, he'd earned some secret-keeping by now. But ever since the fight with Callum and Nerea and the agreements they'd come to in its aftermath, he knew he had to tell them sooner or later. Preferably, sooner. But just because telling his parents was the right thing to do, didn't mean he wasn't terrified. Jamie being queer was one thing. His mum had always been relatively easy with it, and his dad had wanted him to be happy and as safe as possible. But being bi, and dating a married couple who were both twice his age, were on two very different ends of the Things His Parents Would be Okay With spectrum.

But his parents loved him, and it would be fine. Which Jamie repeated to himself as he waited at the baggage claim for his suitcase. It was going to be fine.

～

Things at home were not fine.

His dad picked him up from the airport and drove to the house with a set to his jaw Jamie didn't know how to interpret. Jamie wondered if his parents had already heard about Callum and Nerea; he just had no idea how. There had been no buzz on the internet or in tabloids about Jamie appearing at Nerea's gallery opening. He had checked.

But, he realized as soon as he stepped inside the house, whatever was going on had nothing to do with him. His mother greeted him with a hug, but she was clearly distracted. In the kitchen Aoife was at the counter, red-eyed and drying dishes with a mutinous expression on her face.

Aoife hugged Jamie fiercely. Jamie held her tight and looked over her shoulder to where their parents stood in the doorway, watching them and looking worried.

"What is going on?" Jamie said to Aoife.

"Patrick and I want to move in together," she said, stepping back and scrubbing a hand over her face.

"And that's a problem why?" Jamie asked.

"Ask them," Aoife said. "Or listen to the voicemails I left you. You never called me back."

"How about we all sit down," their mother suggested. "Jamie, do you want some coffee? Anyone else?"

Five minutes later, seated all around the living room and fortified with coffee, Jamie demanded again of his parents why Aoife wanting to move in with her boyfriend was a problem. All worries about his own troubles and confessions he needed to make were gone in the face of his sister's situation. He had no idea why his parents would object. Aoife and Patrick had been together for years. Hugh and Maureen were Catholic, sure, but had always worried more about good sense and kindness than any adherence to doctrine. And Beth had lived with her husband for six months before they'd gotten married. Though they'd been engaged at the time.

"She's — you're so young, Aoife," his mother said.

"I'm twenty-two. You were married when you were twenty-two," Aoife pointed out.

It was clear they'd had this argument many times. Jamie felt like an absolute prick that he hadn't returned Aoife's calls or even listened to her voicemails. He'd assumed if it was really important she would have texted or emailed to remind him.

"I know this has nothing to do with me being young," Aoife said.

And there it was. Jamie looked at his parents, who looked worried but resolute. And who were saying nothing.

"Are you telling me," Jamie said, "that you don't want Aoife to have a relationship with someone she loves because she has Down Syndrome?"

"Patrick and I both do, thank you," Aoife added.

"What I am telling you — and Aoife," his mother said, "is that we live in Ireland, and while there are resources available to help you live independently, I'm afraid you and Patrick won't be allowed to live together unless you're married."

"We're getting married," Aoife said in a tone that suggested she had said it many times before. But the whole room seemed to still. Apparently Jamie's parents had not heard this before this moment.

"I'm sorry, what?" their father said.

"We're getting married," Aoife repeated, sitting up straighter. "So we can live together. We've found a residential services community we like. We can go on the waiting list. We'll move in after the wedding."

Again, silence, as everyone absorbed this.

Maureen was the first to speak. "Why couldn't you have told me this in the right order? Because there are still things we should talk about, but this makes everything very different. And you need to be sure."

"That's what married is," Aoife said, "Being sure. We thought you'd be most upset about moving. And I wanted Jamie to be home to share," Aoife said with a sidelong, almost shy glance at Jamie. "But then we started arguing again."

"Congratulations," Jamie said and stood up from his seat to walk around the table to hug Aoife. Someone had to stop being shocked and say what was right.

"Yes, yes, congratulations," his mum said, and then she and his dad were standing up to join in the hug too. It was a bit awkward, and not just because there were four of them, but because it felt like his parents still weren't certain. But it was probably a lot for them to get used to. Jamie would call them on it if he needed to, but there was no reason to do so in front of Aoife.

"You're going to have an awesome wedding, right?" Jamie asked when they all pulled apart. Although that was as much to make a point to his parents as it was to find out what Aoife wanted. "Because you should have a wedding just like Beth's and Mary's. If you like, of course."

Aoife, delighted now that the worst was over, laughed and stamped her feet with joy. "Yes!" she exclaimed, drawing the word out so that it felt like more than one syllable and wandered through several pitches. "But first I need to get the ring."

"Bring Patrick round this week," his dad said. "We should talk with him and with his parents."

"Whoa. What?" Jamie turned to him. "You can't treat Aoife like a kid. Especially not now she's engaged. Why do you have to talk to her fiancé's parents?"

Hugh looked amused. "Because that's how it works. When two people get engaged, their parents get together to talk about their children and the wedding. Not that you'd know that, Jamie-boy."

Jamie flushed harder than was warranted by the comment alone. Now he was the only one of his siblings not engaged or married. And if he stayed with Callum and Nerea, that situation was never going to change.

He loved Callum and Nerea, and he loved his parents and his sisters, but as he watched his mother — nervous and grateful and surprised — hug Aoife again, he couldn't help but mourn the fact that he might well never share a moment like this with his family.

⁀⁀

The next night Jamie went out to dinner with Aoife and Patrick, where he apologized to both of them for blowing off Aoife's phone calls. He might not have been able to help in any particular way, but he could at least have been an ally to them both while Aoife had worked through matters with their parents.

That evening, up in Jamie's room at their parents' house, the siblings talked for hours. About Aoife's plans for the wedding, but mostly for the life she wanted to build outside of the house she'd lived in her entire life and that their parents had probably thought she would never leave. The transition was going to be immense for all concerned and was going to take time. Now that Aoife had decided, Jamie wasn't clear on how patient she was inclined to be. They were alike in that. They were both a little greedy for all the world could give them, no matter how strange, no matter other people's doubts.

"Can I tell you about something?" Jamie said to his sister after their mum had come in to say good night and admonish them, fondly, not to stay up too late.

"Yes?"

Jamie flopped back on his bed and stared up at the ceiling. "So I told you I'm seeing someone."

"Yeah, even though you refuse to give me any details."

"The someone I'm seeing is actually two people."

"And they don't know about each other?" she guessed.

"No. They're married. To each other," Jamie clarified.

"But they don't know you're dating both of them?"

"Still no. I'm dating a married couple. Like. Jointly."

"That seems confusing," Aoife's face twisted up as she said it. "Who are they?"

"Somebody I met at work. And his wife."

The confusion in Aoife's face turned to judgment. "Who, Jamie?" She was insistent.

"You know how I was in the movie with Callum Griffiths-Davies?"

Aoife started laughing and then didn't stop.

Jamie sat up and waited for Aoife's giggles to run their course. But they didn't seem to be subsiding. Which, if he looked at the situation — both that of his relationships and of this conversation — he could hardly blame her for.

"You're dating Callum Griffith-Davies. And his wife?" she finally managed through gasps of mirth.

"Yeah."

"No, you're not. You're teasing me. Which isn't nice."

"I'm not," Jamie said. He wouldn't. "I mean, I'm not teasing you. I really am dating them."

Aoife pressed her hands over her mouth; the giggles starting again. Then she took a deep breath and very cautiously slid her hands to her cheeks so she could talk. "You're dating Callum Griffith-Davies *and his wife*," she repeated.

Jamie laughed. It was pretty funny to hear it aloud from an uninvolved person. "Yes." Maybe if he was lucky his parents wouldn't believe him either.

"Jamie. Oh my God."

"Yeah. Yeah, I know."

"Have you told Mum and Dad?"

"What do you think? Especially after the fit they threw about you and Patrick? How am I supposed to?"

"You should," Aoife said, sobering. "If you're serious."

"Of course I'm serious! And they're serious about me. Which is why I have this problem now."

"A lot of people would like that problem. He's hot. Mum's going to go spare." Aoife pointed out. Then she went starry-eyed. "Will you bring him to my wedding?"

Jamie dropped his head into his hands and moaned at what was a fair, generous, and likely deeply unwise request.

Aoife patted him unsympathetically on the shoulder.

⁌

Jamie waited until the next evening to broach the topic. He was helping his mum wash the dishes while his dad was out of earshot in the living room watching the news. Aoife was at work. As much as he'd been glad to come to her defense the other day, he didn't want her to have to come to his.

"So, er, I wasn't sure how to bring this up," Jamie said as he scrubbed water droplets from a plate with a towel his mother had had since he was a kid. "But I mentioned I'm seeing someone?"

"You've mentioned. In the vaguest possible terms," his mother said. She looked amused. "Am I going to get details now?"

"Sort of," Jamie said.

"What's that mean?"

"It means they asked me to Spain for Christmas and for a wedding, and I said yes because they're important to me, and I didn't tell you before cause I knew you were going to be mad?"

"This is where you give me a name, Jamie," his mother said after the briefest of hesitations. Jamie noted, with some alarm, that she'd set down the glass she was washing out.

"Callum," Jamie practically squeaked.

His mother's eyebrows went up. "Is this Callum, your coworker, Callum?"

"Yeah."

"I thought he was married. I've seen her in magazines. Pretty Spanish woman."

Jamie nodded. "He is. She is."

"They're separated? Getting a divorce?"

"Um. No."

"*James.*" His mother looked horrified. Jamie shrank back. Nobody called him that, ever, except his mum, and only when he was in very, very deep trouble. "What are you telling me? Is he cheating on his wife with you?"

"No." Jamie kept rubbing the towel over the plate, even though he'd dried it ages ago. "I'm dating her, too."

He had wondered if his mum might yell. He decided the stunned silence that stretched on — and on — was far worse.

"I'm sorry, I think I misheard you," Maureen finally said.

Jamie shook his head. "You didn't or you'd be talking."

More silence. Then she said, "This isn't what we meant by equal opportunity."

It wasn't a joke, not really, and Jamie had to restrain a wild and inappropriate urge to laugh.

"It wasn't like I planned it," he said, knowing that wasn't much of a defense against anything his mother could possibly be thinking. But he needed to stall for time as he looked for the right opening to explain. A petulant *we're in love* was definitely not going to cut it.

"Clearly."

"Look, I mean, I understand why it freaks you out — "

"You do, do you?"

Jamie was dimly aware that she might be working up to that place where she enjoyed her outrage, which definitely wasn't going to help his case.

"It's not typical. It's not what you expected for me — it's not what I expected for me. But why does that matter?"

Maureen set a dish down on the counter with more force than was strictly necessary. Jamie flinched. "Which of my eight thousand objections would you like first? I'm perfectly happy to argue about bad translations and believe the Church is just wrong about homosexuality, but there aren't exactly any three-person relationships lurking in the Bible — "

"Not exactly true," Jamie interjected.

"If you say The Holy Trinity, God help your soul."

"That's not what I was going to say!"

"Good. But there is a list available for this fight, and we should start somewhere."

213

"Fine, what's the list?" Jamie asked, even if he could tell he was irritating his mother even more by being reasonable.

"In no particular order: Age differences will break your heart; Hollywood decadence is a slippery slope toward a hell likely filled with Scientologists; they're married to each other, which gives you no security; and two against one isn't a game anybody wins."

Jamie picked up another wet dish out of the strainer and concentrated on it. He was horribly afraid he was going to laugh at the accidental sexual innuendo of the last item on her list and was well aware that if he did, his mother would lose her mind.

"I bought a book," he blurted, because it was better than laughing.

Maybe not that much better, he reflected, as his mother turned disbelieving eyes on him. He didn't have the heart to tell her that Callum's reaction had been the same.

⁓

"Jamie!" Nerea exclaimed, when she picked up the Skype call. "We weren't expecting you to call so early."

"Are you in the middle of something?" Jamie asked somewhat helplessly. It didn't look like they'd been in the middle of sex, but then, Jamie knew firsthand how well the two of them could put themselves back together in cases of unexpected interruption.

"No, no. We're glad to see you. What's going on?" Callum asked. He and Nerea were sitting in bed. From the lack of books or tablets scattered about, Jamie assumed they'd been watching a movie.

"Can you take me off the big screen?" He kept his voice low. His mother did not need to know he was making this call. Whatever confrontation she might eventually have with his lovers, Jamie was not up to today being the day that happened. "Callum's right, it is really weird to have you look at me like that."

"Of course, just a moment." Callum reached for a remote.

The view on Jamie's laptop changed to the couple sitting together, their faces both looking down at what he presumed was Callum's tablet.

"What's going on?" Callum asked.

Jamie hunched forward, not even able to relax in his own room. If he could have dived through the screen to be with them he would have. "I know I'm not supposed to come to Spain until next week, but would you mind if I came early?"

Callum and Nerea exchanged a look. "Of course not," Nerea said. "How early?"

"Tomorrow?"

They exchanged another look.

"What's happened, Jamie?" Nerea asked, her voice serious.

"Can I not talk about it right now?" Jamie had thought he'd be able to explain. But now that he had Callum and Nerea in front of him and also several hundred miles away, he was horribly afraid he was going to burst into tears. "I promise I'm okay; everything's okay; I just need to see you."

"You're always welcome here," Callum said, "but you're giving us the one sentence version of what's going on before you book a flight."

"Callum," Jamie whined. He couldn't help it. It was the only manner of expression he could find that wasn't going to make everything in his head and his parents' house significantly worse.

"Like everyone else in this relationship, you are an equal until you don't tell us what we need to know to be useful," Callum said sternly.

"I told my parents," Jamie blurted.

Nerea gave a little gasp and covered her mouth.

"How did that go?" Callum asked, even though Jamie thought the answer should have been apparent.

"With my mum, 'bout like that," he said, pointing to Nerea on his screen. "With my dad, kind of worse."

Chapter 26

Callum offers Jamie some advice

Callum was worried. He and Nerea had woken up to an email from Jamie with his flight information; he'd be landing just before noon. Which made today a busy one for arrivals, as Thom was due to arrive that morning and Piper was getting in later that afternoon.

Callum had wondered for some time what would happen when Jamie told his parents about the three of them, but he had assumed things would be more or less all right when that eventually came to pass. Jamie's parents, from everything he knew, seemed like reasonable people who loved their children. But Jamie fleeing home in tears right before Christmas seemed like an unmitigated disaster. Whatever was going on was more serious than when Jamie stormed out of their flat after Nerea's gallery opening.

Nerea was uneasy too, which unnerved Callum, if possible, more. While Callum tidied the living room and his study, she checked her mobile every five minutes, as if waiting for a call or a text even though Jamie was surely in the air by now. Nerea was the calm one, the one who didn't overreact. If she was worried, things with Jamie and his family might be very bad indeed.

Thom arrived before breakfast. He had taken the earliest possible flight and, having flatly refused to be picked up at the airport, rented a car to drive over to the house. He'd declared he didn't want to be carless while sharing the house with a horde of people, most of whom he neither knew nor spoke the same language as. Callum, once a stranger here too, could hardly blame him for wanting to be secure of the means of occasional escape.

Callum met Thom in the driveway to say hello and show him where he could park so he wouldn't get blocked in by later arrivals. Thom looked tired and also worried, more so than would be justified by traveling during the holiday season.

"What's wrong?" Callum asked, after they'd exchanged a brief hug.

"Nothing," Thom said dismissively.

It was rude to pry, Callum decided. Perhaps something had happened with Katherine. And if nothing else Thom was allowed to feel less than in top form for his first holiday season following his divorce. Still, as Callum led Thom into the house, he couldn't shake the sense that something else was off. He'd known Thom all through the bitterness and misery of the divorce proceedings. This mood now didn't feel like that.

Callum tried to push the nagging worry to the back of his mind. He had enough else to fret over.

Nerea was waiting for them in the living room. "You're first, so you get the pick of the guestrooms," she told Thom as she hugged him hello.

"Any room but the one Jamie had last time."

Nerea laughed. "Deal." She seemed to sense that something was wrong with Thom, too, because she shot Callum a worried, questioning glance while she took Thom's coat to hang it up. Callum shrugged and shook his head.

"Are you okay, Thom?" Nerea asked.

Thom nodded.

"Really okay?" Nerea pressed.

"Yes, of course. Why do you keep asking?"

"Because you look terrible," Nerea said bluntly.

Thom did chuckle at that, but said nothing about whatever it was that was bothering him. Callum thought about pressing further, but suspected that if Nerea couldn't get the matter out of him, no one could. Once Thom got settled, he ate breakfast with them in the kitchen which was already under siege with preparations for the upcoming wedding and holiday.

Callum felt overwhelmed by the chaos and had no idea how Nerea didn't. Crates of pine boughs were stacked in a corner with spools of gold ribbon balanced precariously on top. The island was piled with provisions for everything that needed to be baked or cooked that wasn't coming in from Antonio's company. And one half of the big kitchen table was covered with candles, pine cones, and yet more winter greenery for the centerpieces.

After breakfast Callum wandered around looking for his keys so he could go to the airport to pick Jamie up. Thom tailed him, chattering about nothing, which seemed like an improvement. Callum had originally considered having Thom wait at the airport and drive Jamie over himself, but whatever Jamie's current circumstances were had precluded that.

"When does everyone else get in?" Thom asked as Callum opened the hall closet so he could dig through the pockets of various coats.

"Jamie'll be here as soon as I can get him back from the airport. Leigh and Sam don't get here 'til tomorrow, because they're taking the ferry over and then driving." No keys in the closet; Callum went back to the living room to look around. "Piper's getting here this afternoon. As for the rest of the relations and friends, I have no idea. Nerea has a spreadsheet. I think. I don't even remember who's staying with us."

"Ah. Can I talk to you then? Thom asked, his hands in his pockets and his shoulders uncharacteristically slouched. Something was definitely going on with him.

"Sure," Callum told the sofa as he shifted cushions. "Ahah! There they are. I'm going to get Jamie now, come take a ride with me?" Maybe he could get Thom to spill the matter on the drive out.

"Ah. No. No, thanks," Thom put his hands up and took a step back. "That's okay."

"We're not going to pull off the side of the road and have sex in the car," Callum said.

"Not actually my concern."

"What is it, then? Come on, or Nerea's going to put you to work."

"That's okay, I should help out anyway, since you two are putting me up and everything." Thom continued to back out of the room.

Callum, puzzled and worried, watched him go and then turned to find his sunglasses.

⌒

After making the drive to and from the airport twenty times a year for more than two decades, the road and the scenery were excessively familiar to Callum. When he arrived in Spain and was driving to the house, it was his favorite road in the world. Other days, when he was leaving again, he hated it. Today, with dry roads, not too much sun, and the prospect of seeing Jamie at the end of it, the drive was a pleasant one. Even taking into account Jamie's distress and his adjusted timetable. Callum was confident they could work out whatever needed to be worked out. In the meantime he was not going to complain about getting a few more days' worth of Jamie.

He started to reconsider that opinion when Jamie appeared at the international arrivals exit, dragging his suitcase behind him. He had sunglasses on. Callum was about to tell him to take them off — it had clouded over and there was nothing so attention-catching as huge sunglasses in an airport — when Jamie took them off himself, folded them carefully, and hooked them in the collar of his shirt. His eyes were very red.

"Can we go home?" Jamie said, making no move to hug or otherwise greet Callum.

"Okay," Callum said and reached for Jamie's suitcase. He didn't react — out loud — to Jamie's use of the word *home*.

They drove for half an hour in silence before Jamie started crying. Without saying anything, Callum pulled over to the side of the road, under a stand of bare trees. As soon as his hands were no longer occupied with driving, Jamie fumbled off his seat belt and buried his face in Callum's shoulder. Callum stroked the back of his neck and murmured comforting nothings in his ear until Jamie's breathing evened out and he straightened back up.

"That bad?" Callum asked. He leaned over Jamie to pull open the glove compartment and fish out a packet of tissues to press into Jamie's hands.

Jamie scrubbed one of the clean, if crumpled, tissues over his eyes and blew his nose. "I have *never* had a row like that with my parents."

"Do you want to tell me about it?"

"Will it change anything?"

"Sometimes talking helps."

Jamie gave a noise that was probably supposed to be a snort but came out more as a sniffly squelch. He blew his nose again. "There was yelling."

"They didn't take it so well," Callum surmised. Jamie had said as much before.

Jamie shook his head. "I thought it was getting better, that Mum was starting to listen to me. But then — I don't know, maybe I said something I shouldn't have, maybe she totally freaked out, but next thing I knew we were just yelling at each other. And Dad didn't say anything, which — that's how we always knew we were in deep with him when we were kids. I stalked off to my room to call you before I really said something I regretted and now I'm here. In Spain. And I won't be home for Christmas, which was the plan, but not like this. And…." His voice trailed off.

Callum's hands tensed in his lap. He didn't want to imagine what could follow that *and*.

"My little sister's getting married," Jamie said so softly Callum had to strain to hear him. "I'm worried I won't be at the wedding. And — you don't have to say anything to this, I'm not asking for anything — I'm worried I'll never get married myself."

Callum was terribly, guiltily glad Jamie had said he didn't have to say anything. Because what was there to say to that? Nothing. Absolutely nothing. He reached out and took Jamie's hand in his instead. Jamie clung with a frightened strength.

"Your family's reaction isn't your fault," Callum said.

"No," Jamie said. "But I should have handled it better, should have told them sooner. How am I ever going talk to them again? I just packed up my stuff and left."

"You did that to us and we're still talking to you," Callum said.

Jamie gave him a doleful look.

"Okay. Bad example," Callum admitted. Even if — and he wasn't going to say this to Jamie, not in this state — it was probably a fair one.

"I'm okay," Jamie said. "You can keep driving."

Callum nodded, put the car back in gear, and pulled back onto the road. Next to him, Jamie belatedly pulled his seat belt back on.

"How did your parents react?" Jamie asked after a few moments. "To the news that you and Nerea — you know?"

"Were dating, or were poly?"

"The second one."

"We've never actually had that conversation. Can you imagine? Talking about feelings and personal lives? Terribly un-British."

Jamie cracked a smile. Callum counted it a victory.

"Nerea's parents, though — I'm not sure what they were most angry about. That I'd gotten her pregnant before I married her, that I was English, or that we were both still seeing other people. The end of her university career was also not appreciated. She tried, but the circumstances were too chaotic."

"She was pregnant before you were married?"

"Oh yes. It's why everything happened so quickly. There was respectability to be maintained," Callum said dryly.

Jamie's mouth started to twitch up at the corners. "You had a shotgun wedding!"

"No, we didn't," Callum protested.

Jamie was grinning full out now. "Yes, you did. Oh my God. Why doesn't anyone know this?"

"The internet wasn't around back then, and it can't do math now." It was Callum's turn to be sulky, or at least act sulky, because it seemed to make Jamie smile. "What happened was, I told her I'd marry her. She said that was lovely. And told me exactly what she was going to expect of me, regardless of our marital status. If I hadn't been head over heels in love with her already, I would have been then."

"Wow," Jamie said.

"Mhmm. Mind, I broke most of those promises within a year. Except for the ones about financial stability and sexual freedom."

"Has Nerea forgiven you for that yet?"

Callum sighed. He was glad to hold Jamie's hand for this conversation and also glad he didn't have to look at him while he admitted these things. The countryside spread out before them, brown and green and gold in the winter light. The road was busy with holiday travelers. Callum tried to imagine a life without these things — without Spain and Nerea and the home they'd built together — and couldn't. The mere prospect was bleak and terrifying.

"I'm not sure she ever will," he said. "I don't want you, or anyone else, to get the wrong idea. I didn't introduce her to polyamory, because the fact is I happen to be made of relationship failure, or I was for a long time. I was sleeping around and behaving terribly while she was a woman with complex relationships and a lot to teach me."

"Don't shame yourself," Jamie said.

"I'm not ashamed of what I was doing, just how I was doing it," Callum clarified. "And frankly, I was talking foolish risks."

"Huh?" Jamie shook his head as if to clear it.

"It was the eighties."

"Oh. Shit. Sorry."

Callum shrugged. What else was there to say about that?

"But you and Nerea are happy together, right?" Jamie frowned like he was trying to puzzle that out. "You didn't marry her because you were scared."

"I've never been scared enough of anything," Callum said. "We're together because we're together. And very happy. And we were then, too. Our marriage has never been bad, although there were rough patches."

"What kind of rough patches?" Jamie asked, half curious and half wary.

Callum sighed. There was no better illustration of the point than the argument that had followed the wedding when the girls were little. He was ashamed to relate his dreadful behavior to Jamie, but Jamie deserved to know the bad of his history as well as the good.

Jamie listened without interruption.

"I had to learn to be more responsible and more present," Callum said once he'd retold the story. "And the credit goes to

Nerea for giving me the chance to learn how to do both of those things. It's part of why you running here, as delighted as I am to get my hands on you, worries us. Well, me. Nerea too, but I won't speak for her. You can't solve problems where you aren't.'"

"I also can't solve problems if no one is listening to me," Jamie said.

"Here's the thing," Callum said with a reassuring squeeze to Jamie's hand. This boy was wonderful and wanted to do everything so right. But he was going to have to learn how to fix situations when he made royal messes of them. Callum had taken far too long to absorb that lesson himself, but maybe he could save Jamie a few decades of pain and regret. If so, Callum's own screw-ups might have been worth it. At least a little.

"You're going to hate this," Callum continued, "but no one is obligated to listen to you. Which is something it's going to get harder and harder for you to remember, the older you get and the more successful you are. You let your parents know what is happening in your life, you remind them you're willing to discuss any questions they have, and you stay in touch so they realize you're the same person you were yesterday, just maybe a little more mature."

"Do you think it would help if my parents met you?"

"Right now — and I say this as a man with three daughters who tries not to be a boorish, archaic, misogynist twit but sometimes is — probably not. I've spent time hating everyone my kids have dated. If your parents are uncomfortable with your relationships, they're uncomfortable," Callum said honestly. "But you know them, and I don't."

Jamie shrugged. "The only thing I know is that I don't want to lose any of you. You and Nerea or my family."

"I can't promise you that's going to be possible," Callum said, because a life of poly had taught him that keeping everyone happy was never guaranteed. "But don't put off calling home again. It'll only make things harder in the long run."

Chapter 27

Nerea hears an unexpected confession

Now that the kitchen was needed to make food in large quantities for the house guests that would soon be arriving, Nerea moved her command center for wedding operations into Callum's office. It was comforting to sit at his desk to work and be surrounded by so much that reminded her of him, with the room's muted colors and the fragrance of old wood and paper. The spines of the books, some gleaming in faded jewel tones, others with battered jackets and covers, stretched from floor to ceiling. There was a stack of books on the windowsill that Callum had pulled out, presumably titles he thought Jamie might like or otherwise felt necessary for him to read.

With Callum gone, all Nerea could do was keep busy until he and Jamie returned. She did her best to stay occupied with working on the centerpieces for the wedding, but she was too distracted and upset to concentrate and kept making mistakes. Thoughts of Jamie's distraught face kept creeping back into her mind.

Nerea had just ruined an attempt at a centerpiece, again, when Thom rapped on the door frame with his knuckles.

"Yes?" Nerea looked up from her sad excuse for handiwork.

"Since I'm having a devil of a time talking to your husband, would you mind if I talked to you?"

Nerea frowned at him. She didn't do Callum's relationship management for him, but she'd had the sense all morning that something was wrong with Thom. Thom's face right now did nothing to allay her fears, and she didn't like that one bit.

"Have a seat," she said cautiously.

Thom pulled a chair over from the table by the window, but didn't sit down. "It's about, well." He rubbed his fingers over the worn carving on the back of the chair. "It's about — "

"Thom, a word of advice."

He looked up at her, his eyes a bit wild.

"The longer you delay, the worse I think this is."

"I'm dating your daughter," he blurted.

Nerea blinked. "Which one?" She had a single daughter, a married poly daughter, and a monogamous daughter who was about to have her wedding. She could only hope Thom wasn't dating that last one.

"Piper," Thom said desperately.

"Thank goodness that's the least complicated answer. Now sit down."

Thom, obediently, sat.

"So this is what's had you on edge all day."

"All day, all week, all month." Thom looked miserable.

"Callum's going to burst something when he finds out."

"I know," Thom moaned.

"How long has this been going on?" Nerea asked.

Thom picked up a pinecone that was meant for the centerpieces and rolled it between his palms, not looking at her. "Since May."

"It's December now."

Thom said nothing.

Nerea leaned back in Callum's desk chair. "That explains the company she had over that she wouldn't talk about. Callum may punch you though."

Thom let out a deep sigh. "Believe me. I know."

"Have you tried to tell him?"

"I've been trying for months!" Thom protested.

"You should have tried harder!"

"Yes, and he should be able to recognize that other people have lives even when he's distracted by his newest fling."

"Is he ever not distracted by a fling?" Nerea asked.

"No, which is why we're having this problem now!"

Nerea started laughing. Mainly because there wasn't much else she could do. He and Piper were both adults, and, in truth, Thom hardly deserved to be yelled at. Making him more afraid also wasn't going to help him do what he needed to do, which was to talk to Callum before he found out on his own.

"I'm not going to tell him for you," she said eventually, once she had stopped laughing and once Thom had slumped down miserably in his chair again.

"I didn't think you would. Just — God, this was not how I was hoping to have this conversation."

"Yes, you were hoping not to have it at all. Now. I'm not going to rage at you like Callum will. But," she pointed her pen at Thom. "I have some concerns."

"I am ready and willing to hear them," Thom said.

Nerea was fairly sure she could get him to say or do absolutely anything right now, which was the sort of power she wasn't sure she should be trusted with. Yes, she was the responsible one, but even she had her limits.

"Good," she said. "For one, she's fifteen years younger than you."

"Sixteen, if you want to be brutally honest, but Jamie's twenty years younger than *you*," Thom protested.

"Closer to twenty-five, the world is different for women, and don't talk 'til I'm done."

Thom snapped his jaw shut.

"You've just gotten divorced. It is finalized now, yes? Please tell me yes." Last Nerea had heard from Katherine, it had been in the final legal stages.

Thom nodded.

"*Tell me.*"

"Yes, it's finalized."

"So you've just been through a messy and painful divorce from a woman I've known for years and consider a friend. That's awkward enough as it is, but we can cope with that. But now you're rebounding, and the woman you picked for a rebound is my daughter." It was funny, sad, and worrying, and Nerea couldn't help but think about telling Tonio about this whole mess. Piper had once been very much like a daughter to him and Nerea was absolutely certain he would laugh at the vengeance the universe was apparently wreaking on Callum with this turn of events.

"It was an accident. I didn't even know who she was when I met her."

"Do we want to discuss how this implies you either have latent attraction for myself and Callum or you slept with my daughter without knowing her last name?"

"Can we go for neither? I'd like to go for neither," Thom said, pained.

"Also, house rules. I don't care if you sleep together under my roof. In fact, it would be easier if you did, because if I can

231

put both of you in the same room it'll make guest arrangements easier. But you have to tell Callum before any of that happens."

Thom nodded.

"Unlike Callum, I will not penalize either of you for the fact that women like sex too. But Thom, for the love of God, whatever you're doing, be clear with her. And make her be clear with you too. Her worst qualities are all Callum's."

"And her best are all yours?"

"See, now we're getting back to that latent attraction issue. Seriously, though. Communication. And if you're going to have an epic meltdown with her, for any reason whatsoever, try to keep it out of my house and avoid the day of the wedding?"

"I'll do my best," Thom said.

"I'd appreciate it."

"Callum's going to murder me, isn't he?" Thom said morosely.

"I'm afraid so, and you damn well better tell him before everyone gets drunk at the wedding."

Chapter 28

Jamie finds an ally

Nerea met their car in the driveway. Jamie kissed and hugged her and then clung. He inhaled the scent of her perfume and the warm, familiar smells of the house. It helped steady him, if only a little.

"Do you want to go upstairs and lie down?" she asked as Callum carried his bags into the house.

Jamie shook his head. "Do you have stuff I can do?" He wanted to stay busy, not be left alone in idleness with his own thoughts.

"Oh darling. Christmas and the wedding are in a matter of days. I have so much for you to do."

Jamie spent the rest of the morning sweeping, dusting, and vacuuming. The only other person in the house beside Callum and Nerea was Thom Abbott, who Jamie had met briefly at Nerea's gallery opening. Thom was quiet, made intelligent conversation, and didn't fuss at all about the fact that Jamie was dating both his best friend and his best friend's wife. Thom also kept to himself enough that Jamie didn't feel weird about occasionally taking a break to snuggle up to Callum or Nerea.

All through the morning Aoife sent him frantic texts, asking him why he had gone and why he wasn't calling. When he finally worked up the courage to go out to the back garden to call her, she was in tears. Jamie felt like the worst person on the planet. But, as he explained to Aoife, he couldn't go home. Not yet. Not until he felt more sure of himself, his place in the world, and had come up with something like a plan to make everything okay again.

At least Aoife was willing and even eager to talk to him. He wasn't sure the same could be said about his parents. Or his other sisters. None of whom he had heard a word from. He assumed that Aoife would tell their mother he was safe.

⁓

Callum and Nerea's youngest daughter Piper arrived after lunch. This time it was Nerea — in her seasonably inappropriate convertible — who went to meet her at the airport.

Jamie's first impression of Piper, when they arrived back at the house, was of a girl about his age who looked like Nerea and talked like Callum, two traits that combined to make her highly unsettling, at least to Jamie. He worried Piper might react sharply to his existence as Margarita had at first, but to his pleasant surprise she greeted him warmly and didn't ask any awkward questions.

Jamie discovered exactly why she had been so magnanimous when he barged into the last room at the very end of the second floor hallway carrying an armful of sheets to make up the spare room beds. There was Piper — and there was Thom. With their tongues down each other's throats.

Thom, once they'd pulled apart, looked like he wanted to sink through the floor. Piper looked like she wanted to kill Jamie. Jamie restrained his impulse to laugh and instead backed out of the room slowly to let them at it.

Given that neither Callum nor Nerea had mentioned the fact that Thom and Piper were dating, Jamie assumed they didn't know. Maybe they hadn't told or maybe he had walked in on the worst-timed first kiss. He didn't particularly care. He just didn't want to be the messenger of any further family relationship drama.

Half an hour later, Piper banged into another guest room where Jamie was struggling to get a possibly too-small fitted sheet on a double bed.

"Oh good," she said. "I was looking for you."

Jamie straightened up and blinked nervously at her. As he did, the wretched sheet popped off the mattress again. "I'm not going to tell them." He didn't want to incur Piper's wrath, and what she did was none of Jamie's business. Or her parents' if she chose not to tell them.

"Tell them what?"

"Oh, nothing. I mean. I didn't see anything, so how could I tell them anything?

Piper narrowed her eyes at him. Then she looked at the sheets, and Jamie's miserable efforts to get the bed made. "Why should I trust you?"

"Your parents already like me, and I'd prefer to keep it that way. Not playing the messenger."

"All right," she said cautiously. "Why are you here early?"

"I'm, er, having drama with my parents."

"What kind of drama?"

"My baby sister's getting married, and I shacked up with a movie star and his wife."

235

"Ah," Piper said delicately. She watched Jamie struggle feebly with the sheets, "Do you want help?"

"Please."

They worked in silence for a few moments. Then Piper spoke again.

"What part of Dublin are you from? One of my uni flatmates was Irish so I went a few times."

Jamie smiled, not at the small talk, but at the offer it represented. They were going to be allies. And what Jamie needed, as he sorted out the mess of his own family relationships, was allies.

⁘

Of the five people around the dinner table that night — Callum, Nerea, Jamie, Piper, and Thom — Jamie suspected that only three of them knew how awkward a meal it really was. Unperturbed by anything more than the details of the upcoming holiday and wedding, Callum and Nerea made easy conversation. Nerea asked Thom what he'd been up to in London, and Callum ribbed Piper about some long-running inside joke. Neither of them seemed to have the least idea that Piper and Thom were together. And Thom and Piper, sitting at opposite ends of the table, barely even glanced at each other throughout the whole meal.

Although Jamie felt some wariness about what would happen when it all came to light, the situation was an oddly welcome distraction from his own family woes. Even so, he kept an eye on his mobile lest he miss any more texts or calls from Aoife. He tried not to text at the table in deference to Nerea's rules, but she gave Jamie an encouraging smile when she caught him flicking on the screen to be absolutely sure he hadn't missed anything. Clearly, whatever he had to do to be in touch with his family would be fine. Jamie was grateful, but he still didn't know what to do about his parents.

After dinner Thom mumbled something about being tired from the flight and made a hasty retreat upstairs. Jamie watched as Piper made a similar excuse and escaped to her own room, or so Jamie assumed. Whether she and Thom were going to find some way to spend the night together, he did not want to know. He already felt strange keeping the secret from the people he was seeing.

Jamie found Callum in the living room, flicking through movies on the TV.

"Nerea kicked me out of my office, apparently I was getting in the way of her decorations," Callum said with a rueful smile. "Want to watch something with me?"

"Depends on what you're watching."

"I haven't decided yet. Do you have a preference?"

Jamie suspected he was being indulged, but he decided he didn't mind as he curled up under Callum's arm on the love seat. Doing nothing but sitting and watching a movie — and not having to speak to anyone — seemed like absolute heaven. The solid warmth of Callum's body pressed against his didn't hurt either.

⁓

One morning before the rest of the guests were due to arrive, Jamie sat on the end of Callum and Nerea's bed wrapped up in a blanket and watched Nerea brush out her long hair. The room was dim in the grey light of early morning. Callum was in the bathroom shaving. The door was open a crack, and Jamie could see a sliver of his face in the fogged-over mirror as he worked. The sight made Jamie wish he could paint, to capture the soft lines and moody atmosphere of the room.

"I have a question," Jamie asked. His own voice sounded soft in the pre-dawn stillness.

"What's that, love?" Nerea met his eyes in the mirror over her vanity.

"What are you going to tell your families about me? Both of you," he added, raising his voice so Callum could hear as well.

"What do you want us to tell them?" Nerea asked.

"That wasn't what I asked." After the gallery debacle he wanted to hear their plans and assumptions. But more than that, they knew their own families best. He hadn't succeeded in telling his own parents without making a mess, which meant Jamie had no idea how to tell anyone else's.

"But it matters," she said.

"I don't know," he confessed. "In an ideal world, I do want you to tell them about me. But I don't want to cause more drama with your family. I already screwed up well enough with mine."

"If it makes you feel any better," Callum said, coming to stand in the doorway while he patted his face dry. "My parents will ignore whatever makes them uncomfortable."

"Have they met many of your lovers?"

"Besides Nerea? No. That is, no one they've known I was sleeping with."

"What about yours?" Jamie asked Nerea.

"Yes. Tonio, mostly. There's been one or two others. There was a lot of yelling from my mother at the beginning, but they've more or less given it up now. I think the grandchildren helped. My sister, though, knows everything."

"You were open and honest with your parents about us." Callum sat next to Jamie on the bed. "We owe it to you to do the same with our own families. The girls, obviously, already know. And if you want to avoid more drama and for us to not tell our parents, that's fair, too. But even with our best efforts this isn't the sort of relationship that can be hidden forever. And sooner may be better than later."

"Then, yes. I guess you should tell them." Getting it over with seemed best. At least they were all together. Jamie felt reassured by Callum and Nerea's calm, even if he was still nervous about meeting their families. "I never expected this to get so complicated," he confessed. "I just really liked spending time with Callum. And with you," he said to Nerea.

"Jamie, darling," Callum said, pressing a kiss to Jamie's temple. "I'm afraid complicated is what life and love is."

<hr />

The rest of family and guests arrived three days before Christmas.

Nerea's sister Delores was first. She flew in from Madrid and drove herself from the airport, getting to the house just before lunch. Jamie set down the silver he, Thom and Callum had been polishing and went to say hello.

If Jamie had thought the resemblance between Piper and Nerea was uncanny, the resemblance between Nerea and Delores was downright spooky. Same height, same build, same dark hair.

"It's odd, isn't it," Callum murmured to Jamie as he stared at Nerea hugging her sister hello.

Jamie nodded, but before he could say anything else Delores turned to Jamie and put a hand on her hip.

"So this is the Irish boy," she said with an amused smile.

Jamie had picked up enough Spanish to understand her and reply in the affirmative. But whatever she said next Jamie didn't catch.

She pursed her lips and switched to English. "You're cute, but that's probably not going to make up for all the trouble you're going to cause."

Callum's parents arrived after lunch, followed shortly afterward by Callum's sister, brother-in-law, and nephew. A very pregnant Leigh and her wife Sam rolled in not long after that, and for a brief while everything was chaos. Cars cluttered the driveway, and the front hall was so clogged with luggage it became difficult to navigate without tripping.

Sam, Jamie decided, was awesome. He won points with her and with Leigh immediately upon arrival by helping them haul their luggage up to their guest room and then fussing over Leigh.

"You're eager," Leigh said, amused.

"Nah. Just, I have two nieces and when my sister was pregnant she trained me well."

Both Leigh and Sam laughed.

"I don't need anything," Leigh said. "But you'd win points with my father and my wife if you keep them apart from each other."

Jamie must have looked as wary as he felt, because Leigh hastened to add, "They get along perfectly fine."

"But I find his charm annoying and he finds I threaten his masculinity," Sam put in cheerfully.

"Now, both of you, go and let me sleep," Leigh said, already crawling into bed. "That ferry ride was awful and I am very tired of hauling around a miniature human."

Once Jamie and Sam went back downstairs Nerea put them to work. They spent an easy hour sweeping the patio and raking the short grass in the back garden. Sam, like Jamie, seemed happy for something to do, and Jamie found her good-natured ribbing and her easy manner soothing. Jamie decided — though he kept the thought to himself — that Callum found Sam threatening because they were remarkably similar.

It was especially nice to have another friend, because Jamie wasn't sure what to do about Callum's parents. They arrived as Sam and Jamie were coming back inside, laughing at a joke Sam had just told, their cheeks red from the chill outside. The upside of Callum's parents, Jamie decided quickly, was that they spoke no Spanish and so he had two more people to talk to. The downside was that they had never been confronted with one of Callum's lovers in close proximity before. They regarded him with a reserved British pleasantry, when they had to regard him at all, and ignored him the rest of the time.

It was funny, in a way. It was also perfectly awful. Although Jamie could mostly ignore their coolness, it was much harder to ignore the distinct disapproval he — and Nerea — received from various friends and neighbors.

Nerea's parents, along with a group of neighbors Jamie didn't know, arrived after dinner. With the help of Google Translate and Piper when she was in earshot, he was able to put together most of what the women were saying about him. The most flattering of which, from the neighbor lady who'd spied on him and Nerea through the shrubbery, was *I knew she was carrying on with him but didn't think she would flaunt it.*

Jamie was offended on both Nerea's behalf and his own. Before he could formulate a reply Piper tugged on his sleeve and whispered in his ear.

"Tell her — " Piper rattled off a sentence in Spanish Jamie understood part of but not all of. Repeating it was manageable, however.

The women turned as one to stare at him.

"Wait. What did I say?" Jamie asked Piper in English.

"'She's not flaunting me, I'm just too cute to get rid of,'" Piper responded, her eyes dancing with mirth.

Jamie was torn between horror and amusement. The group of women seemed to catch on to what had happened and began laughing. After a moment Jamie couldn't help joining in.

"Well," he said. "It's not like that's not true."

Jamie and Piper fled the group only to run into Margarita. Piper peeled off, leaving Jamie and Margarita together. When he apologized, cautiously, for all the gossip and judgment flying around the house she waved him off. To his relief and no small surprise.

"The neighbors blame my mother. I blame my father. You're just the poor soul who got dragged into all this."

"It's not entirely their fault," Jamie pointed out. "I said yes to being here. I didn't mean to overshadow your wedding with our drama."

"Sweet of you," Margarita said. "But useless. I've known my parents a lot longer than you have. If it wasn't this, it would have been something else."

By the middle of the next morning Jamie was feeling overwhelmed. He was used to big family gatherings, but the house full of complete strangers was a bit much. Callum seemed to sense his mood.

"I have to go pick up the truly ridiculous quantity of wine we ordered for Christmas and the wedding," Callum said while he cleared the dishes from breakfast and Jamie and Nerea cleaned the kitchen. "Do you want to come with me?"

"Oh God, yes," Jamie said.

He slumped with relief in the passenger seat as they drove away from the house.

"How are you holding up?" Callum asked with a smile.

"So. Many. People."

"But no one's yelling yet."

Jamie rolled his head to the side and narrowed his eyes. "I'm not sure your standards for positive social interactions are the same as anyone else's."

Callum laughed. "You're just realizing that now?"

Jamie and Callum retrieved the wine, stopped for a cup of coffee at a café in a town nearby, and spent an hour just sitting and talking about nothing in particular. It was fun, lovely, and exactly what Jamie needed. By the time Callum pulled into the long driveway that led up to the house Jamie was feeling much more philosophical about the ordeal ahead. Tomorrow was Christmas Eve. Then there would be Christmas, and the wedding the day after. Everyone had plenty to fuss about that wasn't him.

When they got out of the car and popped the boot to begin unloading, a number of the men came out to help them carry in the cases. It was jovial, even if Jamie couldn't understand most of what they were saying. He could lift a case of wine, and that was all anyone cared about.

"Where's my wife?" Callum asked, as he left the last crate stacked by the back door of the kitchen.

"Upstairs, she said she wasn't feeling well," one of the men answered. Another said something in Spanish that Jamie didn't catch at all, but that made Callum start. A third, disregarding everything going on, pointed at Jamie. "Who is this?"

Callum shot Jamie a look that was an indicator to introduce himself.

So he did. "Hola," he said as Callum ducked out of the kitchen and upstairs. "Me llamo Jamie and my Spanish is terrible."

Chapter 29

Callum definitely didn't see this coming

Nerea wasn't in their bedroom, but the door to their bathroom was closed.

"Nerea?" Callum called.

He got a muffled reply and the sound of a toilet flushing in response.

"Are you okay?"

"No. Fool." That much was distinct. There was the sound of water running, then Nerea pulled the door open. Her face was flushed, and her hair was pulled back in a messy ponytail.

"You look terrible."

"Love you too, dearest." Nerea walked past him and crawled up on to the bed, collapsing face-first into the pillows.

Callum immediately curled up beside her, murmuring apologies for having left her alone all day and asking whether he could get her anything. When she shook her head, he started rubbing circles on her back. "Flu?" he asked. "Food poisoning?"

"Maybe."

"Define maybe," Callum said cautiously. Was this somehow not one of those despicable sudden onset stomach bugs that circled the world every winter?

Nerea flopped over onto her back with a groan. "Yesterday morning when I woke up I felt terrible. And the morning before that."

"Why didn't you say anything?" Callum was appalled.

"Because it was gone by breakfast and there was so much to do it was easy to ignore. Nerves or living on coffee or too many baked goods. Don't worry, love, I was fine."

"If it's getting worse, you should go to the doctor, before they close for the holiday."

"If it were getting worse I wouldn't keep being this damn ravenous."

That stopped Callum in his tracks. "Take off your shirt," he blurted.

Nerea rolled her head to the side so she could look at him. Her eyes were wide. Callum wondered if she hadn't thought of this possibility herself or just hadn't wanted to.

"What is wrong with you?" she demanded.

"Take off your shirt," he repeated, going for the buttons on her blouse.

She batted his hands away, and they settled at her hips, thumbs just brushing her belly.

He watched as she stared at his hands and then returned her gaze to his face. He saw the moment realization overcame any denial she'd been clinging to.

Then she cursed, shoved him out of the way, and ran for the bathroom again.

Callum sat on the edge of the bed and waited, a behavior Nerea had trained into him long ago, when she'd been expecting Leigh, until she reemerged.

"I can't believe this," he said.

"Good," Nerea said, sitting down next to him, "Because it might not be anything at all."

"When was your last — ?" Callum cut himself off.

"Two months ago."

"Ah."

"It's not like it's a regular event anymore," Nerea snapped.

She had a point. Her getting pregnant hadn't been at the top of their list of worries for some time. They were careful, usually, but they also didn't lose sleep about it when they weren't. They were much more disciplined about safer sex in their more casual relationships.

"So," he said.

"It's probably nothing." Nerea studied her hands.

"You think?"

Nerea was silent, which was generally not a good sign.

"Okay, you don't think so," Callum said. "What do we do next?"

"Go find Jamie," she said very quietly.

"What?" Callum was startled, but Nerea was thinking logically and he wasn't. This was not a situation — no matter how possibly wonderful — he had imagined them confronting. "Aren't you two careful?"

She looked up at him. "About as careful as I am with you," she said. "Which you'd know, since you're often there."

Callum thought suddenly of Jamie and his ridiculous, *infuriating* book and his desire to do everything right. Which had included getting tested for STDs — which Callum had appreciated — and then several rounds of totally unprotected sex, which he had also appreciated. The problem with birth control, of course, was that no one really enjoyed using it.

"The time we…."

"Possibly. Probably." Nerea was apparently remembering the same thing he was. "Now. Will you go get our boyfriend?"

Callum pulled his mobile out of his pocket with his other hand. *Come upstairs when you can?* He texted Jamie. Nerea leaned her head on Callum's shoulder, and Callum stroked her hair while waiting for the sound of footsteps.

Chapter 30

Nerea sends Jamie on an errand

Nerea turned her face into Callum's shoulder and ordered herself to breathe. Bursting into tears would not help the situation. Hyperventilating would only make it worse. Callum wrapped his other arm around her too and buried his face in her hair. She clung to him, grateful for his strong arms and his steady presence.

Jamie burst in a few minutes later. He stopped short when he saw Nerea and Callum sitting on the bed together.

"What's wrong?" he asked.

Nerea sat up straight, smoothing back loose wisps of hair off her face. She was grateful when Callum left an arm wrapped tightly around her shoulders.

"Come sit down, Jamie," she said and patted the bed on the other side of her.

Jamie's face went pale under his freckles. "Is everything okay?" he asked, but didn't sit. "Oh God, did I offend somebody? Is it your parents? I'm so sorry, I can apologize —"

"That's not the problem," Callum said maybe more sharply than was necessary, but Nerea supposed he was having a shock.

"You haven't caused any new and shiny drama. Come sit." Nerea patted the bed next to her again.

Jamie finally sat, warily, tucking one knee up under himself so he could face them.

Nerea felt Callum kiss the side of her head. *Your show.* She took a deep breath.

"You know how I am too old for you but not totally ancient?" She was not sure her attempt at humor would keep the tears at bay.

Jamie's face said he had no idea where this was going. "Yeah?"

"I've been wanting to throw up for days and now I actually am," Nerea said. Saying it out loud didn't make it seem any more real. This was too unlikely, too absurd. "No one else in the house is sick. So I am going to draw you a map and you are going to drive to the one pharmacy open today in the next town over and buy me a pregnancy test. And you are not going to get into a car crash along the way despite the fact I just said that. Also, we like our cars so please don't damage them."

Jamie blinked. Rapidly. "Okay."

"Okay?" Nerea asked. She hadn't known what Jamie's response would be, but she had hoped for something she could interpret.

"Yeah. Okay." Jamie blinked again. He was as white as a sheet. "Can I ask questions when I get back?"

"You can ask questions now," Nerea said after a glance at Callum. They'd been so lucky to find each other and become so serious together about their relationships. But this was not the kind of luck any of them had been hoping for.

"No. I'm good," Jamie said. His breathing was too quick. "I'm going to — yeah. Map?" He said, standing up again. He swayed a little. Then, "Does this mean I can take your convertible?"

"No." Nerea said firmly. "You can take Callum's car."

"Are you okay to drive?" Callum asked.

"I was carrying the wine, not drinking it," Jamie blurted.

"You're reacting like a person in shock," Nerea said.

"Medical shock," Callum clarified.

Nerea could see why clarification was necessary. Metaphorical shock was a given.

"I'm trying not to have a reaction about something hypothetical," Jamie said. He sat down again and took a deep breath. "But I do need a map. I hope you can draw well."

"Jamie," Nerea said, "I'm a painter."

Chapter 31

Jamie gets lost

Jamie appreciated the offer of Callum's car, even if it wasn't as fun as Nerea's, but when he reached the garage it was blocked in behind a half dozen other vehicles. He decided that getting air would be better for thinking through everything at hand, so instead he dragged out Callum's bicycle.

Finding the village wasn't hard. He'd been there before, and Nerea's map was clear. Focusing on the directions gave him something to do other than panic. Because if his parents were angry with him now, the part where he was going to have to explain that his girlfriend was pregnant — possibly with his baby, possibly with her husband's baby — was only going to lead to something worse.

As Jamie walked into the pharmacy the few staff working turned to look at him as he made his way to the counter. Which was probably about the lack of business on the holiday and his being an unfamiliar face, but he couldn't help feeling that they all knew exactly why he was here. Embarrassing was an understatement.

He'd made Nerea write out the Spanish he would need, but he couldn't make out her handwriting. He ultimately sighed and passed the note over to the girl behind the counter. She looked wildly amused but didn't ask him any questions as she rang up the transaction.

"¡Feliz navidad!" she said, waving merrily, as he collected the bag and his change. The same people who had stared at him as he walked in, watched him walk out as he awkwardly tried to shove the bag with the test into his jacket pocket.

Heading back to the house would be easy. He'd gotten this far; surely he could retrace his route. But when he went to retrieve Nerea's map from his pocket, it wasn't there. Nerea had written the Spanish he'd need on the other side of it, and he'd accidentally left it with the girl at the counter. Jamie didn't think he had the nerve to go back for it. No matter. He could find his way.

Or so he thought. Although Jamie was fine for the first few turns, the green barn that was supposed to be one of his landmarks never materialized. Jamie turned around and attempted to retrace his route, looking for the missing turn.

Twenty minutes later he had to admit that he was totally, utterly, lost. He fished his mobile out of his pocket and prayed that there would be a signal strong enough to consult the mapping feature. No luck. But there was — barely — enough to make a call. The ring back tone was weak and staticky. Jamie bounced anxiously on the balls of his feet hoping one of them would pick up.

"Jamie?" Callum sounded worried.

"Hi. I got the pregnancy test but now I'm lost. Help?" Jamie said in a rush, afraid that at any moment the call would drop.

"What do you mean you're lost?"

"I mean I took your bike, lost the map, my smartphone isn't being smart, and I'm pretty sure I'd have to ride through a garden and over the top of some warehouse to even have half a hope of getting back," he concluded desperately. "Come fetch me?"

"It's a good thing we like you," Callum said.

⟁

Jamie didn't feel less embarrassed when Nerea screeched up twenty minutes later in her convertible, the top up in the December chill. She yanked her door open and marched around to where he was standing on this random bit of Spanish countryside with Callum's bike. He braced for her to start scolding him, but all she did was rip the bag from the pharmacy out of his pocket and shove her car keys at him.

"You're driving," she said and then marched off behind a bush.

Jamie was just about to open the boot of the car to see if he could get the bike in when he realized what the plan was.

"Oh my God, no, we cannot do this here."

"We can't do it in my house," she said and kept going.

To be honest, Jamie didn't see why not. But now was not the time to ask.

Jamie opened the boot, got the bike in with a bit of wiggling and prayer, and then slid into the driver's seat. He folded his hands on the steering wheel and pressed his head against them. He was possibly hyperventilating. And he was definitely, absolutely, going to panic. However, as he forced his breathing to even out, Jamie was conscious of a different set of emotions.

In his prior relationships, he'd always been careful to use protection for the sake of everyone's health but also to avoid a moment just like this. He'd always imagined that if he ever did end up waiting for a woman's pregnancy test to show a result — and he wasn't married to her — he'd feel nothing but dread and regret. But despite the adrenaline pumping through his system, Jamie felt no such thing. Terrified? Yes. Overwhelmed? Definitely. Nervous? More so than ever before. But for all that uncertainty, he also felt excited. There might be a baby. The prospect was wonderful.

"Don't say anything," Nerea hissed when she got back to the car, slamming the door after her.

Jamie turned his head to her but kept it pillowed on his arms. He cracked an eye open. "Well?"

"Well, we have to wait three minutes. And you're not allowed to react."

Outside a car whizzed by. "Earlier you wanted me to react."

"Earlier I was worried you were going to pass out. But everyone has to have their own feelings about this without feeling pressured by anyone else."

Jamie rather thought she sounded like the book she and Callum still teased him about. "What are we going to do, write notes to each other?"

"Yes," Nerea said softly, staring at the little plastic stick in her hand.

"Seriously? You two are crazy. I mean, obviously, because this is happening, but — "

Nerea passed him the stick.

He stared at it. "Oh. You mean *yes*."

"Don't react," she said sharply and burst into tears.

Jamie cursed under his breath and started the car.

255

By the time they got back to the house with Nerea giving directions for the long way around, her eyes were dry, her makeup was repaired, and Jamie had pocketed the positive pregnancy test. Callum gave him a wary look when Nerea cheerfully greeted everyone and darted upstairs. Jamie intercepted him before he could follow.

"How is she?" Callum demanded.

"Take a guess," Jamie said. "Oh, and you're not allowed to react." Apparently that was all it took for Callum to get a clue and drop into a chair in the kitchen.

"Really?" he asked, looking so pleased Jamie felt dizzy.

"Seriously. She said you're not allowed to react. We have to write it down or something."

"Okay," Callum levered himself out of the chair. "Can you please make nice with everyone while I go check on my wife?"

Jamie didn't miss the possessiveness in Callum's word choice. He put a hand to his chest to stop him from going. There were things that he needed to say, and they needed to be said now. "We need to get on the same page with this, you and I."

"Is that so?" Callum asked. "Which page are you on?"

"The one where my opinion doesn't change based on whose it is."

"Good." Callum gave a tight smile and leaned down into Jamie's space. "So let me be clear now. I don't care whose baby it is. But I've been with Nerea for thirty years, and the page you need to be on is that she is the top priority here. What she wants — and what she needs — is what she gets. Clear?"

Jamie nodded. "Clear." He refused to look nervous in the face of Callum's display. The masculinity drama they were having was not about jealousy, but about commitment, and Jamie could live with that.

"Excellent. Now, seriously," Callum squeezed Jamie's shoulder fondly, "I need to see my wife."

Chapter 32

Callum manages to be an adult, surprising no one so much as himself

Callum found Nerea in the bathroom brushing her hair.

"Oh good, there you are," she said, setting her brush down and picking up a hair tie.

"Jamie told me," Callum blurted. "And that you'd prefer we don't react."

"Yes." Nerea nodded.

"What do you need from me?"

"I need to get through the rest of this day as if nothing is happening. So I need you not to say anything — or do anything — out of the ordinary. I also need you to finish packing up the centerpieces so they don't get in anyone's way on Christmas, and please make sure all the lights in the garden are working, I think one of the strands blew out."

"Do you mind if I kiss you?" There was so much to be worried about, Nerea's health and that of the baby's not the least of it. But even with those concerns Callum wasn't sure how to contain his happiness. The decision to keep the baby or not was, of course, entirely up to Nerea. But wise or not, Callum was already all in.

Nerea turned to face him with an exasperated, but fond, smile. "If you must." She wrapped her arms around Callum's neck eagerly, though, and kissed him for several long moments before she pushed him away with a reminder of everything they still had to do today.

Callum was a trained actor; so was Jamie. Still, in Callum's opinion, Nerea definitely won the day's prize for pretending nothing out of the ordinary was happening in the chaos that was overtaking the rest of the house. People were even beginning to lose interest in Jamie's relationship with them. Which was a relief, but possibly a short-lived one. As much as anyone judged him and Nerea for having a boyfriend, that judgment was going to pale in comparison to what would happen if and when everyone found out Nerea was pregnant with a baby very possibly not her husband's.

Callum didn't want to worry about any of it. While Nerea holed up in the bedroom and Jamie walked around dazed and wide-eyed, Callum couldn't help but smile as he submitted obediently to Nerea's well-organized to-do lists. He spent the rest of the day putting up lights, hauling tables around the garden, and doing his best to avoid both Nerea's parents and his own. Sure, it might be hard, but Callum loved kids. His career had maybe gotten in the way of him spending enough time with his daughters when they were young, but he'd relished every moment he had with them. Having a baby in the house again would be a joy.

It was after midnight by the time the three of them were finally able to go upstairs for the evening. They faced each other, comically wary, from different sides of the bedroom: Nerea by the bathroom door, Jamie hovering by the window, and Callum at the foot of the bed just wanting to go to sleep.

"Are we going to talk about this now?" Jamie asked. He looked even more nervous than when he'd asked Callum about being bisexual in public, over dinner at Callum's club. Callum wished he could calm those nerves now as easily as he had then, with a touch of his hand and a smile. He'd known from their first meeting that Jamie was special, but then he'd just thought the boy was destined to be a star. He couldn't have known just how marvelous Jamie really was.

Nerea started taking her hair down from its bun. "We could. We probably should," she said in answer to Jamie's question. "But none of us have the energy for it, and I still feel awful."

Jamie looked beseechingly at Callum, but he wasn't sure what, exactly, Jamie was beseeching for. Did he want them to talk about it? Did he not want to talk about it? To have exhausted sex and fall asleep in a heap?

Callum shook his head. If Jamie wanted something he was going to have to ask for it more clearly. And regardless of what he wanted, Nerea had spoken.

⁂

Callum woke the next morning to find only Nerea in bed, curled up on her side as she tapped at his tablet one-handed. Her hair was tousled and she was wearing a wrinkled T-shirt of Jamie's. There were dark circles of sleeplessness under her eyes. Callum wondered if she'd been ill again or just too worried to rest. Either way Callum's heart ached at how lovely she was even in exhaustion.

"Where's Jamie?" All he wanted to do was stay in bed with the two lovely human beings who for some reason wanted him in their lives. Unfortunately, one of them was currently missing.

"I don't know. He wasn't here when I woke up."

Callum threw back the covers. "I suppose I should go find him." He was still worried about Jamie's lack of communicativeness last night. Callum wanted to address and at least try to solve whatever it was Jamie needed.

Nerea shook her head. She let the tablet fall forward onto the mattress and looked at Callum.

"Give him space and time. We could all use some of that."

"What are you doing?" Callum nodded toward the tablet.

"Googling."

"Googling what?" he asked tightly.

"Everything."

❧

Callum found Jamie an hour later entirely by accident. Nerea had sent Callum up to her studio to grab some odds and ends necessary for decorations. There he found Jamie, sitting backward on an old wooden chair, his arms folded across the back and his chin resting on his crossed wrists.

"I was wondering where you'd got to," Callum said mildly as he shifted things about looking for craft glue and a very particular pair of scissors he'd been sent up to find.

"I just needed some quiet," Jamie said. His voice was dull and his eyes, Callum noted, were rather misty and red. Next to him on the floor was an open sketchpad, and on the page —

"Is that you?" Callum asked, squinting down at the sketchpad.

Jamie glanced at it. "Yeah."

"Nerea's work?" Callum thought about picking the thing up for a closer look, but didn't want to intrude on whatever distance Jamie needed right now.

"Yeah," Jamie said again. "I saw the painting she did of you. When I was here over the summer. I asked if she'd do one of me, so." He nudged the sketchbook gently with a socked toe. "Things were simple back then, huh? Relatively speaking."

"Only by comparison," Callum said. "I know you don't want to hear this, but life was only ever going to get more complicated. If it wasn't this, it would've been something else."

"Maybe." Jamie sounded doubtful. "But I'm pretty sure this is the most complicated it could possibly get."

Callum couldn't disagree. He left Jamie with a squeeze to his shoulder. "Take as much time as you need."

≈

Getting ready for Christmas Eve mass that night, Callum dressed in the bathroom still warm from the steam of their showers while Nerea helped Jamie with his cuff links in the bedroom. Buttoning up his own shirt, Callum thought back on all the Christmases he'd spent here over the last three decades.

There had been holidays in London, of course. Especially when the girls were little and they'd tried to rotate Christmas between his parents and Nerea's. But more recently this house had become the center of all things holiday and celebratory. It was hard to believe that any of it — the food, the language, the hymns — had ever been strange to him. This is what Christmas was: Huge meals with the neighbors, relatives too much underfoot; mass at church; and the sheer joy of the season.

As they had each Christmas spent here, they and all their guests walked to the church. Despite it being more than a mile away, it was festive to troop down the road with their family and friends in the crisp evening air. Nerea looped her arm through Callum's. Jamie, with a tentative glance at both of them, took her other arm and was rewarded with a dazzling smile. Whatever else was in store for the three-possibly-four of them, Jamie could make Nerea smile like that. As far as Callum was concerned, that was worth almost anything life could throw at them.

Jamie was fine at church, cheerful as he smiled and nodded and was generally enthusiastic in conversation to make up for the fact that he could hardly understand anyone. Even the neighbors had surrendered to the spirit of the season and refrained from snide comment, at least within Callum's earshot. But walking home afterward he trailed behind them, texting furiously into his mobile. His sister or a parent, Callum presumed and didn't press. If Jamie wanted to tell him what was going on, he would when he was ready.

Back at the house everyone sat up eating baked goods and talking. Jamie, however, withdrew into himself. Once they all went upstairs long after midnight he dropped into the chair beneath the window and then sat rigidly on the edge of it, responding to all inquiries in monosyllables.

"Jamie, please come to bed," Callum finally huffed. Having emotions was all well and good, but this was ridiculous.

"I'm not cuddling while we discuss this." Jamie gripped the arms of the chair for dear life. Callum struggled not to laugh at him, or curse in exasperation.

Sitting up in bed against a stack of pillows and wrapped in one of Callum's shirts, Nerea ran her hands over her face. "Can you please stop acting as if we aren't all on the same side?"

"Fine. Then explain to me how that works," Jamie said. "Because the way I see it — and I've now spent more than a day thinking about this — either you and Callum are having another baby, which means there's not really room for me; or you're having my baby and Callum's going to be gracious about that, which also means there's not really room for me; or you're going to have an abortion and then we'll all be pissed off and sad and awkward 'til we break up. So excuse me if I don't feel like being in your bed for this disaster that I've ruined my relationship with my parents for. Also it's Christmas Eve and who has conversations like this on Christmas Eve? People are supposed to be all into baby Jesus, not worried about an actual baby."

"Jamie — " Nerea tried to cut him off.

"What?"

"You are being an awful human being right now," she said.

"So?" he retorted.

"Where is this coming from? You've been so sane."

"Yeah and then I had to spend all day around your families, who still don't know what to do with me, and not talking to my family, who still aren't speaking to me."

Nerea and Callum exchanged a look.

"What?" Jamie demanded.

Callum frowned. "Get your arse out of that chair and sit on this bed right now so we can have this conversation with you the way it needs to be had."

He sighed in relief when Jamie got up and slunk over.

"Fine," Jamie said when he sat down.

"Can I rewind?" Callum asked Nerea, who only made an irritated gesture in response.

Callum took Jamie's hands in his own. "You're having a panicked meltdown about this, regardless of any complicating factors. I have been there. I get it." In a way, Callum — both present and past — was grateful to have someone to share this particular experience with. Jamie's sullen belligerence in the face of life's vagaries, while concerning, was well-earned.

"Okay, fair and all, but when you knocked Nerea up you got to marry her and feel responsible. What am I supposed to do?"

Callum boggled at Jamie. It was, in its way, a fair question, but Callum had no idea how to respond.

Nerea, though, giggled. When Callum and Jamie turned their heads simultaneously to look at her, her giggling turned into outright laughter. Callum started to chuckle himself; her mirth was infectious and the stress and absurdity of the situation demanded some sort of outlet. Jamie caught it, too, and before long the three of them were tangled in a laughing, hysterical heap on the bed.

"Okay," a breathless Jamie finally said. "I'm done being a prick. For now. I think."

Nerea swatted him lightly on the arm. "Good."

"Sorry about that," Jamie said.

Nerea smiled. "I think we've learned never to let you stew about anything."

Jamie sat up. "I still have questions."

Nerea kissed him gently and then settled back against the pillows. "Ask away."

"You and Callum got married, he said, 'cause you gave him a list of conditions when you got pregnant with Leigh."

"He told you that, did he?" Nerea turned a fond gaze on Callum. Callum couldn't help but smile back.

"So if you do have this baby, do you have a list for me?"

There were times when Callum couldn't believe that Jamie was real. What had he done to deserve someone so lovely to share life, and Nerea, with?

"I think it's helpful, not to mention necessary, to remember that I'm forty-eight and the chances of me carrying a baby to term are very low," Nerea said. "Assuming that's something I want to do."

"Should I be assuming that?" Jamie asked carefully.

"We are sitting here worrying about it," she said. "It's a terribly romantic notion, but I don't know. I like my life, Jamie. I like my marriage; I like our relationship; I like my body; I like my career. Pregnancies change all those things."

Callum kept his face studiously neutral. Now was not the time to gush about how much he wanted a baby.

"What do you need from me if you don't have the baby? For whatever reason?" Jamie asked.

"In that case, I want your support in whatever happens and whatever choice I make. If it's too much for you, or too hard, you're welcome to leave, as you would be in any relationship."

"And in the other case?" Jamie asked, hesitantly and with a flash of hope he was trying, and failing, to conceal.

Nerea looked at Callum before she turned back to Jamie. She took Jamie's hand in one of hers and laced the fingers of her other hand through Callum's. "I can't be a single parent again. Not at my age, and also, not ever again. So I would need commitments, from both of you that at least one of you is going to be present at all times. If — and I can't emphasize enough how big an *if* this is — if there's a baby, I don't want to be the primary parent. Not at six months, not at six years, and not at sixteen. I've done my time."

Jamie, to Callum's deep pleasure and utter shock, nodded instantly and even eagerly. "I can do that," he said.

"Can you really?" Nerea looked as surprised as Callum felt.

"Of course I can. I mean, I won't have much clue of what I'm doing, but my sisters have kids and you guys were probably as clueless as me when you had Leigh, right? So — yeah. Yeah. I want to be with you. *Both* of you. And if this happens to be a part of that life. I'm not going to say no."

"That's very generous of you," Callum said. And it was. Possibly more than it was wise of Jamie to offer. "But you have a brilliant career opening up. Wanting to be a parent and present is all well and good, but just how much of your job are you willing to give up? Because, speaking as someone who knows, either way, you're going to have to make sacrifices."

Jamie fell silent, but it was the silence of thoughtfulness and someone making a plan, not of regretting offers made.

Callum turned his attention back to Nerea. There were plans and promises he wanted — needed — to make too. "I'm content with any decision you make," Callum said. "I know I've screwed up before, but if there's an opportunity for another chance, it would be the joy of my life to make up for that."

Nerea looked between the two of them and briefly pressed a hand to her breastbone. "That's sweet, both of you. It really is. But Callum, how you feel and what you can do aren't necessarily the same. And Jamie, Callum's right that you need to consider your career. Speaking of which, aren't you both scheduled to go on a contractually obligated press tour in eight months? Together?"

Callum looked at Jamie, who was staring back at him with a look of utter horror on his face.

"Oh," Callum said.

Jamie turned to Nerea. "Is that a reason you don't want to have a baby, or a reason you'd be annoyed about having a baby?"

"Start of a long list. After which comes *I'm forty-eight*," she said. "That's a concern both for my sake and a baby's. The risk of complications increases, the risk of birth defects increases — "

Jamie's head snapped toward her. "Birth defects like what?"

"Oh, God, any of them. Congenital heart problems, Down Syndrome — "

Jamie had leapt up from the bed and started pacing. "No. No. No, no, no, no, no," he said, agitated.

Nerea looked at Callum, baffled, but Callum had no idea either. He shrugged.

"Jamie, I'm afraid that's the science," Nerea told him.

"No," Jamie said again. "That's not what I mean."

"Then what do you mean?" Nerea asked.

"You know Aoife? My sister?"

Callum's heart sank. He could see where this might be going. And if he was correct, Jamie was going to have every right to be upset with what Nerea had just said.

"You've mentioned her," Nerea said. "The one who just got engaged, yes?"

"Yes." Jamie nodded. "She's my favorite person in the whole world. More than you, more than Callum. And she has Down Syndrome."

Nerea covered her mouth with her hand. Shock, Callum thought, that somehow neither of them had known and together had been callous for it. Jamie could be so forthcoming, and yet there was always more. He was so kind, and yet always seemed to keep so many secrets in his life so unbearably close. Callum suddenly wanted to know about all of Jamie's sisters. He felt chagrin for all the times he and Nerea had never asked. Callum wished for Jamie to trust them with the whole of his world, but Callum could see now why that hadn't happened yet.

"And that," Jamie said, angry, "is why my very decent but imperfect parents freaked out about her engagement and then had a meltdown when I told them about you."

"We didn't know," Callum said uselessly.

"And you shouldn't assume that every family is like yours!" Jamie exclaimed. "I love my sister. When I told her about you she couldn't stop laughing. She didn't believe me! I told her I was dating a movie star and his wife, and she thought what I was saying about the three of us sounded too good to be true. So if you don't want to have a baby, I guess that's fine. But if you don't want to have a baby like Aoife — because you think it's too hard or not cool or you're too busy or famous or whatever — that I can't do. I can't be here for that."

"Why didn't you tell us sooner?" Nerea asked.

"Because I shouldn't have to say any of this? Because she's a person, and I wanted you to meet her first?"

"I'm sorry, Jamie. I didn't know." Nerea echoed Callum.

"Well, now you do." Jamie stopped pacing and dropped into the chair again.

"Perhaps I am coming at this with a set of biases I didn't even realize I had." Nerea took a deep breath and glanced at Callum.

He nodded at her. As he kept saying to Jamie and himself, Nerea came first. Whatever her feelings were, she should express them without checking them with Callum.

"I'm willing to acknowledge that and to learn from you and your family," she said. "But the reality is, while you may want a baby regardless of what type of baby, my age restricts my ability to care for a child who in any way needs long-term care. It wouldn't be fair to me, and it wouldn't be fair to them."

"Aoife's getting married," Jamie repeated. "She and Patrick are getting a flat in a community that can support them. Don't assume what someone needs from you when you don't know."

"I'm learning Jamie. I'm trying, I really am. I am, once again, only one of three potential parents here," she added. "Regardless of any of these issues, I can't be the primary parent. I've said that before and I have a feeling I'm going to keep saying that until this plays out one way or another. So that ball is in your court, boys. It's also only one of our many problems."

"But you could love a Down Syndrome kid? As long as we did all the work?"

"Of course I could love her," Nerea said. "That's not in question. Not to me. And not, I hope, for you."

"What are the other problems?" Callum asked, circling back to the remark that had been half-buried by the crisis of the moment.

"Our lives, our schedules, our homes," Nerea said. "Jamie. You split your time between Dublin, London, and — if we continue this pattern — Spain. Callum and I split our time between London and here. We are three adults with time-consuming careers and somewhat itinerant lives."

Callum wondered how they hadn't talked about this before. But then, there hadn't been an immediate need to. Not like this.

"This international jet-setting lifestyle is compelling in theory," Nerea went on. "But in practice, it's not an arrangement that's sustainable. And that's true whether I'm having a baby or not. So if you need to find some new reading material to occupy you, Jamie, start brainstorming solutions as to how we're going to fix that."

Callum said nothing. He wanted to see what Jamie's response would be.

"That's easy," Jamie said. "We're all just going to have to move."

Chapter 33

Nerea is grateful for drama that does not involve her

Christmas morning dawned cold and clear with a sharp wind that whistled down the terraced hillside. Nerea woke before either Jamie or Callum and had no interest in lingering in bed. As much as she loved them, she needed a few minutes just to herself.

She crept downstairs, aware that the rest of the house was still asleep. She did not want to rouse any of her guests. She supposed that was one advantage of not having young children around anymore: Quiet mornings and moments alone, even on Christmas Day.

In the kitchen she made tea and sat at the table by the window, watching dawn grow over the hills. She would miss this house terribly if and when they left it. She struggled to imagine it not being part of her life, not just at Christmas and for great family celebrations, but on the quiet, ordinary days meant for just her and anyone else she chose to include in her life. She had so many fond memories here, from when she was a girl and from when her daughters were children.

No matter how foolish, she could even picture herself here next Christmas with a new baby. Callum would burst with pride to show it off to their family, and Jamie would be the sweetest and most attentive parent. She herself would not just have joy in the baby, but also triumph over the neighborhood and all its judgment of her. In an ideal world she would be able to raise it here, on her family's land and surrounded by the history that was so much a part of her life. It was a beautiful daydream, and it hurt to think how unlikely it was to come to pass.

She wasn't surprised to see Callum padding down the stairs fifteen minutes later. Even with Jamie in the bed, he could tell when she wasn't there. And after the events of last night, small wonder that he'd seek her out for a quiet moment alone together.

He sat down across from her and slipped her mug out of her hands, his fingers cool against hers.

"Get your own." Her hands chased his, and she wound up with his hands wrapped around both her slender fingers and the mug.

"How are you?" he asked quietly.

"To be honest, I hardly know," her voice was nearly a whisper. "There are so many decisions and so many things to think about. Where am I supposed to even start?"

They were interrupted by a clatter at the doorway. Nerea and Callum turned to see Thom stagger into the kitchen. He started opening cupboards at random until Callum cleared his throat.

Thom jumped. "Jesus," he moaned. "Sorry. Didn't see you there."

"Coffee's in the cupboard to the right of the stove," Nerea told Thom. In spite of everything, Nerea shot Callum an amused look.

"Mm. Thank you."

There was a brief interval while Thom got the machine running, stood humming under his breath until it was done, and then took a mug and, to Nerea's discomfort, the whole pot with him. She suspected the rest of that pot was for Piper, and this was not the moment for Callum to find out about any of that.

"Where do you want to start?" Callum asked once Thom was gone.

It took Nerea a moment to refocus. "I don't know. But I can't stop thinking about the fact that I'm forty-eight."

"You keep saying that. And?"

Nerea did not say that she was repeating herself because, apparently, Callum and Jamie needed to hear things over and over again to absorb them. "And, I did not anticipate the possibility of having to care about someone's every need until I turn sixty-five."

"You'd have help. I meant every word I said last night."

"Sixty-five, Callum. When do I get to come first?"

Callum said nothing.

"Yes, you see, there's no answer."

"What do you want me to say?" Callum tried.

Nerea ignored him. "And that's to say nothing of the next nine months. What about complications? Or miscarriage? I'm too old for this to be smart, and the likelihood of this ending in tears is very high."

"You've always had easy pregnancies," Callum pointed out. Nerea couldn't yell at him because he wasn't trying to talk her into anything, just stating the facts. But he made it seem possible. And he made it seem desirable. Which wasn't helpful.

"Easy pregnancy is a relative concept!" she protested. "And I don't want to even think about trying to lose baby weight at forty-nine."

"That doesn't matter."

Nerea sighed. She didn't have the energy to explain the unpleasantries of her reluctant life in the public eye right now. "Yes, because you have a prick. Which is how we're in this mess."

"You think it's mine?" Callum asked.

Nerea shook her head. "I don't, but I couldn't tell you why."

"Me neither."

"Does that change how you feel about it?" she asked.

"No. I mean, yes, but not like you think."

"How then?"

"We talked. Jamie and me. In the car on the way from the airport. What was really cutting him up — I mean, aside from him being scared he won't be able to go to his sister's wedding and that his parents will never speak to him again — is the idea that he'll never get married. Not in a way that means something to other people. Not if he stays with us."

"Oh," Nerea said. She should have thought of that herself. But somehow, in the recent chaos, she hadn't.

"And," Callum said, bracing himself. "If Jamie's really in this, this may be his one chance to be a father."

Nerea dropped her head down against the table and moaned incoherently.

Callum rubbed a hand through her hair. "And he did seem to leap at the chance last night. But he should sleep on it for more than a day."

"Rather," Nerea said. "He's also horrifyingly right that we all need to move. God, this is hard enough when there's just one of you around."

"Do you need some space?"

"That is why I came down here." She was exasperated, but she didn't want to scold Callum for making sure she was okay. "I need to not make this decision right now. Our daughter is getting married in," she glanced at the old kitchen clock. "Approximately thirty hours. Our other daughter is about to go into labor at any moment. And I have a house full of guests and a neighborhood full of women whose favorite pastime is judging me and my choices. I don't want to make any promises I can't keep."

"No matter what else comes out of my mouth, I want you to make the choice that's right for you."

"I know. Thank you." Nerea straightened up. "Now, will you — "

She was interrupted by the appearance of Piper, carrying the coffee pot Thom had carried off before, now empty. Nerea could see the moment when Callum noticed it. Piper wasn't carrying a mug, but she was wearing —

"Piper," Callum said. He sounded slightly strangled.

Piper looked up. "Oh, hey. Good morning."

"Piper," Callum repeated. "Whose shirt is that you have on?"

Piper looked down at herself, then up at them. "Um."

Nerea said nothing. She just curled her hands tighter around her mug and braced for impact.

"Because Thom was just down here, to get coffee," Callum said, sounding dazed and more than a little horrified. "He was wearing a shirt very similar to the one you have on right now. One might even say identical."

"Oh. Huh. Weird." Piper returned the coffee pot to its proper spot in the coffeemaker and turned to go. Rapidly.

Nerea held her breath. If Piper could just get out of the room Nerea stood half a chance of distracting Callum. Before she got to the doorway, though, she was stopped by the roar of Callum's voice.

"Thomas! Thomas Charles Abbot! Get your arse down here right now!"

Piper had stopped in her tracks, her eyes huge. Nerea clapped her hands over her mouth so as not to burst out laughing at the ridiculous timing of it. Voices murmured upstairs, but there was no sound of footsteps, so Callum roared again.

"He's not coming down now," Nerea pulled her hands away from her mouth to tell Callum. "I imagine he's crawled out the window and is running across the fields for France."

"Did you know about this?!" Callum pointed at Piper.

"Are you going to yell at me?" Nerea raised an eyebrow.

Callum swore and pushed himself up from the table. With his robe flapping about his ankles he strode to the door, past a still-dumbstruck Piper, and pounded up the stairs.

"If it helps," Nerea told her, as she went to rinse out her teacup. "Today might be the one day in all days he won't actually kill him."

&

When Nerea climbed the stairs to see the confrontation unfold for herself she discovered Thom hadn't climbed out of his bedroom window. Mainly because he wasn't in his bedroom.

For years to come Nerea knew the entire family would tell the story of the Christmas morning when Callum — father, brother, uncle, son, boyfriend, and internationally acclaimed movie star — banged open the door to his daughter's bedroom to find his best friend huddled, in true romantic-comedy style, under Piper's lavender-colored flannel sheets.

All the occupants of the house, eager for any and all drama, roused themselves and gathered in the hallway, chattering at each other in a mixture of English and Spanish while Callum hollered himself nearly hoarse at Thom, who stayed in bed under the covers because he was naked. Because Callum's daughter — Callum took many pains to stress that point — was wearing Thom's clothes.

Nerea smiled when she saw Jamie hovering at the back of the pack, looking torn between horror and amusement. Then she sat at the top of the stairs and laughed until she cried.

⤳

Soon everyone was in the kitchen, too many bodies in one reasonably large room as Nerea orchestrated the multi-person operation that was making breakfast. This many English people in the house meant making English breakfast for them all, even if she herself had never quite understood the appeal of beans so early in the morning. In the middle of setting the table Jamie, apparently done being put out by other people's judgment, kissed her soundly on the mouth. Nerea laughed, delighted by the sparkle in Jamie's eyes.

Piper and Thom both appeared at breakfast, although only after most everyone else had already eaten. Piper looked defiant and Thom looked nervous, but he stayed close to Piper as they got plates and settled in on adjacent stools around the kitchen island.

Nerea couldn't help herself. Thom gave her a wary look as she approached them, but she placed a reassuring hand on his back before wrapping her arms tight around Piper.

Piper protested, but she didn't look displeased and she did hug Nerea back.

"I didn't get a chance to say how happy I am. For both of you," Nerea said, looking between her daughter and Thom.

"Really?" Piper looked uncertain.

"Of course. Thom, you know how fond Callum and I both are of you. Despite his threats this morning. He'll get over them. I promise. And Piper, you know we just want you to be happy."

"And to fuss over me."

"Of course. Which reminds me," Nerea said with a saccharine innocence. "I'll be back in London once Leigh has her baby and I'm sure we'll be seeing plenty of each other then."

"Great," Piper affected sarcasm but looked pleased nonetheless. Nerea hugged her again. Thom still looked as though he expected the sky to fall down on him at any moment, so Nerea hugged him, too.

There was much laughter and clatter of furniture as people arranged themselves around the tree. It was now Thom, rather than Jamie, who was the focus of people's teasing, but neither of them seemed to mind the change. Piper grinned at Thom and steered him to a chair and then sat down on his lap in triumph. Thom, with an arm resting easily around her waist, looked happy. Though he did throw an occasional look of half-laughing alarm at Callum, who seemed to be taking such a sight in stride, or at least trying to.

Jamie darted upstairs but soon reappeared, creeping over to where Nerea was half-sitting, half-lounging against Callum on the couch and held out a box for them, wrapped in simple brown paper stamped with snowflakes.

"Thank you, Jamie," she said, taking it. "You didn't have to."

"I know." Jamie perched on the arm of the couch next to Callum. "But I wanted to."

Nerea peeled back the wrapping to reveal a set of glasses. Not two or four, as were common for gifts, but three.

"Jamie," she breathed, her fingers tracing over the design etched on one of them. It was Celtic knotwork, one continuous line tracing a tri-pointed shape.

"It's a trinity knot," Jamie said. "It's meant to represent, well. The Trinity and all that. But I thought it worked pretty well for us too." His voice was steady and there was a look in his eyes that spoke assurance. He'd grown so much over the past year. Not into being an adult — he'd been that already — but into a man who was confident in himself and his relationships. Nerea loved him, deeply and with a ferocity that startled her sometimes. There had never been anyone else, except Callum, who she'd wanted to devote so much time to.

"They're absolutely beautiful," she said.

"I remembered that story you told me, about being at Callum's and him not having any glasses." There was a spark of mischief in Jamie's eyes, though the rest of his face was serious.

"You didn't," Callum said to her.

Nerea squeezed his knee with her free hand. "I did."

Jamie went on. "It made me think about how we — the three of us, but anyone really — are always changing. We had lives before, and we all put effort into building the ones we have now, individually and together. And now we have to work out what we want from ourselves and each other in the future. And no matter what we do there's always the things we used to be or aren't yet. And I just wanted to make sure there was some marker of this moment, no matter where we go next," Jamie said, his voice hushed and emphatic. "Which, I guess has gotten a lot more complicated in the last forty-eight hours."

"Jamie." Callum set down his coffee cup and gently lifted one of the glasses out of the box Nerea cradled on her lap. His eyes were a bit watery, and he cleared his throat before he spoke again. "I don't know what to say."

Jamie looked incredibly pleased with himself.

"We have a gift for you, too," Callum said. His voice was choked. "On the mantel over there, Jamie," he pointed. "I'd get it for you myself, but," he nodded his head toward where Nerea was still lounging against him.

Jamie retrieved the package with such eager curiosity that Nerea had to laugh. When he tore back the wrapping paper, his mouth fell open in a small O.

"We got that for you before any of this week's chaos," Callum said. "I suppose we were also trying to mark a moment." He reached out a hand to pull Jamie down on the couch on the other side of him. Jamie dropped down next to him, his knees tucked up next to Callum's.

Nestled in the box was the watch Nerea and Callum had chosen for him. Almost reverently, Jamie picked it up. It glinted in the winter sun pouring through the window. The face was black, with gold numbers around the edge. The gear work was visible, ticking solidly along, and the leather strap lay warm and soft across Jamie's palm.

Callum put his hand on the back of Jamie's neck, his fingers pushing into the short hair there. "Whatever else is true about us and our relationship, we want this time to be the beginning of something," Callum said. "This week has made that, whatever it's going to be, more fraught, but it hasn't made it less true."

"Do you want help putting it on?" Nerea asked, as Jamie's fingers fumbled with the buckle. He was trembling.

Jamie nodded, his cheeks flushed and his eyes wide and awed.

"I love you. Both of you." He looked up, his eyes darting between their faces. "I know we've said that before. But it feels like more now. And maybe that's just the drama talking, but I like what it's saying."

⌒

For the rest of the day whenever Nerea's eyes found Jamie in the bustle of the house she caught him fiddling with the watch, a smile on his face. And every time he looked up to see her looking, a broader, brighter smile broke out.

"You made the right choice," she murmured to Callum as everyone gathered around the dining room table for Christmas lunch. She nodded toward Jamie.

"The watch or the boy?" Callum whispered back.

Nerea nudged her elbow into his ribs. Callum laughed and wrapped his arms around her waist to pull her in for a kiss.

The rest of the day was a Christmas that Nerea knew would live on in her memory as one of the very best. For all that had gone awry, everyone was getting along now, talking and laughing and working together. By the time Nerea went to bed that night she was exhausted but happy. Callum and Jamie seemed to feel the same, snuggling up on either side of her and chatting about the day and last minute logistics for the next. Whether there was going to be a baby or not, the three of them were building a family together, not just with each other, but with their extended relations and friends. Margarita's wedding would cement that even further.

Nerea fell asleep with her head on Jamie's chest and Callum's arm around her waist. Her last thought before she drifted off was that she wasn't worried about the future at all.

~

Nerea woke the next morning before her lovers, climbing out of bed as carefully as she could to avoid disturbing them. As she stood at the window looking out at the quiet morning stealing over the fields there was a rustle as a still-sleeping Jamie moved into the warm spot she'd vacated. Nerea thought again about a life not just where she might have a baby, but where this place was no longer home. The thought of giving up the house made her want to weep. But it also didn't feel as wrong as it had a few days ago. Just another change in a life full of agreements and adjustments.

Nerea took a deep breath and went to shower. She had so much to get done and not enough time to dwell too long on what had been or what would be.

She was the first one downstairs, but not for long. Soon she was joined by Leigh, who complained good-naturedly that it was impossible to sleep in her condition, and by her own mother, who was happy as ever to be involved in wedding preparations while ignoring everything else going on.

We could give the house to Margarita, Nerea thought, when her daughter tripped downstairs, still in her pajamas and glowing with bridal joy. Margarita had a Spanish name, a Spanish life, and she could use a Spanish home. The house had been passed down from mother to daughter for Nerea didn't know how many generations. Perhaps now it was time to pass it on again.

But those logistics could wait. For now, Margarita needed to get dressed. And for that, Nerea needed her bedroom. Callum and Jamie hadn't appeared downstairs yet, and while Nerea was grateful they were staying out of the way, she needed them to be elsewhere.

"All right, time to get out," Nerea announced at the bedroom door. Jamie and Callum were awake and thankfully not in the middle of anything other than reading.

"Where would you like us to go?" Callum asked, as Jamie grumbled and extracted himself from the warm covers.

"Anywhere that's not here. Actually, take anyone who wants to go and make sure everything at the church is in order."

"Shall we?" Callum asked Jamie.

"Yeah." Jamie nodded. Now that he'd conquered the step of getting out of bed he looked excited. "You know," he said to Callum as the two pulled on clothes and tromped out of the room, each pausing to kiss Nerea goodbye, "I've never gotten to set up a church for a wedding."

"Not even for your sisters' weddings?" Nerea heard Callum ask as they reach the hallway.

"Nah," Jamie said, but whatever else he offered in the way of explanation Nerea didn't hear.

She was soon joined by Margarita and her bridesmaids. Margarita sat at Nerea's vanity while Nerea brushed her hair the way she had when Margarita had been just a girl. She curled and braided it while Margarita's bridesmaids flitted around them getting ready themselves, their excited chatter filling the room. Nerea was so lucky to have all this happiness, none of which had been certain or even possible when Margarita was a child and Callum had never been home. Then there had been Tonio followed by Callum trying to fit himself back into their lives. It had all been so difficult.

But somehow, they had arrived here. Callum was older but wiser, making up for the past by thinking thoroughly of the future. And now they also had Jamie. Sweet, earnest, steadfast Jamie, who tried so hard and wanted so much. It was mad, how willing he was to devote himself to her and Callum individually and as a couple. But it had been just as mad when she was twenty, pregnant, and terrified and had demanded safety and security from the English boy who was already halfway to being movie star.

Taking her own wedding veil — that her mother and grandmother had worn at their weddings before her — down from the closet where it lay safe in layers of tissue paper, Nerea wondered about all the weddings that might take place in the future. For Margarita's children, for Leigh's. For the baby she herself carried.

Chapter 34

Jamie has an idea

Jamie had been to a lot of weddings. His sisters', his cousins', even some of his schoolmates'. He'd attended with friends and, once or twice, with a girlfriend. But attending a wedding as the boyfriend of the parents of the bride was another matter entirely.

He had offered to sit discreetly back in the pews with the rest of the guests. Under different circumstances he would have made a fuss about any attempt to hide him, but this event wasn't about him. But Nerea had refused and Callum had shaken his head and looked almost upset that he had offered. So here Jamie was, sitting at the end of the row reserved for family, next to Leigh and Sam. He watched along with the rest of the congregation as Miguel's best man walked Nerea down the aisle, followed by the bridesmaids Piper and Lucia, and then Margarita on Callum's arm. Callum looked so proud and so happy, and the lace of her veil could not hide the smile on Margarita's face.

Nerea slid into the pew next to Jamie as Callum lifted Margarita's veil. Nerea squeezed Jamie's hand as Callum kissed Margarita on the cheek and shook Miguel's hand, before retreating himself.

The mass may have been in Spanish, but Catholicism was Catholicism. Jamie could follow along well enough. But his mind wandered. If he stayed with Callum and Nerea he would never have a wedding. Not like this. Not legally or in the Church, not to the both of them. And not to one of them unless there was a divorce or a death. Marriage equality had passed in Ireland by a landslide with the help of Jamie's own vote, which Callum had made it possible for him to cast. But despite that overwhelming sentiment for equal rights under the law, public sanction of the happiness he had now seemed as if it might be too much to hope for.

Would it be worth it? As Miguel and Margarita exchanged vows, Nerea dabbed tears from her eyes. Even Callum look a bit watery. A wedding, after all, was just a day. A lovely day, to be sure, but still. And a marriage was built much more on trust and love than on ritual and paperwork.

Besides, he thought as the congregation stood for the *Our Father*, Faith and the Church were what one made of them. His parents had taught him that, and Jamie had grown up believing it ever more firmly as he realized all the ways Church doctrine differed from who he was and the kind of person he wanted to be. Jamie had long since come to his own relationship with the idea of God. There was no reason he could not do the same with marriage. He didn't need priests or lawyers. He just needed the commitment of his own mind and heart, freely given and gladly received. Which he had. Which he did.

The important question now was whether Callum and Nerea felt the same? Jamie was nearly certain that they did. But that was a conversation they very much needed to have. Relationships could not be sustained on assumption alone.

At the Sign of Peace, both Callum and Nerea kissed him, chastely but unhesitatingly. Jamie clung to their hands until the final hymn and smiled with the rest of the congregation as they departed again down the aisle after Margarita and Miguel. As he merged with the crowd flowing out of the church, his thoughts went from himself to his parents. Would his mother be disappointed if he never got married in the Church? Would his father? Maybe. Maybe not. But he'd once been afraid that his parents would be angry he was bi. They hadn't been, not really. But they were obviously angry — or at least frustrated — about his current relationships.

They'd understood before. Maybe they would again. But Callum had been right; Jamie needed to put in the hard work to make that happen.

⸙

At the reception, while Nerea danced with Antonio on the floor that had been set up under the bare fruit trees and Callum charmed his way through the guests, Jamie sat on a low wall at the corner of the garden, thinking hard. Eventually he slipped off into the leafless winter vineyard, the noise of the party fading behind him as he made his way deeper down the rows. It was colder away from the heat lamps and the crowd, but the air was bracing and the sky above shone with stars.

His fingers shook as he scrolled to his parents' number and clicked *call*.

"Hello?" His mother answered the phone after two rings. Jamie was relieved at that until she repeated her greeting, sounding confused when he didn't answer, and he remembered his parents' home phone didn't have caller ID.

"Hi, Mum," he said as he walked, scuffing old leaves under his feet. "It's me."

"Jamie!"

"Hi," he said again. "I'm sorry I didn't call earlier, I just…."

"Are you okay?" his mother demanded.

"Yeah. Yeah, I'm okay, Mum. Happy Christmas, by the way, I should have called yesterday."

"You should have," she agreed. "But I should have called you, too. I was going to, but then…."

Jamie smiled wanly at the similarities between them.

"Is everything okay there?" Jamie asked. Maureen sounded worried, which might have been over himself or might have been over Aoife or might have been something else entirely.

"To tell the truth, we had a bit of excitement yesterday." Now she sounded rueful. "We had to take Vegetables in to the animal hospital."

"What? Why? What happened?" Jamie demanded, his heart clenching. After the events of the last week he'd never thought to worry about the dog. Was he going to have to deal with a dead pet on top of everything?

"He's fine now," his mother said quickly. "He got into the chocolate icing — with the help of your nieces — and needed some attention from the vet. But he's home now and right as rain, just very put out he's not allowed in the kitchen anymore. I'd meant to call yesterday, but by the time we got home it was too late. And then this morning," she hesitated. "I wasn't sure you would want me to."

"Of course I wanted you to!" Jamie said louder than was necessary. His voice faded into the still, cold rows of the vineyard. "Why would you think I wouldn't want you to?"

"There was the small matter of us having a row and you packing up and leaving the house with barely a word," his mother said. Jamie could tell she was trying to keep her voice light and her tone dry, but it didn't quite work.

"Ah. Yes. Jesus, Mum, I'm so sorry for running out. I completely bollocksed that up."

"Don't swear," his mother said automatically. She didn't otherwise respond to his apology. Jamie tried not to take that as a bad sign, but it was hard. "Where are you right now?"

"I'm at a wedding. Not my wedding," he added hastily, at her sharp intake of breath. Though he did wonder who, precisely, she thought he might be marrying. "Margarita's — Callum and Nerea's daughter. She got married today."

"Oh. Congratulations to her," his mum said. Jamie thought she sounded rather taken aback, but then, the last time they'd spoken they'd been in the middle of a shouting match. "Now, where are you?"

"I'm in Spain,"

"And how long have you been there?"

"Since I left your house. I flew right here." Jamie felt another stab of guilt that his mother hadn't even been sure of where he was.

"With your...." She apparently couldn't finish the sentence.

Jamie swallowed, knowing well that a wrong move here might make the situation even harder, if not impossible, to fix in the future. But if he couldn't say these things, how could he ever expect his mother to? *I can't respect your interests if you're not going to protect your interests.*

The face of his watch glinted in the moonlight. Jamie stared down at it and thought about the three glasses, one for each of them, now sitting in pride of place in the china cabinet in the dining room.

"With my partners, yes."

He heard her take a deep breath. "And how are they, Jamie-boy?"

The next five minutes of small talk was slow, almost painfully hesitant. He had never found it hard to talk to his mother before now, and Jamie didn't quite know how to do it. But he tried because he had to.

"I know you're worried about me," he said after a long pause in the conversation that was stretching from tentative to awkward. "But I'm okay. I really am. They're good people."

"It's not just that," his mother said.

"Then what is it?"

"I've spent the last ten years worrying about you. About whether you would be able to build a life with the person you love. This summer, there was Home to Vote, and I thought — yes. Now Jamie will be able to stand up and declare to the world who he loves, no matter who he loves. You were going to be able to have a wedding," his mother said. "Just like Beth and Mary and now Aoife; I never thought that would happen for her, and I guess that's my fault." She sounded close to tears.

Jamie blinked rapidly himself.

"And now — none of that is true anymore, and it will never be true. Not if these are the people you're going to spend the rest of your life with. The world's come a long way, but it hasn't come that far."

"So you're not upset with me?" Jamie asked, still frightened of the answer but far less so than he had been an hour ago.

"Oh, I'm furious at you. But not for loving anyone. Not really. And if I am, that should be my problem, not yours."

"What about Dad?"

Maureen hesitated. "Give him time."

"That doesn't sound good." Jamie rubbed his fingers against the roughness of the nearest vine. He was surrounded by roots and branches discussing his family, past, present, and future. The universe had a sense of humor.

"If you want the truth — "

"I sure don't want anything else."

"I think he's more upset you kept the secret than what the secret's been."

Jamie could see the logic of that. He and his father had always been close, had trusted each other to be friends as well as family. But he hadn't exactly handled this situation with Callum and Nerea that way.

"So how much time do I give him?" he asked. He wanted a blueprint. He wanted his mother to put his father on the phone.

"I don't know."

He had one more question, and it was the one he was most afraid to ask, especially knowing that his father wasn't ready to speak to him yet. "After the holidays," Jamie said. "Can I come home? To visit?"

"James Hugh Conway," his mother said firmly, although he could still hear the touch of tears in her voice. "No matter how hard it is for you, or me, or us, to deal with your life, ever, you will *always* have a home here."

Jamie's scrubbed his tears away with the back of his hand. "Yes, Mum," he said.

"And now, would you like to speak with your sister?" his mother asked. She sounded a bit sniffy herself. "I believe she has some news for you."

"Good news?" Jamie asked anxiously. He could hear his mother muffle the receiver and call for Aoife to come to the phone.

"She and Patrick have a wedding date," Maureen said, returning to the phone. "And I do believe she wants you to help her plan."

For a long time after Jamie stayed in the vineyard, walking up and down the rows of vines in the crisp night air. Moving helped him think, and the quiet let him focus. He would return to the reception, eventually, but he had things to figure out first. There was little he could do about his father other than wait and try his best. His mother had said so, and she was generally right about such things. What were his other options? He had none — not any that were constructive, at any rate.

But if he'd learned anything from the conversation with his mother, it was the importance of being honest. About who he was, what he was doing, and what he wanted. And what he wanted was to build a life and a family with Callum and Nerea. One that worked beyond saying *I love you* and spending the holidays together; one that worked despite the demands of their careers, families, and individual passions. As scary as it was, as uncertain the outcome, it was time for Jamie to speak the world as he wanted it into being. Even if he was just a man, too young, too flawed, too inexperienced to hold that sort of faith in himself. But part of growing up was reaching, and it was time to reach.

The reception was still in full swing by the time Jamie returned and would surely last well into the night. He wound his way through the crowd to where Callum and Nerea were tucked together at an otherwise empty table, watching the celebration.

"I have an idea," Jamie said as he dropped into a chair next to Callum.

Callum blinked mildly at him, his long fingers playing with the stem of his wineglass. Nerea, Jamie noticed, wasn't drinking. Jamie smiled to himself, feeling more certain of what he was about to do knowing that she was seeing a baby as a possibility.

"What is it?" she asked. A wisp of hair had fallen out of the elaborate knot she had twisted it up into for the wedding; she looked tired, but happy.

"Well, like I said last night — the only way this can work is if we all move. And the only place we all have in common, and where our working lives are, is in London. So what if we all lived together in London?"

"Jamie," Callum said lazily. Jamie flicked his gaze to Callum. He felt as nervous — and as resolute — as he had that night he'd demanded to have that conversation with him about being bi in public. While Jamie had had his fantasies about Callum even then, he'd never imagined they'd lead to a conversation like this.

"Yes?"

"Are you asking to move in with us?" Callum's voice and face said that Jamie was being too forward and that he loved everything about that.

Jamie glanced at Nerea to gauge her reaction. "No, I'm asking you to move in with me. Or, more accurately, for us all to move in together as our current London flats just won't do."

After a pause that made Jamie feel like his heart would stop, Callum laughed. He rolled his head toward Nerea.

"See? I told you he was wonderful."

"I'm carrying a baby that's possibly his. I'd say I got the message."

Jamie frowned at Callum. "I thought we weren't supposed to care whose it was."

Callum shrugged. "I don't."

"Okay. What do you think then? About my plan, I mean," he made a gesture he hoped would be interpreted as 'not paternity issues'.

"Callum hates that awful ceiling beam he's always hitting his head on," Nerea offered.

Callum chuckled. "It's true, I really do."

"And your flat is wretched," she added. "No offense."

"None taken," Jamie said. He wasn't in love with his flat either. "So we should get a place together." Jamie was gaining courage, and now that he had started talking he couldn't stop. "The three of us. Big enough for us, and. Well. Anything else we might need space for. And I know you might not think it's a good financial arrangement, because you're both established, and I'm twenty-four, but I have money from this movie and I have other projects coming up."

"You're going to be the most in-demand actor under thirty when this picture comes out," Callum said.

Not a yes, Jamie noted, but not a no. And possibly an encouragement to keep going. He smiled. Disparities of age, experience, money, and opinions were going to be inevitable, but Jamie needed this to be a partnership, and he needed to be able to contribute.

"What do you think?" Jamie turned to Nerea.

"I think the three of us living under one roof will go a long way toward making it easier for the two of you to make good on your promises to help with a baby. If I have this baby," she added sternly. "And, Jamie, as hard as I think it will be — Callum and I have our routines — I do want you to have the security I needed when I was your age and also very much in love with Callum."

"Is that a yes? I know this is a question where yes just brings up a whole lot more questions, but as a start?" Jamie wondered if this was what proposing felt like — frightening and exhilarating — to people who got to have that in their lives.

Callum glanced at Nerea. "What do you think?"

"I think we shouldn't make decisions when we're emotional and you're drunk," she said to Callum, "But I also think I'll want space for a studio and spare rooms so we can all have some breathing space when we need it. Or when people come to visit. And a California king because Jamie darling, I love you, but you kick."

"Sorry." Jamie grinned. That sure sounded like a yes to him. "Callum?"

Callum's only response was to lean across the table and kiss him soundly. With tongue.

Chapter 35

Callum continues to be an adult, which continues to be surprising

"It's good to have the house just to ourselves again," Callum declared, flopping naked onto the couch. Nerea tutted at him, but she was curled up in an armchair reading a book and only wearing one of Jamie's T-shirts, so as far as Callum was concerned she didn't have much grounds to complain.

"Wanna have shower sex?" Jamie, wrapped in Callum's big fluffy robe, crawled up onto the couch with him.

"You'll still steal the hot water and I'll still be a foot taller than either of you whether anyone else is in the house or not. I will happily watch, though."

"I'm not that short!" Jamie protested.

"It doesn't always seem that way."

Jamie humphed. Nerea tutted again, the sound fond. It was all so domestic and comfortable that Callum could almost forget the rather large promises they had made one another and the logistics that still needed to be discussed. Time enough for that in the new year, though.

Nerea put a scrap of paper in her book to mark her page and set it aside. "All right, both of you."

Jamie and Callum both turned to look at her. Callum shifted his legs so Jamie, still settling himself into place on the couch, wouldn't accidentally knee him in the groin. Jamie's face tightened with nerves and Callum couldn't blame him. He felt apprehensive himself.

"You both keep telling me that you'll support whatever decision I make," Nerea began, her face so studiously calm that even Callum couldn't entirely read it. "Which is decent of you, since it's my body, life, and career that are going to be affected the most by any theoretical pregnancy, no matter what you two swear to do for me after a baby is born." She paused.

Jamie nodded solemnly, probably because he, like Callum, knew not to interrupt her at this point. At least he, unlike Callum, had some sort of clothes on, and so some sort of dignity to cling to.

"Because, to be honest, a baby being born is not likely. You both know I'm not young."

Callum's heart clenched. Nerea's face continued to be solemn, almost unreadable, and he still had no idea what was going to come out of her mouth next.

"I have, remarkably, had a lot of time to think over the last few days. About what I've loved about having children, as well as what I've hated. The bad parts are not small, and all the good behavior in the world from the two of you can't change that. But I also thought about what I'm doing with my life, the challenges I'm willing to face, and all the questions I've had lately about how. I did not expect this pregnancy to answer more questions than it's raised, but it has. Having three children and a famous husband didn't stop me from becoming a very successful painter. So, as long as I can face this with the two of you, and the universe continues to think my body can do this, then yes, we're having the baby."

It was, Callum noted, the first time she'd used the definite article to refer to it.

The next thing he noted was Jamie going utterly rigid and then practically leaping off the couch with a whoop of joy.

Callum felt stunned all over again. He'd hoped, of course, but Nerea wasn't wrong — reason and logic were against this decision. He would have died rather than not support her in her choice, whatever it was. But this — he watched Jamie's shining face as he stopped his wild sprawl across the room to look almost reverently into Nerea's face — this was everything he hadn't quite hoped to dream of.

Nerea looked between them, amused but also emotional. "I suppose there's no point asking either of you what you want to do."

Jamie, still hovering in front of her like he was afraid this might not all be real, had tears running down his face and the brightest smile Callum had ever seen. Slowly, Jamie stooped, and with one hand on the arm of Nerea's chair and the other on the back of her neck, kissed her so gently and with such tenderness that Callum looked away to give them this moment together.

He turned back again at the sound of Nerea calling his name. He looked at her helplessly, his heart too full to be able to express even a fraction of it. He knew she understood, though. Standing, he crossed the room to where Jamie and Nerea were now curled up together in the chair, and wrapped his arms around them.

"I love both of you," he said, his own voice threatening to break. "More than I can possibly say."

Callum didn't remember hey-Nerea's-pregnant celebratory sex to be quite so celebratory. But then, the last time they'd had it had been a long time ago. And Jamie, of course, hadn't been involved.

After, none of them could sleep.

"I've been thinking," Callum said.

Nerea, the covers folded around her, said, "For a change."

"What's that?" Jamie asked.

"As you both know I made a lot of promises to Nerea a long time ago, and I didn't exactly keep all of them," Callum said. "I can't do anything about the horrific timing of the press tour for this movie — although I'm going to try — but other than that, I do want to live up to those promises. And Jamie, your willingness to make sacrifices is noble — "

"And the right thing to do," Nerea interjected lazily.

"And the right thing to do," Callum echoed with a smile. "But you also deserve to have your career. You have so much promise, so much opportunity — moments like this don't come twice, and I can't let you squander this one. So I want to take some time off. A year, two, maybe even three. Completely off," he added, just to be entirely clear. "No projects, no press tours, nothing." When the idea had first occurred to him, he had felt frightened and worried about how he was going to pick his career back up again after the break. But now, as he said it, it all seemed simple, a good and right thing he could only look forward to.

"That's very thoughtful of you," Nerea said. "And I'm certainly not going to say no. But what about your work? It's not as if you don't love what you do."

Callum shrugged. "I have this movie coming out, other things in production — the projects will be rolling out for a while after I stop making new ones. No one will even notice I'm gone. And if they do — well, a baby at my ripe old age is a rather good excuse."

"The media's going to be way too interested in this, you know," Jamie put in.

"Mhmmm," Nerea agreed, running a hand back through Jamie's hair. "I do know. And as I hope you can guess now, all the terrible things are going to be said about me."

"That's bollocks," Jamie said, his face darkening.

"It is," Callum agreed.

"And if you want me to do what you do, Callum, where you just sort of quietly terrify people who are awful to Nerea — I guess I can do that. But I also don't want to be your friend, or whatever, forever. I'm okay with taking some time to figure out what the official story is, but I do want to be a part of it. The story is already trickling out, surely, and we should just get this done."

"Jamie," Nerea said. "I have been, in my neighbors' words, flaunting you before God and everyone for the last week. What makes you think that's going to change once we're back in the real world?"

Jamie seemed to take a moment to absorb that. Then he nodded. "Yeah. Okay. Good."

"Believe me when I say it's going to be absolutely excruciating, when word of this does get out," Nerea said. "It's a minor miracle that the Tate show hasn't had major fall out. We won't get lucky like that twice."

"Which is why we should make a plan now," Jamie said. "So we can be prepared."

"And control the message," Nerea agreed.

"So," Callum said, "What about my incredibly generous offer to take a few years off?"

He laughed in delight at the exasperated look his wife and his partner gave each other. Whatever else was changing — and rapidly — in their lives, the relationships between the three of them were only going to grow stronger and deeper. But the little everyday joys that had made him fall in love with Nerea and Jamie in the first place were still there.

"We think it's very generous, entirely appropriate, and definitely appreciated," Nerea said, turning back to look at Callum. "Was there some other response you were looking for?"

"No," Callum smirked. "But if Jamie gets credit for being decent and noble, so do I."

"Ugh, you're both insufferable," Nerea said, but she was laughing.

Jamie made a noise of protest. And then he squeaked as Callum rolled over on top of him, pinning him with his weight. Jamie wriggled happily under him.

"Oh no. No no. You're not keeping him all to yourself," Nerea said and draped herself over the both of them.

"Oi! Heavy!" Jamie protested, but Callum was pretty sure he'd never seen him look happier.

Chapter 36

Nerea attempts to mother from a healthy distance

Once Jamie was down in the kitchen, the friendly clatter of dishes floating up the stairs, Callum scooched toward her on the bed, his curls a mess and the sheets tangled around his long legs.

"Nerea," he said very gently, his big hand splayed over her heart. "Are you sure?"

Nerea didn't hit him with a pillow only because she was too lazy and comfortable to move. "If you ask me that even one more time," she said fiercely, "I will divorce you, marry Jamie, and move to — I don't know where, but somewhere far away from you, your ego, and your need for reassurance."

Callum didn't draw back his hand or recoil, not that she'd expected him to. He just smiled the very gentle smile that had always been just for her. She felt her irritation melt.

"Just checking." he said.

Nerea reconsidered hitting him with a pillow. "You're impossible."

"Yes."

"But I love you."

He smiled and leaned down to kiss her with a combination of such gentleness and thoroughness that she thought she might come apart in his hands. "I love you too," he breathed into her mouth.

⟿

Being in London in the first days of the new year was a breath of fresh air; a return to real life after a strange, dreamlike interlude. Which was odd, because Spain had always felt the most real to Nerea. Except now, that seemed to be changing. Jamie kept most of his things at his flat in Lambeth and even stayed there for a night every so often when the cramped conditions of Callum and Nerea's flat got to be too much for all of them. The situation provided plenty of impetus for looking through the dozens of property listings Jamie found after a protracted conversation about what their financial arrangements could reasonably be.

Leigh's baby was born in the second week of January, a healthy, smiling boy named Daniel. Nerea hadn't told Leigh or indeed any of her daughters that she herself was pregnant. There was no call to, not until it was more certain, and besides it was bad luck this early. But as she watched Callum hold their own first grandchild with an expression of awed joy and devotion, she couldn't help but imagine how that conversation would go. Dramatically, in all likelihood.

Nerea stayed with Leigh and Sam for the first two weeks of the baby's life. Now, she could be useful without being unduly smothering. She told Leigh, at three one morning when the baby was determined to be loud and awake, that she and Callum were in the process of making London, and not Spain, their home base, and that the house would go to Margarita. Margarita had been thrilled at the news, both because it meant the old house would stay in the family and because it would significantly alleviate the financial concerns of starting a life together with Miguel. Leigh, however, looked less overjoyed. Nerea couldn't tell for certain in the dim light coming from the nightlight in the baby's room, but Nerea rather thought her face went pale.

"Not to smother you," Nerea said. "Or hover over the baby or anything like that. But it's time to make the adjustment."

"Are you moving because of Jamie?" Leigh asked keenly once she'd recovered herself.

"Yes. That's part of it," Nerea admitted.

"I spent a lot of time talking to Antonio at the wedding," Leigh said. "He and his wife invited me and Sam and Danny to come out and visit them, whenever we want."

"That's very good of them," Nerea said. "Will you go?"

"Will Dad be awful about it?"

Nerea smiled. "I highly, highly doubt it." One of the very many upsides of this situation was that Callum was not about to repeat any bad behavior regarding Nerea's history with Tonio.

"I think they invited Piper too, but Piper's been kind of. Um. Scarce, since Christmas."

Nerea sighed and shared a commiserating smile with Leigh. "Yes. We're working on that."

⁓

It took Callum until the first week of February before he saw Thom again. Nerea suspected that was more out of not quite knowing how to act with him than actual lingering anger, but either way, it was good when, at her and Jamie's combined urgings, he went out to meet Thom on neutral ground for a pint and whatever manly chat they needed to have.

Callum arrived back home late and slightly drunk. Jamie and Nerea were in bed together watching a house hunting show on Jamie's laptop — for inspiration, Jamie claimed, but Nerea suspected he was just a homebody who liked looking at other people's houses — while Nerea worked on sketches.

"How did it go?" Nerea prompted, when Callum flopped onto the sofa looking distraught. She wondered if she'd been wrong; maybe Callum had been appalling to Thom. The look on Callum's face didn't suggest their meeting had gone well.

"He asked my permission," Callum said. His voice was barely audible.

"Permission for what?" It was far too late, not to mention inappropriate, for Thom to ask Callum for permission to date Piper.

"To marry her."

Jamie's jaw dropped open.

Nerea burst out laughing, in disbelief at the statement as much as at the look on Callum's face.

"Seriously?" she said when she could finally breathe again.

Callum slumped lower in the sofa. Even his curls looked dejected, lying a bit limp around his ears.

"Seriously."

"But she's so young!" Nerea said.

"She's older than me," Jamie pointed out.

Callum groaned and covered his face with his hands.

"What did you say?" Nerea demanded, crawling out of bed and dropping onto the sofa next to Callum.

Callum didn't take his hands away from his face. "I told him not to be medieval and chauvinistic and that my daughter could marry whoever she wants. He said, *thank God*, because they've been engaged since New Year's."

Nerea started laughing again. "Are you two going to be okay now, or are you going to threaten fisticuffs anytime he comes near you?"

"We're fine," Callum told his palms. Jamie, who'd also gotten out of bed, stood behind the sofa and started massaging his shoulders gently, with an immense grin on his face. "We're never speaking of this again, and we're meeting for dinner next week. Just like normal."

"So if Thom's your best friend," Jamie asked, in a tone of exaggerated pensiveness as he dug a thumb in behind Callum's shoulder blade, "does that mean that you're going to be the best man at your daughter's wedding?"

Nerea clapped her hands over her mouth to cover her shriek of delight at that image. Jamie shot her a smile, pleased with himself.

Callum swore.

Chapter 37

Jamie makes a phone call

In March, they started talking a lot less about hypotheticals and a lot more about plans. Callum and Nerea took Jamie with them to a meeting with their solicitor to make, as Nerea rather euphemistically called them, *arrangements*. A civil union between the three of them was obviously outside the realm of possibility. The next best thing they could do for Jamie, as Callum explained, was to make sure he had as many of the rights and protections of marriage as they could give him — and that he did the same for them, where he could. There were wills to amend, powers of attorney to write, contracts to negotiate and sign. Jamie spent a day feeling overwhelmed and then devoted himself to learning everything he could about any laws relating to situations similar to theirs.

There were more than a few, and with the help of Callum's solicitor, Jamie learned to understand most of them. It at least gave him something to read on set of his new movie that wasn't horrifying stories of high-risk pregnancies. Which was good, because Nerea had threatened to kick him out of the flat if he kept doing that.

The day the last of the papers — for now — were signed, Callum, Nerea, and Jamie went out for lunch together and then went to look at yet another flat. The housing market in London was more intimidating than any lawyers' papers.

From the moment Jamie stepped inside he knew this was the right one. From Nerea's soft gasp and Callum's voice murmuring to the estate agent, Jamie suspected he wasn't alone in that assessment. There would be renovations needed, of course, but that just meant the final product would be more theirs. As Jamie stood in the kitchen — warm and bright the way the kitchen in Spain was — he found himself unexpectedly overwhelmed.

"Do you mind if I step outside for a moment?" he said to no one in particular.

Nerea, with a worried glance at his face, shook her head. Callum offered to go with him, but Jamie demurred.

He walked down the street a little way until he found a bit of park that would be perfect to take the baby to once it was born. Four, almost five months in, and Nerea was just starting to let them say *when* instead of *if*. They'd agreed, also, to tell Piper, Margarita, and Leigh about the pregnancy once they'd found a place to live and settled all the arrangements. Aside from reiterating that Jamie should tell his parents, Callum and Nerea had left Jamie to share that news himself on his own time.

Despite the lovely conversation he'd had with his mother at Christmas, Jamie had been avoiding his father. He was a gentle man, but Jamie hadn't been able to shake the dread he'd felt at his mother's pronouncement that his father wasn't ready to speak with him. Jamie never wanted to disappoint him and was afraid he already had. Until now, he'd called home only when his father was at work.

Jamie sank down on a bench under a big tree that was just starting to bud and pulled out his mobile. He flipped through his contacts, not to his parents' home number, but to his father's mobile. It was time to face this.

"Jamie? Is that you?" Hugh answered. Jamie's heart clenched at the worry in his voice.

"Yeah. Yeah, it's me, Dad."

"Are you all right, Jamie?" His father asked when Jamie said nothing else.

"Yeah, Dad. I'm fine. Listen. I owe you an apology. A lot of apologies. I also have some stuff I need to say. If you want to listen."

"Foolish boy," his father said, worried and fond all at once. Jamie wondered what he'd done well in a past life for his father to speak so kindly and easily to him when they hadn't exchanged two words since December. "You know your mother tells me things."

"I know, but you should hear it from me. And there's some new news."

"I'm listening," Hugh said. He sounded apprehensive, which didn't help Jamie's unsettled state. But still, his father was speaking to him again, and that was more than he might have hoped for. "I can't promise I'll like it," his father went on. "But I am listening."

His mother had said much the same thing every time he'd called since Christmas. The conversations had been calm and affectionate, but there were often long silences as they both tried their best. Jamie found it exhausting. He had no idea how his father had been taking any of it. He'd been scared to ask.

"Good. Thank you," Jamie said. He closed his eyes and leaned back against the slightly-damp slats of the bench. "Are you sitting down?"

"Are you all right?" his father asked again, but this time his voice was sharp.

"No. I mean, yes, I'm fine and it's not anything bad. It's fantastic, really, but it's not small, and I'm almost sure you want to be sitting down for this one."

"Out with it," his father said as sternly as he ever had when Jamie had come home guilty-faced over typical teenage transgressions.

"Nerea's pregnant," Jamie said.

"Oh," his father said. His voice was strangled. "Is it yours?"

"I — we don't know. And if we did, it wouldn't matter. Not to me or Callum or Nerea. I — we're in the middle of house hunting. Like, right in the middle. I think we've found the one actually. Callum had that look on his face, and then I just had to step outside and call you."

"For my approval?" his father sounded, of all things, amused. Jamie tried to remember if he had ever once asked for his father's approval for anything in his life. He suspected he hadn't.

"No," Jamie said. "But you should know you're going to have another grandchild."

"I didn't know something so normal could feel so unexpected," his father said, his voice awed.

"Welcome to the last year of my life." Jamie hoped his father wouldn't question that, wouldn't make him explain that falling in love was an obvious, easy thing, no matter how complex or unusual the circumstances.

"You planning to introduce us to them any time soon?" his father asked. It sounded like a challenge.

"Do you want to meet them?" His mother, in all their calls, had never asked. Jamie had assumed she wasn't ready yet and had worried she never would be.

"Yes, I want to meet the people my son is making a life with," his father said indignantly. "What kind of question is that?"

"Well, yours didn't sound like a real happy one," Jamie said matter-of-factly.

"It's a lot Jamie. Who's going to be on the birth certificate? Whose last name will the child have? Are you going to raise it Catholic — "

"Dad, all I'm worried about right now is a healthy baby. And that's all complicated. Really complicated."

"You should have something that's yours," his father said firmly.

"I do," Jamie said. "I will. And it's still complicated. I have spent so much time with lawyers lately. We need to be as protected as we can; we know that."

"Then you bring the baby up here and baptize it."

"You want to run interference with Father Donovan on that? Because I sure don't." Jamie couldn't even imagine how that conversation would go.

"You come up here, with your partners, and make proper introductions to the rest of your family," his father said. "It'll be good for Aoife, to meet them before her own wedding. Since I assume you'll be bringing them."

"Do you have any idea how much chaos that will make?" Jamie asked, even as he reeled a bit with relief. Not only was his father not yelling at him or hanging up on him, he was demanding Jamie stay a part of the family and welcoming Callum and Nerea into it too.

"Because there's three of you or because you're with a movie star?" his father asked.

"By the time the baby's born, I'll be a movie star too," Jamie said.

His father gave a muffled laugh. Jamie could picture him shaking his head.

"Your mother is going to have a lot to say about this. And that's before she has to worry about the notice in the church bulletin."

Jamie grinned. Then he asked, "Is she going to be embarrassed?" That possibility was a lot less funny.

"What's church for if not gossip?" his father admitted.

Jamie tried to imagine that, his mother enjoying the whispers and stares of her friends and neighbors as she carried her grandbaby to church. Now that he thought about it, his mum and Nerea might have a lot to talk about, and wouldn't that be both strange and wonderful?

"I've told you before," Hugh said into Jamie's silence. "If you just walk with your head high, like you've done nothing wrong — because you haven't — people won't say a word. Not people who matter. No one, and no one's family, is perfect. Who has the right to say anything to you?"

"I thought that was about me being bi, not about me being in a relationship with a married couple with a baby on the way," Jamie blurted.

This time, his father laughed out loud. The rich, warm sound reminded Jamie of everything he loved about his family, home, and Dublin.

"One contributed to the other," his father said. "And that's life, Jamie-boy. Too many surprises — some of them good — and then wanting to spare the people you love pain. And if you think you know that already, there's depths still coming. Once that baby's born, you'll do anything for it. You think you're ferocious now."

"And that's a good thing?" Jamie asked. "For me to be even more all the ways I've always driven both you and Mum mad?"

"Of course it is," Hugh said. "Your child happy and truly himself? No father can ask for more than that."

"Well," Jamie said as he thought about how he was going to relay this conversation to Callum and Nerea. He blinked eyes suddenly damp with tears. "I can definitely promise you I'm happy."

More by These Authors

Visit www.Avian30.com to join Erin and Racheline's mailing list and get information about new releases!

A Queen from the North

It may be the 21st century, but in a not-so-united kingdom the wounds of the Wars of the Roses have never healed. The rivalry between the Yorkish north and Lancastrian south has threatened to pull the nation apart for over 500 years.

While the modern world struggles with fractures born of ancient conflict, Lady Amelia Brockett faces far more mundane problems. Known to her family as Meels, this youngest daughter of a Northern earl is having the Worst. Christmas. Ever. Dumped by her boyfriend and rejected from graduate school, her parents deem her the failure of the family.

But when her older brother tries to cheer her with a trip to the races, a chance meeting with Arthur, the widowed, playboy Prince of Wales, offers Amelia the chance to change her life — and Britain's fortunes — forever. Hunted by the press — and haunted by Arthur's niece who fancies herself the kingdom's court witch — Amelia finds herself adrift in a sea of paparazzi, politics, and prophecy.

With few allies beyond her allergic-to-horses sister-in-law, her best friend who has a giant crush on the prince, and the cute young receptionist at Buckingham Palace that calls himself her Royalty Customer Service Representative, Amelia must navigate a perilous and peculiar course to secure Arthur's love and become A Queen from the North.

The Love in Los Angeles Series

Starling, Book 1
Doves, Book 2
Phoenix, Book 3
Cardinal, Book 4
More coming soon!

Love in Los Angeles is a queer romance series, with elements of magical realism, set in and around the TV and movie industry.

When J. Alex Cook, a production assistant on *The Fourth Estate* (one of network TV's hottest shows), is accidentally catapulted to stardom, he finds himself struggling to navigate both fame and a relationship with Paul, one of Fourth's key writers. *Love in Los Angeles* is the story of Paul and Alex — and of their friends and family — as they navigate love, and life, both in and beyond Los Angeles.

The Love's Labours Series

Midsummer, Book 1
Twelfth Night, Book 2
More coming soon!

42-year-old John Lyonel has never been attracted to men before, but falling for 25-year-old Michael Hilliard is actually the least screwed up thing that's happened to him in years. Even if sometimes he thinks Michael's a changeling.

About the Authors

Racheline Maltese can fly a plane, sail a boat, and ride a horse, but has no idea how to drive a car. With Erin McRae she writes romance about fame and public life. She is also a producer and writer on Tremontaine, Serial Box Publishing's adventure of manners, swordplay, and chocolate that's a prequel to Ellen Kushner's gay lit classic, Swordspoint.

Racheline's training includes a journalism degree from The George Washington University, as well as acting and directing coursework at the Atlantic Theater Company Acting School (New York City) and the National Institute of Dramatic Art (Sydney, Australia). Her fiction, non-fiction and poetry has appeared in numerous outlets, and she is a regular speaker on pop-culture topics at fan and academic conferences. Racheline also voiced Desire and Delirium in a benefit performance of Neil Gaiman's The Sandman for the CBLDF.

Erin McRae is a history nerd with a BA in international relations from the University of Toronto and an MA in international affairs from American University. She now lives and works in Washington, DC with her spouse and two cats. She delights in applying her interest in politics to her fiction writing, because conflict drives narrative.